府城榮光
The Glory of Tainan

Tainan Art Museum Grand Opening

臺南市美術館 **1** 館開館展

臺南市美術館
TAINAN ART MUSEUM

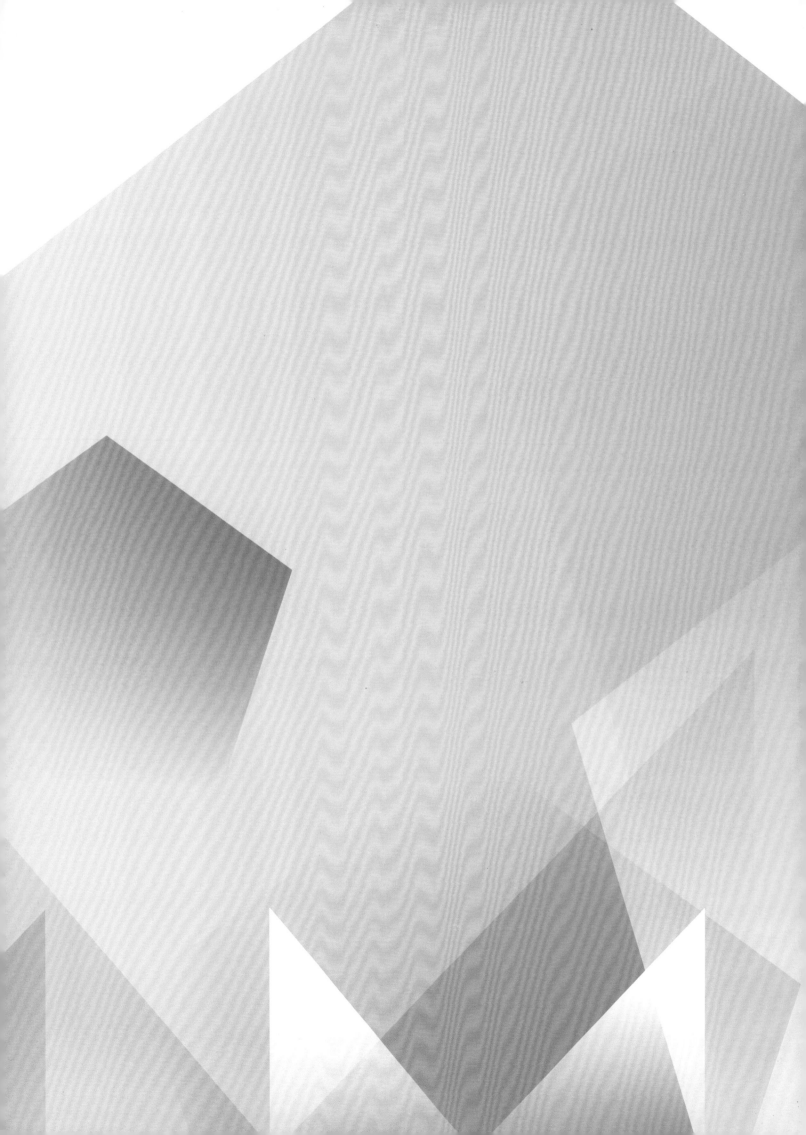

目次 Contents

市長序

2019 年適逢大家期盼一甲子的臺南市美術館正式開館，為因應美術館的第一次開館大展，並為臺南成為臺灣文化首府準備，美術館特別邀請海內外學者專家，共同規劃展覽內容，期許舉辦一次立足臺南，放眼國際的開館展覽。

此次開館展歷經一年多的籌劃，在康乃爾大學美術史及視覺研究學系副教授潘安儀先生、國立臺南藝術大學視覺藝術學院教授張清淵先生、國立臺灣師範大學美術系教授白適銘先生、東海大學美術系副教授李思賢先生等四位國內外專家學者的策劃下，以「府城榮光」為主題，各規劃四個子題 「都市‧新地景‧空間權力」、「府城藝術史話」、「起南風」、「重新詮釋中」，引以展現臺南在地獨特的藝術文化與城市空間發展。「府城榮光」主題旨在彰顯自明清書畫起，府城四百年來輝煌的文化藝術成就，以先前市政府文化局出版的蕭瓊瑞老師主編的三十本《歷史‧榮光‧名作——美術家傳記叢書 I、II、III》為基礎，由臺南出發展出在地創作者的作品，延伸連結至臺灣各地、亞洲各國的當代藝術。各種題材、媒材、裝置、製作將會在這個展覽豐富的呈現，除了府城過去輝煌的藝術，也可看出新世代如何去重新詮釋臺灣文化，藉此透視府城與亞洲各國的歷史與文化關聯。

臺南是臺灣歷史的起點，自荷蘭人於大員蓋熱蘭遮城起，各個階段的殖民統治者及隨之而來的移民在臺南留下無數有形無形的文化資產，來自各方的人帶來不同的文化，以歷史、習俗、語言、生活等的不同方式，相互匯融生息、共生共榮，一方面造就臺南府城成為兼顧經典文化藝術與地方常民色彩的城市；另一方面也創造出臺灣作為一個移民社會豐富多元的文化樣貌。透過此次展覽我們不僅可視作建構臺南美術的契機，也可作為臺灣美術發展的縮影，重新書寫臺灣近代、現代乃至當代在地藝術發展的另一篇重要扉頁。

感謝各界專家學者、藝文好友的協助與諸多文化單位的慷慨借展，我們期待這次展覽除了重現臺南四百年來輝煌的歷史榮光，也能帶著臺南市往前走，以臺南的藝術文化帶著臺灣美術向前一步。

臺南市市長

黃偉哲

A Preface from the Mayor

2019 marks the opening of the Tainan Art Museum, an event that citizens have long anticipated for over sixty years. To celebrate our opening exhibition and prepare Tainan for its role as Taiwan's capital of culture, the Museum invited domestic as well as international scholars and professionals to devise and plan the content of the exhibition. We aim to present an opening exhibition that demonstrates Tainan's international vision as a cultural base.

After more than a year of preparations, curators Associate Professor Pan, An-yi at Cornell University History of Art and Visual Studies, Professor Chang, Ching-yuan at Tainan National University of the Arts' Graduate Institute of Applied Arts, Professor Pai, Shih-ming at National Taiwan Normal University Department of Fine Arts, and Associate Professor Li, Szu-hsien at Tunghai University Department of Fine Arts came up with the theme "The Glory of Tainan" for the opening exhibition. The curators devised four subtopics, namely "Urban · New Landscape · Spatial Power," "Urban Aesthetics — Art Stories from Tainan," "A Southern Wind," and "A Process of New Interpretations" to demonstrate the unique localization of Tainan's art culture and urban development. "The Glory of Tainan" theme aims to exemplify the city's illustrious artistic cultural development over four hundred years, beginning with calligraphy and watercolors from the Ming and Qing Dynasties onward. Based on a collection of 30 books titled "History, Glory, Masterpieces: Artists' Biography I, II, III" formerly edited by Professor Hsiao Chong-ray and published by the Municipal Government's Cultural Affairs Bureau, the exhibition features representative works from Tainan's local artists and extends to a display of contemporary art from various Taiwanese and Asian artists. A myriad of themes, media, installations, and productions are presented in this exhibition. In addition to Tainan's brilliant artistic past, we can see how the new generation reinterprets Taiwanese culture in order to visualize the historical and cultural connections between Tainan and other Asian countries.

Tainan is the starting point of Taiwanese history. Since the Dutch built Fort Zeelandia in Anping District, colonial rulers and immigrants that follow suit left countless tangible and intangible cultural assets in Tainan through different stages of colonialization. Different cultures from people all around the world merged and prospered under various forms of history, customs, languages, and lifestyles. On the one hand, they made Tainan a city that upheld classic cultural art as well as local characteristics; on the other hand, it also highlights the rich and diverse cultural appearances of Taiwan as an immigrant society. This exhibition not only represents an opportunity to construct the Tainan art, but also is a microcosm of the development of Taiwanese art, being an important chapter in the development of Taiwanese modern, post-modern, and contemporary art.

I would like to express my gratitude towards the scholars, professionals, and our friends in the arts field and from various cultural institutions for their generous assistance and for lending their artworks to our cause. In addition to the display of Tainan's glory over four hundred years, I hope this exhibition will also lead our city ahead, furthering the development of Taiwanese art through the artistic culture of Tainan.

Mayor of Tainan City

Huang, Wei-Che

城市文明的美感饗宴——
1 館「府城榮光」展覽序

臺南是臺灣第一座城市，21 世紀臺南終於擁有第一座美術館，是偶然還是必然嗎？

臺南市民已經等待六十年了，臺南市具有豐富的文化底蘊，一代接一代經營了四百年。臺南市本身就是一座生態博物館，大大小小古蹟散佈在全市各地區。只是在如此歲月長河中，臺南市美術館承載著市民無限期許，我們看到 1 館試營運期間無數群眾的到訪，就可以了解到臺南市美術館所具備的吸引力與其背後的感動力量。因為臺南市有悠久的歷史支撐文化的穩定發展。

臺南市擁有悠久的博物館歷史，1901 年臺南即成立臺灣教育博物館，成為臺灣最早的一座博物館，雖然當時設備簡陋，卻已具備博物館雛形。回顧 1984 年擔任蘇南成市長的藝術顧問，協助完成臺南文化中心的空間與藝術品設置計畫，經歷不少苦心方才竣工，不過當時臺北市已經在前一年有了市立美術館。我向蘇市長大膽建議，希望為臺南蓋一座美術館。他說：我已經要奉派去高雄，時不我與！臺南市經歷幾代人努力，卻是不斷挫折，賴清德市長就任之初，即開始籌備臺南市美術館，才有今日「府城榮光」展覽在嶄新館舍呈現。

很高興此次邀請到四位策展人來策劃四個子題，白適銘策劃「都市·新地景·空間權力」、潘安儀策劃「府城藝術史話」、李思賢策劃「起南風」，以及張清淵的「重新詮釋中」。這四項子題包含了府城將近四百年的文化發展脈絡，以及府城與亞洲藝術之間的脈動，雖然我們提供 1 館的有限空間，他們卻盡其可能，納入豐富與多元的作品，試圖探討府城四百年藝術在東亞文化交流中的重要地位。許多作品借展於各大美術館、私人藏家，也有現地訂做，甚而遠從日本金澤這座工藝之都空運來的茶屋。這些藝術作品使得 I 館展場變得豐富多彩，連接起亙古的文化傳統，也連接起亞洲各地的藝術脈動，構成府城在藝術表現、生活美學的豐厚底蘊。

臺灣美術的近代化無可諱言地起於日本統治臺灣之後，但是，在府城，臺灣美術自有其發展脈絡，文人書畫與民間工藝提供豐富的生命力。戰後，經歷許多臺灣前輩畫家的努力，即使美術發展的主導權受到重北輕南的文化政策嚴重扭曲，幸好臺南擁有豐富的文化底蘊，許多優秀藝術家不斷投入創作，臺南沒有在臺灣美術發展的歷史洪流中缺席，代代出現許多優秀畫家，府城榮光不斷昌盛發展。

臺灣以一座歷史悠久的府城文化為典範，一批批優秀的藝術家給這座城市帶來光榮感。我們衷心期許臺南美術館日後成為臺灣美術的發揚基地，成為臺灣藝術家發表美術成果的重要旅程碑，共同建構一部開放而多元的臺灣美術史。

臺南市美術館董事長

An Aesthetic Feast of Urban Civilization :
Preface to "The Glory of Tainan" Exhibition in Building 1

As the earliest city in Taiwan, Tainan finally has its first art museum in the 21st century. Is it by chance or by fate?

Tainan citizens have waited for 60 years, notwithstanding the city's profound cultural deposits that have been carefully nurtured through generations over the past 400 years. Tainan City is an eco-museum in itself, with all sorts of historic monuments scattering throughout different districts of the city. Tainan Art Museum carries the citizens' immeasurable expectations over the stream of time. When we saw the countless visitors coming to the Museum during the trial run of Building 1, we could see the charm of the Museum and its underlying sensational force, because Tainan City has a long history that supports a steady cultural development.

Tainan City also has a long history of museums. The Taiwan Museum of Education, being the first museum in Taiwan, was established in Tainan in 1901; the basic structure of a museum was formed despite the simple furnishings. Looking back to 1984 when I was appointed as Mayor Su, Nan-cheng's art advisor to assist in the spatial and artwork layout plan for Tainan Cultural Center, I completed the task with painstaking efforts. By that time, Taipei City had already built its municipal art museum one year ago. I made a bold suggestion to Mayor Su that Tainan should build an art museum, but he said it was not a good timing as he was assigned to Kaohsiung! Tainan's efforts over a few generations had met with frustrations time and again. Preparation for Tainan Art Museum eventually began at the beginning of Mayor Lai, Ching-te's tenure, and this has led to the presentation of "The Glory of Tainan" in this brand-new hall today.

I am glad to have four curators planning four subtopics for this exhibition, namely "Urban · New Landscape · Spatial Power" by Pai, Shih-ming, "Art Stories from Tainan" by Pan, An-Yi, "A Southern Wind" by Li, Szu-hsien, and "A Process of New Interpretations" by Chang, Ching-yuan. These four subtopics cover the 400 years' cultural development of Tainan, as well as the interaction between Tainan's arts and Asian arts. In spite of the limited space in our Building 1, the curators tried their best to include as many and diverse works as possible, attempting to delve into Tainan's essential role in East Asian cultural exchange over the 400 years. Many exhibits are borrowed from various major art museums and personal collections, while some are custom-made for this exhibition. In particular, the tea rooms are transported all the way from Kanazawa of Japan, the city of craftsmanship. These artworks have enriched and added colors to the exhibition hall in Building 1, drawing on the well-established cultural heritage and connecting the artistic dynamics of various Asian regions. The exhibition truly demonstrates Tainan's bountiful deposits of artistic expression and aesthetics of life.

Modern development of Taiwanese art undeniably emerged since the Japanese rule of Taiwan, but Taiwanese art has seen a unique development in Tainan, where literati's paintings and calligraphy and folk arts have provided vigorous vitality for the arts. After the war, many predecessor artists' efforts have sustained the profuse cultural foundation of Tainan despite the serious distortion of a cultural policy that places priority on the north over the south. Many outstanding artists have devoted themselves to creative work, keeping Tainan's presence in the history of Taiwanese art development. With a generation of excellent painters after another, the glory of Tainan keeps prospering.

The culture of the time-honored capital Tainan has always been a good model for Taiwan. Bunches of excellent artists have brought glory and honor to this city. We look candidly forward to Tainan Art Museum developing into the artistic base for the prosperity of Taiwanese art and an important milestone in Taiwanese artists' presentation of artistic achievements. Let us jointly construct an open and diverse history of Taiwanese art.

Chairman of Tainan Art Museum

Chen, Huei-Tung

回顧過去，前瞻未來——
1 館「府城榮光」展覽序

臺南市民自來以身為府城居民為傲，將近四百年來府城在臺灣的政治、文化、經濟發展中佔有一席之地，府城歷史幾乎也可說是臺灣歷史重要史頁。特別是傳統文化風華，不只能繼承傳統，也蘊藏卓越的豐富傳統，邁進 21 世紀，府城依然是全臺沒有一個縣市可以取代的文化都城。21 世紀的府城，終於有一座屬於自己的美術館，在 1 館舉行「府城榮光」展覽。1 館建築物已經說明一切，融會日本統治時期舊警察州署建築與 21 世紀空間設計，營造出融會傳統與創新的絕佳場所。

在 1 館的「府城榮光」展分別以四個子題進行展示，分別是白適銘策劃的「都市‧新地景‧空間權力」、李思賢的「起南風」、潘安儀的「府城藝術史話」，以及張清淵的「重新詮釋中」。這四個子題呈現出府城將近四百年的文化發展歷程，以及府城與亞洲藝術的發展脈動，相當豐富與多元，足以折射出四百年前府城在東亞文化交流中的重要地位。

臺南在 20 世紀中期以後，在臺灣繪畫發展中彷彿進入沉寂狀態，但是在文化發展的事實上則不然，1984 年臺南文化中心完成，至今依然是全臺最優秀的文化展演空間之一，1996 年設置臺南藝術學院，培育傳統與創新的藝術人才，還有直至今天已經一百二十年的臺南大學，這些文化設施與人才培育場所早已為府城培育許多人才與展示場所，唯一欠缺的是專業美術空間。空間不足無法展現文化發展的市民權與活力，數任市長都將美術館視為施政理念，可惜都一再挫敗，賴清德市長就任開始即將此視為文化建設的首要工作，終於展開新氣象。

我們希望這場「府城榮光」的開館活動，能為府城美術發展脈絡進行清晰地梳理，展現出府城近四百年藝術的燦爛內涵與風華。這次展覽作品包含油畫、水墨、裝置藝術、複合媒材、陶藝及立體茶室，其中茶室展現出臺灣、中國大陸及日本在茶文化當中的詮釋能力與開展面向，此外，府城在經歷四百年發展的濃厚民間色彩與文人情懷，也在此次展覽中以巧妙地方式呈現出來。參與此次展覽的藝術家以臺灣占最大多數，其他國家地區尚有日本、中國大陸、港澳、東亞各國，希望此次展覽能為本館往後發展起定錨作用。

此次展覽於府城藝術而言是嶄新的開始，府城榮光不再是過去式，將因為這座美術館的開啟，啟動府城於 21 世紀呈現嶄新風貌之姿的進行式。府城有許多偉大藝術家及優秀的年輕藝術工作者，可惜此次展覽只能局部呈現，日後有待更多活動來發掘。

謹在展覽前夕，感謝這些策展人及我們館內同仁不眠不休的努力，方能使得這項展覽得以順利展開。希望這場展覽能看見過去，眺望未來。

臺南市美術館館長

Retrospect and Prospect :
Preface to the "The Glory of Tainan" Exhibition in Building 1

The people of Tainan have always been proud of being the ancient capital's residents. For nearly 400 years, Tainan has played a crucial role in Taiwan's political, cultural, and economic development. The history of Tainan is an indispensable chapter in the Taiwanese history, especially when the essence of our traditional culture is not just an inheritance of traditions, but also forms a rich legacy. At the turn of the 21st century, Tainan remains a capital of culture that no other county or city in Taiwan may replace. The 21st century Tainan finally boasts an art museum of its own, currently holding "The Glory of Tainan" exhibition in Building 1. The architecture of Building 1 is self-explanatory of its symbolic meaning, where the former prefectural police headquarters during Japanese rule is merged with the 21st century spatial design to create a perfect example of blending tradition with innovation.

"The Glory of Tainan" exhibition in Building 1 is presented under four subtopics: "Urban · New Landscape · Spatial Power" curated by Pai, Shih-ming, "Urban Aesthetics – Art Stories from Tainan" curated by Pan, An-Yi and "A Southern Wind" curated by Li, Szu-hsien, and "A Process of New Interpretations" curated by Chang Ching-Yuan. The four subtopics illustrate the 400 years of cultural development in Tainan, as well as the artistic pulses of Tainan and Asian arts. The extremely rich and diverse exhibits aptly reflect Tainan's important role in the East Asian cultural exchange 400 years ago.

Tainan seemingly entered an inert state in Taiwanese painting development during the mid-20th century, though that was not the case in terms of cultural development. Tainan Cultural Center was completed in 1984, which remains one of the best cultural performance spaces in Taiwan. Tainan National University of the Arts was established in 1996 to cultivate young people talented in traditional and innovative arts. In addition, we have the 120-year-old National University of Tainan. These cultural facilities and training institutions have cultivated many talented individuals and provided exhibition venues for the city's arts. A professional artistic space is what we missed. Without sufficient space, the citizens' rights or vitality in cultural development could not be adequately shown. Several mayors had made the art museum part of their administrative focuses, but their efforts were in vain until Mayor Lai, Ching-te assumed the mayor's office; he made this a priority of the cultural development task, ushering in a new era.

We hope that "The Glory of Tainan" opening exhibition clarifies the development of art in Tainan and demonstrates The 400 years of brilliant artistic gist and magnificence of Tainan. The exhibits include oil painting, watercolors, art installation, complex media, pottery, and three-dimensional tea rooms. The tea rooms in particular show the interpretive capabilities and approaching perspectives of tea cultures in Taiwan, China, and Japan. Additionally, Tainan's richly folk-oriented arts and literati heritage over 400 years of development are also tactically presented in this exhibition. The majority of artists covered in this exhibition are Taiwanese, while some artists from other countries such as Japan, China, Hong Kong, Macao, and East Asian countries are also included. This exhibition is expected to anchor a direction for the Museum's future development.

This exhibition marks a brand-new start of Tainan art. The glory of Tainan does not stay with the past only; the opening of the Museum will unveil a whole new look of Tainan in the 21st century. There are many great artists and young art professionals in Tainan. Unfortunately, we are only able to present the works of a select few. We eagerly look forward to digging deeper into their works in the future.

On the verge of the exhibition, I would like to thank our curators and colleagues at the Museum for their endless efforts to facilitate a successful opening to the exhibition. It is my sincere hope that this exhibition will provide an insight into the past and an outlook into the future.

Director of Tainan Art Museum

Pan, Fan

「府城榮光」策展總論述

白適銘／撰稿人・策展人（國立臺灣師範大學美術系教授）

　　城市之發展，代表人類社會由四處散布、居乏定所的原始聚落狀態，逐漸走向系統化、結構化及效率化空間管理之具體結果；同時，隨著空間規模及居住族群之不斷擴增、衍化，城市不再只是純粹的居住地，更成為反映政治治理、市民記憶及空間美學的概念物。17世紀之前，臺灣之山海平地原為原住民各族散居之地，少數外人亦曾渡居於此，然隨著大航海時代之開啟，西方勢力魚貫轉進東亞，臺灣自東海邊陲蕞爾小島、化外之地，一躍成為國際競爭、亞洲新秩序中的兵家必爭之處，地域戰略價值益為彰顯。

　　眾所周知，臺南首府作為臺灣最早都會，由荷蘭東印度公司開啟其建城序幕，原為發展東亞貿易之重要據點，其後，標舉「反清復明」旗幟的鄭成功據有閩南沿海、金門、廈門等地，並於1661年起兵攻打臺灣，最終迫使荷蘭退守，屯田於嘉南、高雄平原等地，養兵待時，正式占領臺灣西南地區。鄭經即位後，明鄭勢力即全面撤出閩南，建立「東寧王國」，都於安平。康熙年間，清政府翦除明鄭餘黨之後，正式占領臺灣並設一府三縣——臺灣府（臺南）及臺灣縣（臺南市南部）、鳳山縣、諸羅縣，臺南遂成臺灣首府。

　　明末以來，因實施海禁政策之故，片板不得入海，清政府繼之占領轄管臺灣之後，統治者視為邊疆彈丸之地，甚為忽視，二百餘年之間故未積極經略，臺灣隔著海峽與中國遙遙相望，關係至為疏遠。直至最後的二十年間，因西方列強入侵、門戶洞開等燃眉之急，態度始轉向積極。隨著18世紀末葉以來之政令鬆弛，及至最終開放，閩、粵十府州等地漢人遂大舉來臺墾殖，群聚於海岸山丘之間，漢文化於此繁衍日盛，城市發展亦漸次擴及北部、東部。

　　明鄭或清朝時期，因官宦或流寓之故，往來中土與臺灣兩地間之孤臣宿儒、文人墨客漸多，清政府基於治理，在臺推行漢化，於府縣所在地施設儒學，地方人士亦參與書院、義學、鄉堡社學、民學（私塾）、詩社等之興建，藉以教育子嗣投身科考，文教設施由南往北遍及全臺，一時文風大盛。中土文士通常兼善詩書畫，來臺後與在地文人雅士多所交流，詩畫酬唱並共同提倡文藝。俗稱「板橋林家三先生」之謝琯樵、呂世宜、葉化成，除在林本源家擔任教席之外，分善書法、繪畫及金石之藝，可謂當時聞名全臺之藝界翹楚，文人三絕之藝益形發達。

　　此外，自明鄭時期以來，以府城臺南為中心，即已發展出深具臺灣地方特色之藝術風貌。因其與中國南方，尤其如浙江、福建、廣東等地之畫派關係密切，慣稱為「閩習」。「閩習」一詞，雖為清代文人正統畫派對於地方繪畫因襲成風、筆勢具有粗野放逸習氣等的譏評而起，於今反而成為學界廣泛引用、並借稱18世紀以降閩臺地域風格的代名詞。其中，最夙負盛名者為林朝英、林覺、莊敬夫三家，曾獲「閩習三家」之尊稱，三人為居住、活動於臺南首府之在地畫師，其畫名及作品卻廣受全臺讚頌歡迎，反映府城美術之重要歷史位置。

甲午戰敗，中國勢力雖退返大陸，然漢文化已歷經數百年的積澱，成為臺灣進入現代化階段之後的固有精神遺產。日人自統治臺灣伊始，即與中國採取之鎖國政策及純粹漢化不同，藉由各種現代化建設之積極推動，成為治理殖民地、拓展國力之首要目標。日本江戶幕府政府對於西方勢力之東來或外來新知，態度欲拒還迎，採取局部及選擇性之開放，固而蘭學（西學）及漢學興盛於此時。其後復因明治維新之全盤西化，繼而成為亞洲強國，中日在東亞地區發展的主導權上遂出現逆轉。

日本統治臺灣之後，遷都臺北，五十年間積極發展成為現代化殖民社會，並成為其擴展南洋勢力之基地。其間，工業、商業、資訊及教育的普及發達遠甚清朝，與亞洲及世界之連結更形密切，伴隨現代市民文化教養養成觀念之進步，同時造成美術觀念之巨大變革，有別於傳統守舊之「新美術」，逐漸成為彰顯臺灣現代文化價值及時代意義之表徵。尤其是，官辦美術展覽會如臺展、府展的舉辦，更為萌芽不久的臺灣美術帶來成長動力，一時之間名手輩出，成為引介日、歐最新美術思潮流派，以及形塑臺灣地方美術特色之重要旗手。

都市建設及教育普及，皆為日人在臺推行現代化建設之重要手段，透過國民初、中等教育之實施，革除明清以來農業社會陋規，尤其是1919年頒布「臺灣教育令」，全面實施教育改革，確立完整學制，並強調內臺共學。日治期間，全臺廣設師範學校，如臺北、臺南（設於1919年）、臺中（1923）、新竹、屏東（1940），培育諸多知識菁英，成為推動社會前進的主要力量。藝術教育方面，上述師範學校皆設有手工圖畫課程，雖時數不多，卻能引發興趣，建立其理性觀察、體現自我之能力。

來臺推廣新式美術觀念之奠基者，以石川欽一郎、鹽月桃甫、鄉原古統、木下靜涯等四人最為重要，同時更是開辦臺展、府展之主要啟蒙推手。與朝鮮、滿州國類似，臺展、府展為日本文展、帝展等官方美術機制之海外縮影，分為「西洋畫」、「東洋畫」（包含日本畫及南畫）二大部門，可謂臺灣現代美術之發源地及藝術家養成之搖籃。透過日本傳來之西式美術或日本繪畫，皆為明治維新以來逐漸發展定形的現代藝術類型，與在臺「閩習」書畫、文人畫或民間藝匠之封閉落伍，彷若天壤之別。

因為新式美術教育及其觀念之推廣，美術現代化之風潮正方興未艾，傳統書畫因之瀕臨式微，藝匠畫師逐漸退出公眾舞臺，蟄居、沉寂於閭閻之間。然而，其中亦有能積極回應時代衝擊、與時俱進者，如府城畫師潘春源，即率先改變傳統摹稿傳抄路數，兼行寫生，反映現實生活，將傳統師徒傳授之學，轉化為現代公開推展之藝，誠為眾人之表率。

此外，基於府城地區深厚、悠久而豐富的文化歷史積澱，日治時期出身臺南之西洋或東洋畫家更不遑多讓，屢在臺、府展獲得諸多獎項，成績耀眼。其中，如顏水龍曾留學東京美術學校，受業於岡田三郎助及藤島武二等帝展名師門下，其間，為提升臺灣美術研究及創作風氣，並與陳澄波、郭柏川、廖繼春等人合組畫會「赤島社」。學成返臺後，與劉啟祥等人成為極少數曾赴歐洲遊學的臺灣畫家，增進其對西洋繪畫傳統、歷史及技法的認知。此外，並成立「南亞工藝社」、「臺南州蘭草產品產銷合作社」、「竹細工業產銷合作社」等社團，致力於傳統工藝之研究、推廣及教育。

郭柏川亦出生於臺南，臺北國語學校師範科畢業後赴日留學，後轉入東京美術學校西畫科，致力於油畫創作。後旅居中國，復任教於國立北平師範大學、國立北平藝專及京華藝專，成為在陸臺人之重要美術教育家之一。後返回臺南定居，任教於成大建築系，並於1952年創辦「臺南美術研究會」，推展南臺灣美術不遺餘力，使其成為發揚府城文化、藝術及歷史遺產的現代基地。更值得一書的是，郭柏川生前曾大聲疾呼建立美術館的重要性，然基於戰後社會背景所限，未得如其所願，於今，臺南市美術館已巍然成立並對外開放，成為南臺灣文化地標，正可告其在天之靈。

顏、郭之外，劉啟祥同為具旅外畫遊經驗之畫家，早年赴日就讀中學，其後進入東京文化學院洋畫科，受教於當時日本畫壇最前衛的二科會名家門下。其後，偕同楊三郎前往法國遊學，不僅吸取巴黎最新藝術思潮養分，並往返於羅浮宮研究、臨摹西洋巨匠名跡，拓寬眼界，因而畫藝大進。戰後，劉啟祥同樣舉家自日返臺，分別定居於臺南、高雄等地，為推廣美術，曾連結南部諸縣市如高雄、臺南及嘉義等地畫友，輪流舉辦展覽，此即「南部美術協會」，並赴各地寫生，致力描繪臺灣山岳風景、海岸港灣之美。

此外，如陳澄波、廖繼春、薛萬棟等人，雖非出生於臺南，卻因工作或寫生創作等因素旅居、造訪臺南，故而創作出不少描繪當地美景等膾炙人口之佳作，例如陳澄波造訪正任教長老教會中學（今長榮中學）的畫友廖繼春時，即有描繪該校校園〈新樓風景〉等名作；廖繼春居住臺南時描繪自家庭園之〈有香蕉樹的院子〉，曾獲得帝展殊榮，並成為繼陳澄波之後第二位入選的臺籍西洋畫家。薛萬棟雖不像陳、廖等人具備傲人的留日學歷，僅是一名擅長日本畫（今稱膠彩畫）的業餘畫家，因工作關係居於臺南，其後入畫師蔡媽達門下苦心習藝三年，〈遊戲〉一作竟獲府展最高獎項「總督賞」，名盛一時，另為持續創作，亦常前往孔廟等地寫生。

數百年來，臺南歷經政權轉移及人事更迭，雖不再成為政治中樞，然其不僅見證此地過往歷史興衰，經由不同時代藝術家之描繪、留影，更成為臺灣形塑自身政治體質之縮影、文化性格之由來，臺南建城的重要性及象徵意義若此。府城美術背後所蘊藏的美學意涵，不僅在於展現富含地方色彩之自然景觀、民情風俗或生活現實，更從荷蘭、明清迄於日治時代等不同政治治理中，摸索建構自身主體價值之方法、途徑，自然調和傳統書畫、民間藝匠與現代美術之間的鴻溝與衝突，復因藝術家之旅外經驗，灌注再造當地文化榮景的清泉活水，形塑兼具宏觀與微觀視野的府城美學。

非物質文化遺產或美學價值之外，除上述顏水龍之在地復興外，自古以來，臺南即積累如建築、民藝、服飾、生活器用等不計其數之物質性文化遺產。在所有民間生活文化中，飲茶堪稱最具臺灣本地特色重要代表之一，「臺灣茶藝」之形成，更可謂結合潮汕工夫茶與日本茶道、煎茶道等之後，重新詮釋而成的在地文化。尤其是進入1970年代之後，經由諸多茶人、茶會、茶館之鑽研、傳習及推廣，融會美學、哲學、佛學等精神思維及生活情趣，注重茶種、水質、泡煮方式、茶具甚或飲茶環境等因素，體現「道藝一體」真義，並因而形成獨具一格的生活飲茶風習。

在茶具造型及工藝美學方面，隨著現代人飲茶習慣、需求的日新月異，茶道器物的製作不斷精進提升及國際化，新茶器的創新開發，更成為反映茶人藝匠材質與形式上實驗精神的具體表徵。在材質方面，包含對汝窯青瓷釉料的研究及再利用、異材質結合、金屬等，不勝枚舉；此外，在造型或技術方面，臺灣或東亞的現代創作者，一方面各自延續如雕、鑿、鑲、嵌等工藝技法傳統，另一方面則積極連結當下美感需求的各種可能。在林林總總的造形語彙之中，時而表現優雅細緻的文人品味，時而呈現極簡抽象的大膽作風，時而探索材質原料的純粹物性，時而反映不同性別的個人特徵，不僅為茶道具增添多元趣味、形塑全新格局，更呈現當代工藝美術從實用到審美的發展歷程。

隨著解嚴時代之來臨，臺灣社會逐漸走向自由、民主及開放，藝術表現衝撞既有威權體制、突顯個人意志及尋求在地化連結之現象層出不窮，並在追求身分認同及形塑臺灣意識的雙向軌道中，逐步建構其文化主體性。「後解嚴美術」，已成為當今美術史書寫最為關注的課題之一，以1990年代前後作為起點，臺灣當代藝術萌芽此種既紛亂卻又充滿希望的年代，臺南當地美術亦在此種整體環境變遷中，摸索如何跳脫臺北中心之框架，企圖建構以反映在地精神為目標的藝術光譜，呈現兼具歷史縱深、媒材廣度及形式多元於一爐的嶄新局面。

從空間權力的角度來說，臺北及臺南分別代表官方及民間，長期以來凝聚而成的政治意識形態，反映「朝」大「野」小的不對等權力關係。例如在展示場域方面，大型藝文空間多分布於首都及其周邊，經費集中於少數人或單位手中，造成諸多弱勢的藝術家被排斥於官方展覽機制之外。為尋求更多展出機會並突顯藝術概念及主體價值，1980年代末期開始出現的「替代空間」，如臺北「伊通公園」（1988）、高雄「阿普畫廊」（1990）及臺北「二號公寓」（1989）為其中顯例，並可為其註腳，成為臺灣當代藝術建立多元價值、對抗極權壟斷的特殊現象。

臺南當代藝術形式及展陳方式之在地形塑，主要仰賴於獨立營運或此種替代性空間之出現，如許自貴自組「高高畫廊」，另有「邊陲文化」（1992-1995）、「新生態藝術環境」（1992-1999）、「原型藝術」（1998-2005）、「文賢油漆行」（2000-2018）等最為重要，近三十年間雖歷經各種消長起伏，然其勇於衝破體制、完成自我之奮鬥軌跡，已成為最能反映後解嚴精神中的典範代表，臺南在這種大時代的體質汰換及改革運動中並未缺席。此外，甫自國外學成歸國之藝術家帶回全新資訊，透過其在臺南教學及創作的個人經驗，傳遞當代藝術最為前衛而嶄新的視野及思維，為沉浸已久的在地文化注入新血。

新一代藝術家的創作表現，與明清、日治時期不同，隨著當代藝術空間、工具材料觀念之轉向，複合媒材、空間裝置及數位媒體、錄像等複雜多變的形式外貌及展陳方式，已成為時代寵兒。與臺北的方式不同，臺南因應地方人文生態，出現兼具圖書、展覽、演藝、電影及餐飲等不同功能的複合式空間，促進跨領域藝文創作之對話，不僅引領當地風潮，其影響至今猶存。解嚴以來，基於尋求文化主體性之需求，匯聚於臺南地區之當代藝術家，在其仍處邊緣化的境遇中，長期推展有成的「南方美術」，象徵跳脫府城陳舊歷史意象之後，在最前衛、先進的當代蛻變中，完成兼具在地化任務的心靈軌跡與心路歷程。

臺南，作為一個歷經古今變異的臺灣最初首都及重要城市，其歷史或風貌雖幾經改弦更張，而有所變異，然其中積澱已久及正在醞釀發生的，不管其消長關係如何，正形成互為體用的雙關語彙，缺一不可。亦即，古城或古代遺跡之保存護養，得以體現一個偉大城市豐厚飽滿的歷史履歷及人文底蘊，現代都會之建設開發，又為其帶來全新的空間體驗及生活利基，呈現一種看似衝突卻又兼容並蓄的文明奇觀。在進入工業化或後工業時期之前，最能反映人類文明進展總體成就的，不外乎就是城市本身。城市發展，代表人類生活智慧、居住習慣的演變實績，儼然一部由建築材質、空間觀念及地方治理等交錯而成的進化論。

從臺灣城市發展史的角度來說，明清時期之城鎮互不聯屬，交通網絡欠缺，知識經驗難以廣泛傳播，長期處於自足卻封閉的狀態。日治時期，經由數十年間大規模計畫性的都市改造，呈現現代化建設具體成果的「新地景」，已澈底改變明清以來傳統景觀之「地方性」特色，並建構出臺灣近代社會都會生活空間的「公共性」特質，展現近現代市民更為多元、摩登的生活文明及城鎮生活經驗。隨著現代化都市之大規模興起，作為現代生活實驗室、展示場之生活空間，人潮、物資及觀念不斷湧進輸出，孕育全新的社會秩序與運作模式。

現代「新地景」（如政治地景或文化地景）之成立，不僅反映物質建設、空間治理之具體成果，更可經由其象徵意義之形塑，積極傳達主導者的政治意識與文化視野。據此，城市不會只是與鄉村相對的代名詞，城市化亦非單指土地開發程度的有形指標，更是展示地方知識、空間權力及消費欲望的無形場域。舉凡都會文明生活、公共文化發展、社會階級分化、物質流動，甚或環境破壞、災害威脅及居住權、空間權等等，都是探討臺灣自上個世紀以來城市發展所經歷的時代課題，帶動都會生活形塑、城市景觀再現、市民身分認同、當代風景美學建構等的重新思考，由外而內，彼此聯屬。

此種在外觀上不斷被改修、易容或破壞毀棄的結果，正適足反映臺灣近現代都市歷史發展中充滿雜糅、模糊、多元與易變性之特質。從不同時代殘存下來的建築、街道、坊里的遺跡一隅，往昔都市記憶仍不可磨滅。藝術家藉由畫筆、影音探討都市文明、現代生活、住民處境、歷史變遷、城市記憶等的目的，或為記念都發歷史，或為反思居住正義，或為保存集體記憶，反映不同時代中的內在化居留經驗。不同時代、世代所形構的「地景」圖像，都是我們探索臺灣近現代都會生活及公共文化內涵意義，最珍貴且重要的視覺材料。

透過藝術家有關地景觀視、書寫觀點的轉移，突顯其在都市生活參與與市民身分建構上的實際經驗，提供觀看當代城市風景的多重可能模式，再思現代化、都市建設帶來的諸種問題，以及反映臺灣都市視覺意象建構之歷程。這些以城市作為觀察、漫遊、再現或論述對象的藝術作品，不論是平面、立體、裝置、聲光或媒體影像，反映不同時代、世代創作者及其所處都市空間之間的內在化關係，以及在媒材、觀念運用上的「跨地方性」。與政治控制下所產生的「去地方性」、「無地方性」概念不同，「跨地方性」之文化生產，顯示其對於空間權利、地景歷史，以及城市文化記憶重編的主體意識，超越國家、地理、族群或區位框架，呈現當代藝術深具流動、交錯、自主與批判性的狀態。

不論是異鄉客或都會人、本國人或外國人，都市風景反映著個人與居住空間、地理區位、地景歷史及城市記憶等之間極其微妙的權力關係。「地方性」、「地方認同」已成為都市共同居住者之間的交集所在，並在共同經驗與個別履歷等不同形式中，反覆而不斷地被紀錄下來。我們居住的城市或世界，代表身處其中、進行著居住實踐的人們——市民、移民或旅者——共存共構的地方、空間及場域。而美術中的「城市書寫」，不僅針對空間、地景、區位，更可謂來自包含對時代、族群及世界等概念複合理解之結果，自私領域的個人探索實踐，漸次移轉至公領域的集體價值建構。

在上述有關政經、文化等複雜時空背景影響下，臺灣美術歷經萌發、形塑及轉化等不同階段，亦因此融混西方、中國、日本及南島等不同區域族群元素，展現流動雜糅的海國徵候。多重殖民治理及其文明開化經驗之積累，促使臺灣逐漸脫離因襲守舊的俗民社會，進而成為自由開放的市民社會，新興城市儼如現代文化藝術的私人實驗場、公眾展示地。東西文化的競合對峙與不同族群的往返進出，雖帶來不可避免的衝突撞擊，卻得藉此尋思文化身分、建構地方色彩、形塑主體價值等等。從戰前到戰後，臺灣美術可謂一部交織在內與外、西與東、新與舊、自然與文明、朝與野、我者與他者等二元框架中，摸索其現代化可能及不斷尋找自身定位的歷史。

臺南府城豐富的文化積存，包含荷鄭時期以來的戰爭史料、海事地圖、風俗繪卷、生活器用及文人書畫等，反映東西交錯、新舊共存的多重樣態。日治時期迄於解嚴之後，在急速的現代化與走向「世界」、「全球」的過程中，美術雖成為彰顯個人及連結外部之重要表徵，然隨著主體性、在地性建構需求的與日俱增，臺南作為臺灣文化心靈原鄉之地，鳳凰花木、廟宇老街、民俗節慶、飲饌風習等固有遺產及城市記憶，成為本土論述及常民美學的主要依據。於今，在我們除重新探討「府城」一詞的文化內涵之同時，作為其結論，與其說是代表過往的地理、空間或居住概念，毋寧更會是一種突顯在地文化主體價值、反映市民集體記憶，以及表彰市民世代榮光之具體縮影。

「府城榮光」，夾雜著臺灣或臺南古往今來、多義並陳的時空敘事，不論是前瞻或回顧，城市書寫不僅反映於有形的地景構築與空間治理概念，生活於此的世代居民的文化認同與土地經驗等無形遺產之探討，更不可或缺。然而，地方與國族、經濟發展與環境保存、個人與群體、實用功能與美學價值能否兩立？或應如何並存共榮？誠為當下至為緊要之課題。不論如何，臺灣近現代到當代美術的發軔、受容及其擴展、延異，反映一種洄游於上述複合脈絡中的權力構圖，本展覽以城市作為方法，透過相關視覺、物質文化材料，以多元匯聚的統合梳理方式，檢視其主體意識的建構過程與形式內涵，藉以再創府城下一個百年的未來榮光。

The Glory of Tainan: Curatorial Concept

Pai, Shih-Ming/Author/Curator, Professor of Department of Fine Arts, National Taiwan Normal University

Urban development represents the concrete result of human society's progression from scattered and nomadic primal settlements, to gradually becoming a systematic, structured and efficient management of space. At the same time, with the expansion and evolution of space dimensions and ethnic communities, the city is no longer purely a place of residence, but also a conceptual object that reflects political governance, citizen memory, and space aesthetics. Before the seventeenth century, the Taiwanese mountains and plains were originally a land of scattered aboriginal tribal habitats, with a minority of diasporic outsiders. However, with the age of discovery ushering Western forces into Eastern Asia, Taiwan transformed from a marginal and undeveloped island in the far reaches of the East China Sea to a strategic battleground for international competition and the new Asian order. The island's geographical strategic value is evident.

It is widely known that the capital of Tainan is the oldest city in Taiwan. The Dutch East India Company initiated its development, originally as an important base for the expansion of East Asian trade. After Zheng, Cheng-gong(Koxinga)'s successful occupation of the southern Fujian coastline, Jinmen and Xiamen under the banner of "Oppose Qing and restore Ming," his troops attacked Taiwan in 1661, eventually forcing the Dutch to retreat. Zheng established military camps in the Jian-an and Kaohsiung Plains, biding his time while training his army; officially occupying the southwestern region of Taiwan. After Zheng, Jing assumed his father's position, the Ming Zheng forces completely withdrew from southern Fujian to establish the "Dongning Kingdom" in Anping. During Emperor Kangxi's reign, the Qing government officially occupied Taiwan after defeating Ming Zheng forces; inaugurating a central prefecture government and three counties—Taiwan Prefecture (Tainan), Taiwan County (Southern Tainan), Fengshan County and Zhuluo County. Tainan City became the capital of Taiwan.

Due to sea ban implementations from the end of the Ming Dynasty, private maritime trading and coastal settlement were restricted under related isolationist Chinese policies. After the Qing occupied the Taiwanese jurisdiction, the government disregarded it as a marginal frontier and neglected the island's development for over two hundred years. Taiwan was separated from China by the Taiwanese strait, and the relationship between the two became extremely alienated. The Qing government's attitude toward Taiwan only began to actively turn in the last two decades of its reign due to an urgent need for development caused by Western invasions opening China's gates. With a slackening hold of sea ban policies by the end of the eighteenth century to ultimately lifting restrictions, The Hans/Chinese settlers from the ten Prefectures in Fujian and Guangdong provinces came to colonize Taiwan; gathering in the coastal hills. The Han culture flourished and urban development gradually expanded to the northern and eastern areas.

During the Ming Zheng or Qing Dynasties, an increasing amount of bureaucrats, scholars, and literati traveled between China and Taiwan due to the effects of diaspora or administrative change. The Qing government promoted Han culture based on the governance of Taiwan, building Confucianism academies in counties and prefectures while local scholars participated in establishing colleges, free lecture halls, county schools, civil schools (private school), and poetry societies to educate and prepare the next generation for imperial examinations. Cultural and educational facilities spread across Taiwan from south to north, adding to the prevalence of studious pursuit. Chinese literati are usually skilled in poetry, art and calligraphy, adding to their interactions with local scholars in Taiwan as they promote literary culture through song, poetry and art. In addition to teaching the family of Lin, Ben-yuan, the three scholars Xie, Guan-chaio, Lu, Shi-yi, and Ye, Hua-cheng, otherwise known as "three scholars of the Banqiao Lin Family," were also known separately for calligraphy, painting, and the art of engraving. They were the most famous artists of their time, and helped develop the three arts in Taiwan.

In addition, from the Ming and Zheng Dynasties, Tainan has been the center of urbanization and developed an artistic style with Taiwanese local characteristics. Due to local art's close relationship with the painting styles of southern China, especially of those in Zhejiang, Fujian, and Guangdong, this style is often referred to as "Minan-practice." Though the term "Minan-practice" originated from the Qing literati orthodox artists' criticism of local Taiwanese painters' imitative style and wild, undisciplined brush strokes, it is now widely quoted in academic circles and is synonymous with the Fujian and Taiwanese regional style from the 18th century. Amongst artists of that era, the three most famous are Lin, Chao-ying, Lin, Chueh, and Zhuang, Jing-fu, who have been honored as the "the Three Masters of Minan-practice." The three are local artists who live and work in the capital of Tainan, and their paintings and works are widely praised and popular in Taiwan, reflecting the important historical position of Tainan Art.

After the defeat in the Sino-Japanese War, though the Chinese forces retreated to the mainland, Han Chinese culture that was accumulated over hundreds of years became the inherent spiritual legacy of Taiwan that sustained into its modernization. At the beginning of Japanese colonial rule, the Japanese actively administered various modern constructions in Taiwan that were unlike the country-locked policies adopted by China and its singular focus of spreading the Han Chinese cultural influence. Taiwan became Japan's primary subject in colonial administration and the expansion of Japanese national strength. The Japanese Edo shogunate government was hesitant towards embracing the eastern advance of Western powers and foreign knowledge; choosing to adopt a partial and selective openness which led to the equal prosperity of Rangaku (Western learning) and Sinology. Later, due to complete Westernization during the Meiji Restoration, Japan became a powerful Asian country, gradually reversing the Sino-Japanese power relationship as well as dominance over developmental leadership.

After Japan colonized Taiwan, the capital was moved from Tainan to Taipei. Over the next 50 years, Taiwan was actively developed into a modern colonial society and became a Japanese base for expanding its forces into the South Sea. In the meantime, the popularization of industry, commerce, information and education was far more developed and widespread than under Qing rule, whereas the Taiwanese connection with Asia and the world grew in intimacy. With the advancement of the concept of cultivating modern citizen culture, artistic concepts were also greatly changed. A "New Art" that is different from the traditional and conservative arts gradually became a symbol of Taiwan's modern cultural values and represents the significance of the times. Official art exhibitions such as the Taiwanese exhibitions and the Prefecture exhibitions furthered the growth of the budding Taiwanese art. Many famous Taiwanese artists emerged during that period, becoming leading flag bearers in the introduction of latest Japanese and European art trends as well as shaping the characteristics of Taiwanese local art.

Urban construction and popularizing education were key to the Japanese implementation of modernization in Taiwan. Through the administration of national primary and secondary education systems, the Japanese government eliminated and reformed the inadequate agricultural social rules and regulations applied since the Ming and Qing Dynasties. The "Taiwan Education Order" in particular was promulgated in 1919 which fully implemented education reform; establishing a complete academic system, and emphasizing equal education opportunities for Japanese and Taiwanese students. Normal schools were established throughout Taiwan during the Japanese occupation, such as Taipei, Tainan (set in 1919), Taichung (1923), Hsinchu, and Pingtung (1940), cultivating many intellectual elites and became the main force behind social progress. In art education, these schools also offered drawing courses, and though few hours were offered, the classes stimulated interest and established participants' abilities to rationally observe and reflect upon personal abilities.

Amongst artists in Taiwan at the time, Ishikawa Kinichiro, Shiotsuki Tōho, Gobara Koto, and Kinoshita Seigai are the four most important founders advocating new art concepts. At the same time, they are the key promoters initiating Taiwanese exhibitions and Prefecture exhibitions. Similar to North Korea and Manchuria, Taiwan Exhibitions and Prefecture Exhibitions are overseas abbreviations of official art institutions such as the Japanese Art Exhibition and Imperial Exhibition. The exhibition is divided into "Western Painting" and "Toyoga/Dongyang Paintings" (including Nihonga and Nanga) and can be seen as the birthplace of Taiwanese modern art as well as the cradle for artist cultivation. The Western-style art or Japanese paintings that came to Taiwan through Japan are all types of modern art that was gradually developed and shaped since the Meiji Restoration, and worlds apart from the dated and conservative "Minan-practice" paintings, literati paintings or folk artisans in Taiwan.

Due to the promotion of new art education and its concept, the trend of art modernization continued to rise whereas traditional paintings and calligraphy gradually declined, causing its artisans and painters to slowly withdraw from the public stage and go quietly into the night. However, among those were artists who responded positively to impact of trend and keep up with the times. Tainan painter Pan, Chun-yuan for example was the first to diverge from the tradition of imitating the work of old masters to sketch, paint, and reflect upon real life. Pan's work illustrates the shift from taught, traditional skills into modern, promoted art, serving as an example for all.

In addition, based on the extensive and rich cultural historical accumulation of the Tainan area, Western or Japanese painters from Tainan during Japanese colonialization also held their own in the new arts. These artists won many awards in Taiwan and Prefecture exhibitions with dazzling results. Among these artists are Yan, Shui-long, who studied at the Tokyo Fine Arts School and was trained by Imperial Exhibition masters such as Okada Saburōsuke and Fujishima Takeji. In the meantime, Yan formed a painting group with Chen, Cheng-po, Kuo, Po-chuan, Liao, Ji-chun and others to promote Taiwan's artistic research and creative spirit named the "Red Island Society." After Yan returned to Taiwan, he joined Liu, Chi-Hsiang and a small number of Taiwanese painters who had traveled to Europe to study and deepen their understanding of Western painting traditions, history and techniques. Yan also assisted the establishment of "Southern Asia Crafts Society," the "Taiwan Prefecture Soft Rush Product Production and Marketing Cooperative" and the "Bamboo Industry Production and Marketing Cooperative" groups, dedicating their efforts to the research, promotion and education of craft.

Kuo, Po-chuan was also born in Tainan. After graduating from the Mandarin Chinese Normal School of Taipei, he went to Japan to study and transferred to the Western Painting Department of the Tokyo Fine Arts School, where he focused on oil painting. After moving to China, he taught at the National Beijing Normal University, National Beijing Art College and Jinghua Art College; becoming one of the most important Taiwanese art educators in China. After returning to settle down in Tainan, he taught at the Department of Architecture at Cheng Kung University and founded the "Tainan Fine Art Association" in 1952. He spared no efforts in promoting the art of Southern Taiwan, making it a modern base for the development of the cultural, artistic and historical heritage of the Tainan area. What is even more worthy of mention is that Kuo expounded upon the importance of establishing an art museum before his death. However, based on the post-war social background, Kuo was unable to see his dream come into fruition. Today, the Tainan Art Museum stands proudly open to the outside world and has become a cultural landmark in southern Taiwan; an accomplishment dedicated to Kuo's memory.

Apart from Yan and Kuo, Liu, Chi-hsiang was a painter with experience overseas. In his early years, Liu went to Japan to study in middle school, and then entered the Tokyo Cultural Institute's Department of Western Painting (Bunka Gakuin), where he was taught by famous artists of the "Second Branch" art group, the most prestigious, avant-garde art group in Japan at the time. Later, together with Yang, San-lang, Liu went to study in France, not only to absorb the latest artistic trends of thought as nutrients in Paris, but also to study at the Louvre, and to observe the work of famous Western masters and broaden horizons, resulting in a vast improvement in his work. After the war, Liu returned to Taiwan from Japan with his family, to settle in Tainan and Kaohsiung respectively. In order to promote fine arts, he collaborated with artists in the southern counties such as Kaohsiung, Tainan and Chiayi to hold exhibitions in turn. This was the "Southern Taiwan Art Association," where Liu devoted his efforts in addition to travelling around the island to sketch and paint, dedicated to depicting the beauty of Taiwanese mountain scenes and coastal harbor.

Other artists such as Chen, Cheng-po, Liao, Ji-chun, and Hsueh, Wan-tung, etc., though not born in Tainan, have visited Tainan due to factors such as work or for creative purposes, thus resulting in many excellent works depicting the area's local beauty. Chen visited Liao, who was teaching at the prestigious Presbyterian Church Middle School at the time (now Chang Jung Senior high school) and created a masterpiece depicting the school's campus (new building landscape). Liao, Ji-chun painted "the courtyard with banana trees" based on his own courtyard during his stay in Tainan and won the honor of participating in the Emperor Exhibition, following Chen in becoming the second Taiwanese Western painter to be selected. Hsueh, Wan-tung did not have the esteemed academic qualifications of Chen and Liao, and was only an amateur painter skilled in Japanese painting (now called Eastern Gouache). Hsueh lived in Tainan due to work, where he entered the tutelage of painting artist Tsai, Ma-da for three years of painstaking study. Hsueh's "Game" was awarded the highest "Governor's Award" of the Prefecture Exhibition, and he became well known at the time. Hsueh continued to create art, also often visiting Confucius Temple and other places in Tainan to sketch.

For hundreds of years, Tainan has undergone multiple political transfers and personnel changes. Although it ceases to be a political center, Tainan has not only witnessed the rise and fall of local past history, artists of different eras' depiction and photographic images of the city has become the epitome of Taiwan's shaping of its political physique as well as the origin of cultural character. Therein lies the importance and symbolic significance of Tainan's urban construction. The aesthetic implications behind Tainan Art is not only to show natural landscapes rich in local colors and customs of its people or the reality of life, but to also explore the methodology and trajectory of Tainan's subjective value construct and exploration under the different political governances of the Dutch, the Ming and Qing Dynasties and Japanese colonialism. Tainan Art naturally reconciled the gaps and conflicts between traditional painting and calligraphy, folk artisans and modern art; the oversea experience of traveling artists instilling the rejuvenation of local culture, and shaped Tainan aesthetics with both macro and micro perspectives.

In addition to intangible cultural heritage or aesthetic value, above from the efforts of Yan, Shui-long in local reformation mentioned above, Tainan has accumulated countless material cultural heritages such as architecture, folk art, costumes and living tools since ancient times. Among the culture of common living, tea drinking is one of the most important representatives of Taiwanese local characteristics. The emergence of "Taiwanese tea art" can be described as a combination of Chaoshan Gongfu tea, Japanese tea ceremony, and Senchadō and a reinterpretation of local culture. After the 1970s, the continuous study, teaching and promotion of many tea enthusiasts, tea societies and teahouses, merged spiritual thought as well as lifestyle influences from aesthetics, philosophy, and Buddhism to focus on tea characteristics, water quality, cooking methods, tea sets or even environmental settings; reflecting the true meaning of "skill and philosophy as one," thus forming a unique tea drinking habitual lifestyle.

In terms of tea set style and craft aesthetics, with contemporary tea drinking habits and its ever-changing needs, the production of tea ceremony tools are continuously improved and internationalized, with the innovative development of new tools and sets becoming a reflection and actualization of the experimental spirit in craftsmanship, material and form. In terms of materials, the research and reuse of kiln celadon glaze is included as well as the integration of different materials and metal, etc. In terms of styling or technology, modern creators in Taiwan or Eastern Asia on the one hand, continue traditional craftsmanship such as chiseling, sculpting and inlays. On the other hand, they actively connect with the various possibilities of current aesthetic needs: employing a variety of design semantics that sometimes express elegant and meticulous literati taste, sometimes presenting a minimalist abstract boldness, sometimes exploring the pure materiality of material, and sometimes reflecting the personal characteristics of different genders. This not only adds diverse layers to the tools and shape new horizons, but also demonstrates the developmental process of contemporary craft arts from the practical to the aesthetic.

With the lifting of the martial law, Taiwanese society gradually moved towards freedom, democracy and openness. Artistic performance collided with the authoritarian system, highlighting individual will and a search for connectivity with localization; constructing cultural subjectivity through the duality of pursuing identity and shaping Taiwanese consciousness. In the orbit, its cultural mainframe is gradually constructed. "Post-martial law art" has become one of the most discussed topics in contemporary Taiwanese art history discourse. Using the beginning of the 1990s as a starting point, Taiwanese contemporary art budded in a chaotic yet hopeful era, whereas Tainan local art explored and endeavored to break away from the rigid structure of Taipei-centric art and attempted to construct an artistic spectrum that reflects localized spirit, presenting a new landscape in which historical depth, and the broad use of different mediums and form are diverse.

From a spatial power perspective, Taipei and Tainan each represent the official and civil sides of modern society, with political ideologies that has long been condensed reflecting an unequal power relationship between hegemonic political powers and marginal opposition. For example, in the field of exhibitions, spaces for large-scale art display are mostly distributed in and around the capital. Funds are controlled by a select few people or units, causing many disadvantaged artists to be excluded from official exhibition structures. In order to seek more exhibition opportunities and emphasize artistic concepts and subjective values, the "alternative space" that began to appear in the late 1980s such as Taipei's "Yi-tong Park" (1988), Kaohsiung's "Apu Gallery" (1990) and Taipei's "Apartment No.2" (1989) are prime examples of this endeavor and serves as a footnote as well as special phenomenon in the establishment of diverse values and confrontation with monopolization.

Contemporary Tainan art and the construction of localized exhibition mainly rely on the independently managed or the emergence of alternative spaces such as Hsu Tzu-kuey's "Kao Kao Gallery," "Border Culture" (1992-1995), "New Phase Art Space" (1992-1999), "Prototype Art Space" (1998-2005) and "Wen-Xian PAINT HOUSE forum & studio" (2000-2018) were amongst the most important. Though the 30 years after the lift of martial laws have witnessed various ups and downs, the trajectory of struggle in self completion and endeavors to break free from the system has become a model representative best reflecting the post-martial law spirit. Tainan was not absent from the era of philosophical replacement and reformation movement. Artists returning to Taiwan from studying abroad brought back additional new information to convey the most avant-garde and visionary perspectives in contemporary art through their personal experience in teaching and creating in Tainan, injecting new blood into the long-awaiting local cultural landscape.

The creative performance of a new artistic generation is different from the Ming and Qing Dynasties and Japanese colonial rule. With the shift in contemporary art space and the concept of tools and materials, complex forms and visual appearances of composite mediums, space devices, digital media and video recordings are the new darling of our times. Different from the methods of Taipei, Tainan responds to the local humanitarian ecology, and presents compound spaces with different functions that include bookstore, exhibition, performing arts, movies and restaurant use. This employment of space promoted a cross-disciplinary dialogue between art creations that not only led the local trend, but still carries influence to this day. After the lift of martial laws, based on a demand for cultural subjectivity, contemporary artists that converged in the Tainan area have long promoted "Southern Art" even though their situation remained marginalized. Their efforts symbolize a transcendence from the old historical image of Tainan and a contemporary metamorphosis into the advanced and avant-garde, completing the spiritual trajectory and psychological journey of the localization.

As the original capital and important Taiwanese city of that has experienced the differences of historical change, Tainan's history or urban style has undergone many variations with the tides of time. However, the city's accumulated history and current phenomenon, regardless of its growth and decline, it is forming a mutual body of discourse with connotations that cannot exist without one another. That is to say, the preserved care of ancient cities or ruins can reflect the rich history and humanistic heritage of a great city. The construction and development of modern cities brings a new spatial experience and niche lifestyle, presenting seeming conflict that is actually an inclusive wonder of civilization. Before entering the industrialization or post-industrial period, the city itself best reflects the overall achievements of human civilization. Urban development represents the evolution of wisdom in human living and our habits. It is an evolutionary theory that is intertwined with architectural material, spatial concept and local governance.

From the perspective of Taiwanese urban development history, cities and towns of the Ming and Qing Dynasties had no affiliation with each other, the transportation network was lacking and caused difficulties in the wide dispersal of knowledge and experience which led to a long period of self-sufficiency yet closed communications. During the Japanese occupation, "new landscape" that showed the concrete results of decades of large-scale planned urban transformation and modernized construction completely changed the "local" characteristics of traditional landscape in the Ming and Qing Dynasties, as well as constructing the "public" traits of modern urban living spaces in Taiwan; demonstrating a more diverse, modern life civilization and urban living experiences of modern citizens. With the rise of modern cities, living spaces that serve as experimental laboratories and exhibitions of contemporary lifestyles, people, materials and ideas are constantly flowing into an outpour that gives birth to a new social order and operational mode.

The establishment of modern "new landscapes" (such as political landscapes or cultural landscapes) not only reflects the concrete results of material construction and space governance, but also actively conveys the political consciousness and cultural vision of dominant leaders through a shaping of symbolic meaning. According to this concept, the city is not just an opposite definition of village. Urbanization is not only a tangible indicator of the degree of land development, but also an invisible field that displays localized knowledge, space power and consumer desire. Civil life, public cultural development, social class differentiation, material flow, and even environmental destruction, disaster threats, residency rights and spatial rights, etc., all represent discussions pertaining to periodical issues experienced in Taiwanese urban development since the last century. These issues influence the shaping of urban lifestyles, urban landscape representation, citizen identity, and the construction of contemporary landscape aesthetics that are inherently and externally connected.

The result of urban landscapes being constant remodeled, easily accommodated or destroyed and discarded is adequately reflected in the historical development of Taiwanese modern and contemporary cities that is filled with hybrid, vague, diverse and volatile characteristics. From the remains of buildings, streets, and squares that have survived in different eras, the memory of the city's past remain indelible. Artists explore various aspects of urban civilization, modern life, inhabitant positions, historical changes, and urban memory by brush, audio or video, in order to serve as a memorial for the history of urban development, or reflect upon living justice, or preserve collective memory, reflecting the inherent residential experiences of different eras. These "landscape" images created by different eras and generations are the most precious and important visual materials for us to explore the meaning of Taiwanese modern and contemporary urban lifestyle and public culture.

Through the artist's transfer of perspective in landscape and writing, with an emphasis on personal, practical experience in urban life participation and citizen identity construction, multiple possible models for viewing contemporary urban landscapes are provided for us to rethink various issues brought about by modernization and urban construction, in addition to reflecting upon the trajectory of urban visual imagery construction in Taiwan. These works of art depict the city as an object of observation, roaming, representation, or discourse. Whether through the display of graphics, multi-dimensional, installations, sound and light, or media images, these works reflect the internalization of spatial relationships in generations of creators from different eras as well as the "Trans-locality" in the use of media and ideas. Different from the ideas of local alienation or "Placelessness" produced under political control, cultural production through "Trans-locality" demonstrates the subject consciousness of spatial rights, historical history and urban cultural memory rewriting surpasses the state, geography, ethnicity, or location structure to present a form of contemporary art that is fluid, intertwined, autonomous, and critical.

Regardless of outlanders or citizens, natives or foreigners, cityscapes reflect the extremely subtle power relationship between the individual and living space, geographic location, historical history and urban memory. "Locality" and the "local identity" have become a point of convergence for urban cohabitants that is repeatedly recorded in different forms such as common experience and individual encounters. The city or world we live in represents the places, spaces, and fields in which residents carry out living practices—where citizens, immigrants, or travelers—coexist. The "urban writing" in art not only applies to space, landscape and location, but is also the result of a comprehensive understanding of concepts such as temporal reality, ethnicity and the world. A personal exploration of self-realization is gradually transferred to the collective construction of value in the public domain.

Under the influence of the aforementioned complex time and spatial influences such as the economic, political and cultural impact, Taiwanese art experienced the various stages of growth from budding development, formation and transformation, and thus blending elements from different regions and ethnicities such as the West, China, Japan and South Island, demonstrating the fluidity and hybridity of island states. The accumulation of experience under multi-colonial governance and cultural development has prompted Taiwan to gradually break away from the rigid and conservative traditional society and become a free and open civil society. Emerging cities are transformed into private experimental fields for modern art and public display. Competition between Eastern and Western cultures and the coming and going of different ethnic groups, while bringing inevitable conflicts, can also be used to explore cultural identity, construct local color, and form subject value, etc. Taiwanese art can be described as a historical documentation of the binary that is intersected with the inherent and external, western and eastern, new and old, nature and civilization, hegemony and marginalization, self and the other; discerning the possibilities of modernization and the position of a constant self orientation from pre-war to post-war times.

The Tainan area's rich cultural heritage includes historical materials, maritime maps and illustrated documentation of folk customs, daily tools and literati works in paintings and calligraphy that date from the Dutch occupation and Ming Zheng era; reflecting the multiple forms of intersection between the East and West as well as a coexistence of the old and new. From the Japanese colonial rule to post-martial laws, art has become an increasingly important manifestation of personal and external connections in the process of rapid modernization and pursuit of the "international" and "globalization." However, with the increase in demand for subjectivity and constructing locality, Tainan's status as an originating site of Taiwanese culture with its inherent heritage of Phoenix flowers and trees, temples and old streets, folk festivals, culinary customs, and urban memories have become the main basis for local discourse and folk aesthetics. In conclusion to the re-examination of the term "Fucheng" and its cultural connotations, we emphasize the value of local cultural subjectivity, the reflection of collective memory and the epitome of generations of glory, as opposed to the concept of representing past geographical, space or residence.

The glory of Tainan, mixed with the time and space narratives of Taiwan or Tainan, whether looking to the future or the retrospective, urban narration is not only reflected in the tangible landscape construction and spatial governance, but also in the imperative discussion of intangible heritage through the cultural identity and land experience of generations of residents. Yet how can local and national, economic development and environmental preservation, individuals and groups, practical functions and aesthetic values each stand independently? Or rather, how should they coexist? These questions are most pressing in contemporary times. Regardless, the development, tolerance, expansion and extension of Taiwanese modern and contemporary art reflect a power composition that can be traced back into the aforementioned composite context. This exhibition uses urbanization as methodology to review the construction process and formative connotations of subjective consciousness through a diverse examination of relevant visual and material cultural materiality in order to further the glory of Tainan for centuries to come.

都市・新地景・空間權力

白適銘／撰稿人・策展人（國立臺灣師範大學美術系教授）

　　臺灣在進入日本殖民統治之後，殖民政府藉由在體制建構、國土規劃、城鄉開發，以及生活模式改新等方面之持續推動，逐漸脫離傳統守舊的俗民社會，並進而轉型成為具有近代性意義的市民社會。明清時期，山海阻隔，城鎮互不聯屬，交通網絡欠缺，知識經驗難以廣泛傳播，長期處於自足卻封閉的狀態。日治時期，經由數十年間的「現代化」建設，尤其是大規模計畫性的都市改造，促使反映其具體成果的「新地景」四處林立，澈底改變明清以來傳統景觀之「地方性」特色，建構出近代社會、都會空間的「公共性」文化特質，展現近現代市民更為多元、摩登且開放的生活文明及都市經驗。

　　隨著現代化都市之大量興起，作為現代生活實驗室、展示場之摩登生活空間，人潮、物資及資訊不斷湧進輸出，孕育全新的社會秩序與運作模式。舉凡在交通運輸、物質交換、訊息傳布及生活型態上都因此產生巨大變遷，都市適應力及生產力成為檢視市民現代化特質之指標。此外，透過「現代化」之各種手段，造就現代都市文化之形成，透過教育、組織、展示、出版、媒體等公共機制之推波助瀾，快速、廣泛且具流動性的傳播力量，同時形塑整體性的現代新知及個別性的身分認同，彼此交錯。環境變動帶來的外部撞擊，對藝術內部發展產生何種影響，更成為探討美術現代化最重要之議題。

　　事實上，政治、經濟、社會等方面「現代化」所帶來的具體成果，對臺灣近現代美術產生之影響既深且廣，包含很多方面。例如，揚棄臨摹轉向寫生、脫離民俗走入都市、思索何謂臺灣文化、摸索文化身分、建構地方色彩、追求個性、進入世界體系、揉合東西對立、復興民族文化、跨越族群鴻溝、形塑主體性甚或臺灣意識等。這些問題的出現，可謂臺灣歷經新舊文明衝突、族群矛盾、建立價值觀及強化自我意識過程中的必然現象，成為挑戰官方文化威權的第一聲號角，帶動思維革新及文化啟蒙，反映臺灣近現代藝術家建構「時代性」、「民族性」及「世界性」等的思索與苦悶。

　　從都市發展的角度來說，現代「新地景」（如政治地景或文化地景）之成立，不僅反映物質建設、空間治理之具體成果，更可經由其象徵意義之形塑，積極傳達主導者的政治意識與文化視野。據此，城市不會只是與鄉村相對的代名詞，城市化亦非單指土地開發程度多寡的有形指標，更是展示地方知識、空間權力、消費欲望及生活記憶的無形場域。舉凡都會文明生活、公共文化發展、社會階級分化、物質流動，甚或環境破壞、災害威脅及居住權、空間權等，都是探討臺灣自上個世紀以來城市發展所經歷的時代課題，帶動都會生活形塑、城市景觀再現、市民身分認同、當代風景美學建構等的重新思考，由外而內延伸擴展。

西方人文地理學者愛德華‧瑞爾夫（Edward Relph）認為地方經驗具有內在性及外部性，一個人「內在於一個地方，就是歸屬並認同於它，你越深入內在，地方認同感就愈強烈」；反之，外部性導致地方疏離或「無地方性」的產生，地方內化經驗的匱乏，更造成停居者無法形塑歸屬及認同感，並與地方建立真實的關係。都市，作為一個地方，象徵在現代化推動下所產生的權力空間、知識場域或進化機制，置身其中的市民、移民或旅者，在由外而內等不同層面的轉化過程中，皆可產生不同程度的地方認同與地方化結果。地方內化經驗，不論是主動或被動，同時帶來公共參與、集體認知的歸屬感，謀合原有的外來經驗，使彼此產生連結、對話與協商，地方不再侷限於固有的地理及群屬性定義。

從戰前、戰後迄於今日，臺灣城市歷經中國、西方及日本等外來政治強權的多次洗禮，其真正面容已不可復識。換句話說，其背後應具有的地方認同，在政權或政治意識形態急速更迭的狀況下，同時進而產生「去地方性」或「無地方性」的危機。除此之外，大規模的城市建設或土地開發，或許帶來生活或空間上的舒適便捷，然而，卻相對容易造成土地剝削、環境破壞、階級對立、歷史喪失、精神恐慌或自然失調等問題，導致地方認同的弱化與崩解。「地方性」與「公共性」重返對抗局面，前者帶領後者所謂的進步史觀、文明優先論，遂廣遭質疑。

即便如此，此種在外觀上不斷被改修、易容甚或拆解毀棄的結果，正適足反映臺灣近現代都市歷史發展中充滿「雜糅」（hybridity）、模糊、多軌與易變性之特質。從不同時代殘存下來的建築、街道、坊里的遺跡一隅，往昔都市記憶仍不可磨滅。藝術家藉由畫筆、圖像、影音等工具，探討都市文明、現代生活、住民處境、歷史變遷、城市記憶等的目的，或為考掘都發歷史，或為反思居住正義，或為保存集體記憶，反映不同階段中的內在化居留經驗。不同時代、世代所形構的「地景」圖像，儘管如此地形式不一，卻是吾人探索臺灣近現代都會生活及公共文化內涵、意義，最珍貴且重要的視覺材料。

本子題「都市‧新地景‧空間權力」之規畫，企圖透過藝術家有關地景觀視、城市書寫觀點的轉移，突顯其在都會生活參與與市民身分建構上的實際經驗，提供觀看當代城市景觀的多重可能模式，再思現代化、都市建設帶來的諸種問題，同時反映臺灣近現代都市視覺意象建構之歷程。這些以城市作為觀察、漫遊、再現或論述對象的藝術作品，不論是平面、立體、裝置、聲光或媒體影像，反映不同時代、世代創作者及其所處都市空間之間的內在化關係，以及在媒材、觀念運用上的「跨地方性」（Trans-locality）時代特質。與政治控制下所產生的「去地方性」、「無地方性」概念不同，「跨地方性」之文化生產，顯示其對於空間權利、地景歷史，以及城市記憶重編的主體意識，超越國家、地理、族群或區位認知框架，呈現當代藝術文化兼具流動、交錯、自主與批判性的狀態。

城市歷史的變遷，同時來自建設與破壞，象徵主宰力量各行其是的矛盾關係，其意義詮釋呈現兩極化的現象。伴隨政治體制轉變而來之都市開發，主政者在形塑空間權力、勝利者歷史意象的過程中，具有治理、規訓及馴化等象徵意義的政治、文化地景因之崛起，造成住民空間認知及地方經驗的急遽改變。然而，隨著政權移轉或政策之改弦更張，上述帶有特殊象徵意義之地景，容易成為刻意去除化的對象，幾經更迭後或不可復識，或景物依稀、人事全非。改建、拆除或都更等城市再造，象徵此種權力交換中「地方性」（locality）被委棄不顧的不同程度，進而產生「去地方化」、「無地方性」之結果，最終成為居住歷史、城市記憶及地方認同等不斷喪失的主因。（侯淑姿、陳飛豪、霍凱盛）

其次，都市開發雖可造就新穎、有效及更具機能性的生活環境，土地再利用成為活化空間治理的政治資本，進而形成全新的都市文化及社會記憶的再生產。然而，隨之而起的利益衝突、階級矛盾擴大，身處弱勢一方的勞工、低收入戶、殘疾或外來人口，經常成為都市食物鏈下最主要的犧牲者、受害者。都市發展的目的，原應發揮住民共享理想、提供宜居環境、合理分配經濟收益，甚或重建市民的地方認同。空間或土地的剝奪及其資本化擴張，並未造就更多的社會福利，反而導致嚴重的分配不均，無家可歸或居無定所已成為都市開發的最大諷刺。對因此失去空間、地方的弱勢者而言，理想而偉大的城市構圖，儼然只是摩登、光鮮卻虛幻的海市蜃樓。（廖文彬、林書楷）

再者，工業化帶來大量而快速的機械生產，改變人類對於自身及世界形塑的看法，物競天擇的理論只能運用於原始自然，文明演進已由機械（科技）決定，城市發展即其重大成果之一。再現都市或都市建築樣貌所表徵的人類文明，將取決於何種形式元素？反映何種內在化的空間經驗？突顯何種公共意識與地方性？不論是面對個人或人類世界，再現都市發展可能經由微觀歷史的角度，亦可能透過宏觀敘事的結構而被探討，顯示都市與個人間主客觀位置的差異。此種差異，來自個人的選擇立場，都市可能是安身立命之所、他鄉異地，抑或只是反映時代興衰、人事浮沉的工業魅影。（林文藻、羅展鵬）

此外，都市建設經常伴隨著地理擴張，導致鄉村、林地城鎮化的急速變遷，透過現代交通工具的端點連結，帶來人群、資訊與物質的快速移動，城鄉界限的跨越，致使地方性觀念逐步消失，原生地、世居地之概念亦漸次淡化。自此以往，居住經驗來自移動，而非固著，家園概念擺盪於暫留與永住兩極之間。不只城鄉、省市、洲際或國界跨越已成生活日常，故鄉與他鄉反轉位置、互為取代，成為相對性的地方概念。穿越時空，促使人們產生候鳥般的調適能力，自在游移於暫留與永住地之間。都市生活所呈現的，並非侷限於一時一地，而是跨越山海、城郊，在複數城市間往返穿梭的結果。（劉子平、周東彥）

最後，都市建設提供人類庇護，工業化以後的文明進程，造就人類史上最輝煌燦爛之時代。天際線的不斷改易，象徵人類征服天空的物質慾望，以及拓展未來世代的生存需求。然而，自然資源的過度開發，導致生產過剩及環境破壞，隨之而起的災禍如地震、海嘯、洪水、空污等，終究無法避免。人類文明進展的終點，與自然失衡、生態瓦解息息相關，工業社會的摧毀力量源於內部，都市則首當其衝。都市為科技生產、製造及使用之地，兼具受惠及受害雙重可能，然因人口密集、物資集中，一旦災禍發生，損害難以估計。固若金湯的鋼鐵叢林，可能在自然反撲的瞬間化作泥團灰燼。（張永達）

這些反映真實與虛構、過往與當下、自我與他者等錯綜關係的圖像音影，交織著個人與包括社會、國家、世界等在內的外部環境的互動軌跡，清楚勾勒出個人都市、空間論述參與之「跨地方性」結果。不論是異鄉客或都會人、本國人或外國人,都市風景反映著個人與居住空間、地理區位、地景歷史及城市記憶等之間極其微妙的權力關係。「地方性」、「地方認同」已成為都市共同居住者之間的交集所在,並在共同經驗與個別履歷等不同形式中,反覆而不斷地被紀錄下來。我們居住的城市或世界,代表身處其中、進行著居住實踐的人們——市民、移民或旅者——共存共構的地方、空間及場域。而美術中的「城市書寫」,不僅針對空間、地景、區位,更可謂來自包含對時代、族群及世界等概念複合理解之結果,自私領域的個人探索實踐,漸次移轉至公領域的集體價值建構。

Urban · New Landscape · Spatial Power

Pai, Shih-Ming/Author/Curator, Professor of Department of Fine Arts, National Taiwan Normal University

After Taiwan entered Japanese colonial rule, the colonial government gradually converted the traditional Taiwanese folk society to a modern civil society through structural construct, national land planning, rural development and continuously implementing lifestyle reformation. In the Ming and Ching dynasties, Taiwan was self-sustainable yet isolated by the impenetrable mountain and sea barriers; causing a lack of communication and transportation between each secluded region as well as difficulties in a widespread dispersal of knowledge. Through decades of "modernized," strategic construction that emphasized urban planning and urban reform under Japan's colonial rule, "new landscapes" that reflect concrete results were seen across the island, completely changing the traditional landscape and "locality" characteristics of the Ming and Ching era. These developments formed a cultural "publicness" in modern society and urban space, demonstrating the modernity, diversity, and accessibility of civil living and the urban experience.

With the rise of modern cities, experimental spaces that function as a showcase for modernized living have produced a continuous influx of bodies, materials and information; resulting in new social models and order. Transportation, commerce, media and lifestyles have changed drastically due to modernization, making urban adaptivity and productivity a key indicator of modernization in civil character. Modern cities are formed through various steps of "modernization," whereas a rapid, popularized and fluid communicational power is introduced with the advance of public mechanisms such as education, organization, exhibition, publishing and media; converging with contemporary knowledge that shapes conformity as well as individual identity. The external impact of environmental change reflected internally in fine arts has become a key issue in examining contemporary art.

In fact, concrete results created by the "modernization" of politics, economy and society have a profound and widespread impact on modern art in Taiwan that can be seen in many aspects. Replacing the art of imitation with sketching, for example, breaks away from folk customs and enters the realm of urbanism by exploring cultural identity and the essence of Taiwanese culture. The art of sketching captures local characteristics, pursues individuality, integrates world systems, bridges the contrast between east and west, revives national culture, crosses ethnic differences, and shapes subjectivity or promotes Taiwanese consciousness. The emergence of these issues can be described as an inevitable phenomenon which reflects conflicts between Taiwan's new and old civilizations as well as ethnic conflicts in the process of establishing values and strengthening self-awareness. Art visualized the first challenge to official cultural authorities, leading to innovative thought and cultural enlightenment that reflects contemporary Taiwanese artists' thought and struggles in the construction of "period," "nationality" and "the world."

From the perspective of urban development, establishing modern "new landscapes" (such as political landscapes or cultural landscapes) not only reflects the concrete results of material construction and spatial governance, but also actively conveys dominant political consciousness and cultural vision that takes shape through symbolic meaning. Therefore the meaning of urban is no longer restricted to the opposite of rural, and urbanization is not only a tangible indicator of the degree of land development, but also an intangible sphere that displays local knowledge, spatial power, consumer desire and living memories. All civilized life, public cultural development, social class differentiation, material flow, or even environmental destruction, disaster threats and residency rights or spatial rights, etc., are all reflections of periodical issues experienced in Taiwan's urban development over the last century. Innovation in thought toward shaping lives, urban landscape reformation, citizen identity, and contemporary landscape aesthetics construction must extend within from external inspiration.

Canadian geographer Edward Relph believes that local experience is both intrinsic and external. One person is internally in a place they belong to and identifies with. The deeper you internally, the stronger that local identity becomes. On the contrary, externalization leads to local alienation or "placelessness." The lack of experience in local internalization has made it impossible for settlers to shape their sense of belonging and identify with or establish a true relationship with their locality. The urbanized city, as a place, symbolizes the spatial power, field of knowledge or evolutionary mechanisms generated by modernization. Citizens, immigrants or travelers who are in the process of converting the external to the internal can produce different degrees of local identification and results in localization. The local internalization experience, whether active or passive, will simultaneously bring a sense of belonging through public participation and collective cognition that converge with original external experiences to make connections, start dialogues and negotiations with one another. A place is therefore no longer restricted to the definition of inherent geographical and group attributes.

From pre-war, post-war to contemporary times, Taiwanese cities have experienced many baptisms in the hands of foreign political powers such as China, the West and Japan, causing their true faces to be no longer recognizable. In other words, the local identity behind Taiwanese cities are facing "delocalization" or "placelessness." crisis due to rapid changes in political power or political ideology. In addition, large-scale urban construction or land development may bring comfort and convenience to lifestyle or spatial experiences, yet these developments may easily cause problems such as land exploitation, environmental destruction, class opposition, historical loss, psychological panic or natural imbalance, leading to the weakening and disintegration of local identity. "Localness" and "publicness" are once again at an odds, with the former leading the latter's so-called progressive history and civilization priority theories coming into valid question.

Even so, the result of constantly changing, accommodating or even dismantling or demolishing appearances appropriately reflects "hybridity," ambiguity, multi-track and volatility in the historical development of Taiwan's modern cities. From the remains of buildings, streets, and squares that have survived different eras, urban memories of the past are still indelible. Artists that explore the purposes of urban civilization and modern life, as well as inhabitant situations, historical changes, and urban memories, etc. by means of brushes, images, audio-visual tools, etc. in order to explore the history of development to reflect on residential justice, or to preserve collective memory; reflecting the internalization of the experience of inhabitation in different stages. The "landscape" images constructed by different eras and generations, despite their various forms, are the most precious and important visual materials for our generation to explore the modern and contemporary cultural significance of Taiwanese urban living and the essence of public culture.

My sub-topic "Urban ‧ New Landscape ‧ Spatial Power" is intended to highlight the practical experience of urban life participation and citizenship construction through an artist's view of landscape and urban writing in order to provide a comprehensive view of contemporary urban landscape in multiple perspectives. I aim to re-think problems created by modernization and urban construction while simultaneously reflecting the construction of visual imagery in modern and contemporary

Taiwanese cities. These works of art are objects of urban observation, roaming, re-production, or discussion. Whether they are planes, stereos, installations, sound and light, or media images; each reflects the internal dialogue between different eras or creative generations and the urban spaces from which they draw inspiration, as well as depicting the characteristics of "trans-locality" in the use of media and ideas. The cultural production of "trans-locality" demonstrates a re-encoding of subject consciousness in spatial rights, landscape history and urban memory that transgresses the identification borders of state, geography, ethnicity or locality. This re-encoding differs from the concept of "de-locality" and "placelessness." produced under political control, presenting a state of contemporary art and culture that is fluid, intertwined, autonomous and of critical independence.

Change in urban history stems from both construction and destruction, symbolizing the contradictory relationship between conflicting dominant forces each exercising their power, resulting in polarizing interpretations of meaning. With the development of political systems, politicians inadvertently cause drastic changes in spatial cognition and local experiences in the process of shaping spatial power and historical images of victors by constructing political and cultural landscapes of symbolic significance through governance, discipline and domestication. However, with the change of political power and policy, the aforementioned landscape with special symbolic meaning is easily an object of deliberate removal. After several changes made to urban landscape, it becomes unrecognizable though some scenic aspects may remain. Reconstruction, demolition, or the renewal of cities are symbols of the degree to which "locality" in this exchange of power has been abandoned, resulting in "de-localization" and "placelessness.," eventually becoming the main reasons for constant loss of residential history, urban memory and local identity. (Lulu Shur-tzy Hou, Chen, Fei-hao, Eric Fok)

Secondly, although urban development can create new, effective, and more functional living environments, land reuse becomes a political capital in activating spatial governance, further forming a new urban culture and the reproduction of social memory. However, with the rise of conflict of interest and class contradiction, laborers, low-income households, the disabled or disadvantaged immigrants often become main victims of the urban food chain. The purpose of urban development should be to give local residents the opportunity to share ideals, provide a livable environment, rationally distribute economic benefits, or even rebuild civil identification. Instead, a deprivation of space or land and the expansion of capitalization have not created more social welfare, but have led to serious uneven distribution. Homelessness or indeterminate homelessness is now the biggest irony of urban development. For the disadvantaged who have lost space and been displaced, the ideal of great urban composition is just a modern, glamorous but illusory mirage. (Liao Wen-pin, Lin Shu-kai)

Moreover, industrialization introduced large scale and rapid mechanical production, changing the way humanity considers self and the world. The theory of natural selection can only be applied to primitive nature, whereas the evolution of civilization has been determined by machinery (technology), with urban development one of its major achievements. What form or elements will represent the human civilization in the appearance of urban space or architecture? What internalized spatial experience is reflected? What public awareness and locality are highlighted? Whether in face of individuals or the human world, the reproduction of urban development may be explored through a micro-historical perspective, or through a macro-narrative structure, demonstrating the differences between subjective and objective positions of the city and the individual. These differences originate from the individual's choice of position. The city may be a place to live in peace, or foreign land in another country, or an industrial phantom reflecting the rise and fall of times and the people within. (Lin, Wen-tsao, Lo, Chan-peng)

In addition, urban construction is often accompanied by geographical expansion, leading to rapid change in the urbanization of rural and forest land. Through the connectivity of modern transportation, the constant movement of people, information and materials, as well as a transgression of urban and rural boundaries have led to the gradual dissipation of localization and a faded concept of place of origin and ancestral residence. Since then, the experience of living grows from being mobile as opposed to stabilization, and the concept of home fluctuates between the polarizing ideals of temporary and permanent residences. Not only is a crossing of urban and rural areas, provinces and cities, intercontinental or national boundaries becoming daily life, hometown and foreign lands have reversed position and replaced one another, causing local concepts to become relative. Through time and space, people are encouraged to develop the adaptiveness of migratory birds, free to move between temporary and permanent residence. What urban life represents is not the limitation of a single time or place, but a result of crossing mountains, suburbs, and traveling between multiple cities. (Liu Zi-ping, Chou Tung-yen)

Finally, urban construction provides human shelter and the process of civilization after industrialization, creating the most splendid and glorious era known in human history. The constant change of city skylines is symbolic of the material desire of mankind to conquer the sky and develop survival desires in future generations. Yet the over-exploitation of natural resources has led to overproduction and environmental damage, and subsequent disasters such as earthquakes, tsunamis, floods, and air pollution are inevitable. The end of progressive human civilization is closely related to natural imbalance and ecological disintegration. The destructive power of industrial society stems internally, and cities bear its brunt. The city is a site of technological production, manufaction and use, therefore representing both the beneficiary and the victim of industrialization. However, due to dense populations and concentrated materials, should disaster arise, damages cost will be beyond our calculation. Our safe and impenetrable concrete jungle could instantly disintegrate to ashes at the moment of nature's counterattack. (Chang, Yung-ta)

These images and sounds that reflect the intricate relationship between reality and fiction, past and present, self and the other, interweave with the trajectory of interaction between an individual and its external environment including society, country, world, etc.; clearly outlining the results of discussions in individuals, urban and the spatial participation of "trans-locality." Whether visitor or urban resident, native or a foreigner, cityscapes reflect the extremely subtle power relationship between the individual and public spheres as well as geographic location, landscape history and urban memory. "Locality" and "local identity" have become an intersection of urban cohabitants, and are repeatedly recorded in different forms such as common experience and individual encounters. The city or world in which we live represents a mutually constructed place, space, and field in which people inhabit and carry out their lifestyles, a public sphere where citizens, immigrants, or travelers coexist. The "urban writing" form of art is therefore not just restricted to space, landscape, and location, but also a result of comprehensive understanding of concepts such as the temporal, ethnic groups, and the world. The exploration of self and personal domain is now gradually transferred to the collective constructive value of the public domain.

我是十九歲嫁給我先生，
家住新竹縣新豐鄉，先生大我十歲，是相親認識的，
當時台灣人對外省人的風評不佳，
父母原本反對我嫁給外省軍人，
後來發現他人蠻好的才同意。

他那時是個海軍陸戰隊的上尉，我們結婚後先住在台中，
後來分配到左營的復興新村，住了七年，
一家四口吃喝拉撒都在四坪不到的房子裡。

復興新村的鄰居關係好，
我與隔壁的太太常常坐在大樹下打毛衣、聊天，
先生在部隊帶兵，二、三個月才回家一次，
二個小孩上小學後，我就到楠梓加工廠工作，
陸陸續續上了二十幾年的班，也把小孩拉拔大了。

我們在此相遇——鍾文姬與黃克正 01
Here Is Where We Meet - Jhong Wen-ji & Huang Ke-jeng 01
2013 | 數位影像輸出 Inkjet print | 160×90cm

我們在此相遇——鍾文姬與黃克正 02
Here Is Where We Meet - Jhong Wen-ji & Huang Ke-jeng 02
2013｜數位影像輸出 Inkjet print｜160×90cm

侯淑姿 Hou, Lulu Shur-Tzy

在崇實住了四十幾年了，
這兒已是我們的第二故鄉了，
我在老家才住了十幾年，
卻在這兒住了大半輩子。

我們已很習慣這兒的生活，
搭車、上市場都很方便。
當時這一帶都沒有兩層樓的房子，
我們是第一家蓋兩層樓的，
規定不能蓋平頂，要蓋斜屋頂，
結果現在軍港邊卻蓋了十幾層的高樓。

崇實新村這兒很多整修的很好的房子，
好些都住的比我們還久，卻都得搬。
這一路來，為了保住這個家，官司已打了四年，
我們一輩子的心血都在這個房子上，
普改的兩個選項我們都沒有選，
我們也知道可能會一無所有。

我們在此相遇——鍾文姬與黃克正 03
Here Is Where We Meet - Jhong Wen-ji & Huang Ke-jeng 03
2013｜數位影像輸出 Inkjet print｜160×90cm

我的心裡很痛。
眷改的方法很蠻橫，國防部還撤消了我的眷籍，
但我的戶籍就在這個地方，當初也是國防部准我蓋的，
不然我們怎麼敢蓋。
為了蓋自己的房子，我們跟親朋好友借錢，
到前幾年才還完。

老天爺很眷顧我，孩子與媳婦都很爭氣，我已經很知足，
但能否繼續住下去仍是未知，萬一不能住下去，未來的生活無法想像，
除非不吃不喝，如何能買得起高雄的房子，
我們會一直堅持住到不能住為止。

我們在此相遇——鍾文姬與黃克正 04
Here Is Where We Meet - Jhong Wen-ji & Huang Ke-jeng 04
2013｜數位影像輸出 Inkjet print｜160×90cm

陳飛豪 Chen, Fei-Hao

北白川宮能久親王：臺灣縱貫鐵道、荒城之月與臺南神社
Prince Kitashirakawa: Taiwan South-North Railway, Moon over the
Ruined Castle and Tainan Shrine
2019｜19：07，雙頻道錄像 Two-Channel Video

陳飛豪 Chen, Fei-Hao |

低限敘事：臺灣縱貫鐵道
Minimal Narrative: Taiwan South-North Railway
2019｜攝影與歷史檔案
Photography and Historical archive
H80×W80×D3cm

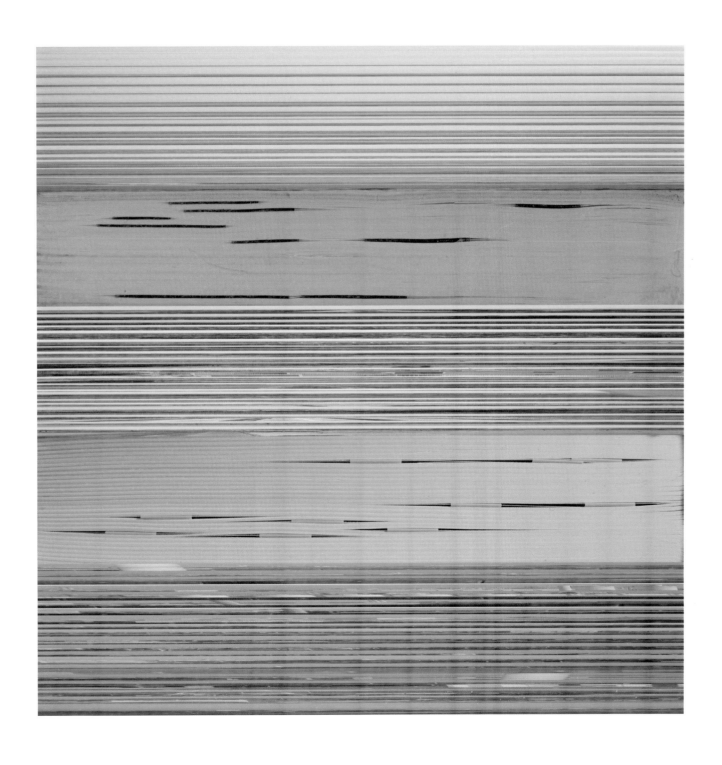

陳飛豪 Chen, Fei-Hao

低限敘事：臺南神社
Minimal Narrative: Tainan Shrine
2019｜攝影與歷史檔案
Photography and Historical archive
H38×W94×D3cm

霍凱盛 Eric Fok |

樂園1582.1　Paradise-1582.1
2016｜針筆畫 Line Drawing｜39×49cm
Yuri van der Leest 收藏
Collection of Yuri van der Leest

霍凱盛 Eric Fok

樂園1582.3　Paradise-1582.3
2016｜針筆畫 Line Drawing｜78.5×108.5 cm
蘇菲亞.C 藝術空間收藏
Collection of Sophia. C Art Gallery

樂園2047.3　Paradise-2047.3
2017｜針筆畫 Line Drawing｜30×60cm
Felita Hui Wai Yin 收藏
Collection of Felita Hui Wai Yin

霍凱盛 Eric Fok

樂園2047.7　Paradise-2047.7
2017｜針筆畫、民國木盒 Line Drawing, box｜H31×W49×D20cm
Yuri van der Leest 收藏　Collection of Yuri van der Leest

樂園 2047.16　Paradise-2047.16
2017｜針筆畫 Line Drawing｜79×108cm
Karin Weber Gallery提供
Karin Weber Gallery provide

霍凱盛 Eric Fok

樂園-Taioan　Paradise-Taioan

2014｜針筆畫 Line Drawing｜56×79cm

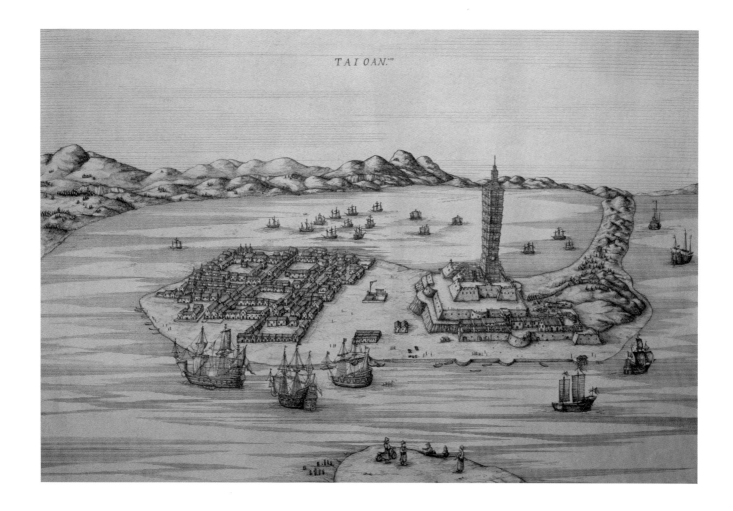

樂園-Formosa　Paradise-Formosa
2016｜針筆畫 Line Drawing｜56×79cm

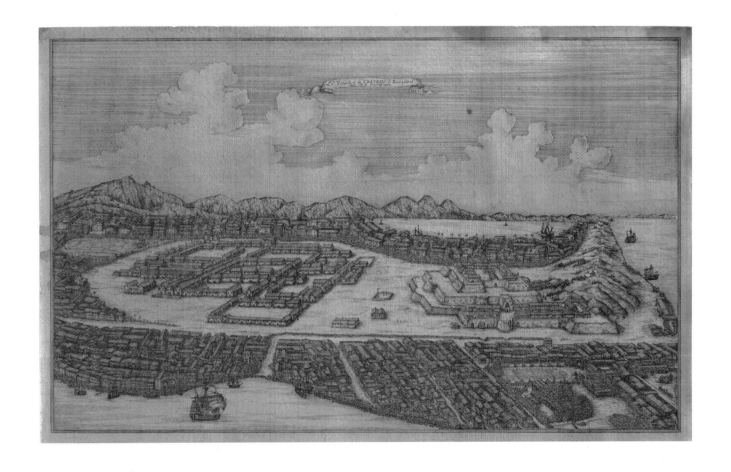

廖文彬 Liao, Wen-Pin

臺灣維納斯　Taiwan Venus
2012｜油彩、畫布 Oil on canvas｜162×112cm

我是一隻牛01   I Am a Cattle 01
2013|油彩、畫布 Oil on canvas|72.5×91cm
私人收藏 / 黑森林藝術空間提供
Private Collection/The Black Forest Art Center provide

廖文彬 Liao, Wen-Pin

我的移動城堡　My Moving Castle
2016｜油彩、畫布 Oil on canvas｜140×200cm
私人收藏／黑森林藝術空間提供
Private Collection/The Black Forest Art Center provide

臺灣維納斯（模型）　Taiwan Venus (figurine)
2012｜紅磚、水泥 Red brick, cement｜H59×W17×D16cm

廖文彬 Liao, Wen-Pin

我的移動城堡（模型）　My Moving Castle (figurine)

2016｜公仔土、油畫 Soil, Oil painting｜H17×W15.5×D10cm

我是一隻牛01（模型）　I Am a Cattle 01 (figurine)
2013｜FRP、布手套、紅磚 FRP, Gloves, Red Brick
H24×W31×D12cm

林書楷 Lin, Shu-Kai

陽臺城市文明系列──夕陽下等待入住的堡壘
The Balcony City Civilization Series-The Castle Awaits for Lodging in the Sunset
2018｜複合媒材 Mixed media｜45.5×53cm
德鴻畫廊提供　Der-Horng Art Gallery provide

林書楷 Lin, Shu-Kai |

陽臺城市文明系列——摩天下滋長的光輝歲月
The Balcony City Civilization Series-The Golden Age
Growing Under the Skyscraper
2018｜複合媒材 Mixed media｜45.5×53cm
德鴻畫廊提供　Der-Horng Art Gallery provide

林書楷 Lin, Shu-Kai

陽臺城市文明系列──被摩天大樓包圍的光輝歲月
The Balcony City Civilization Series-The Glorious Age
Surrounded by Skyscrapers
2018│複合媒材 Mixed media│130×162cm
德鴻畫廊提供　Der-Horng Art Gallery provide

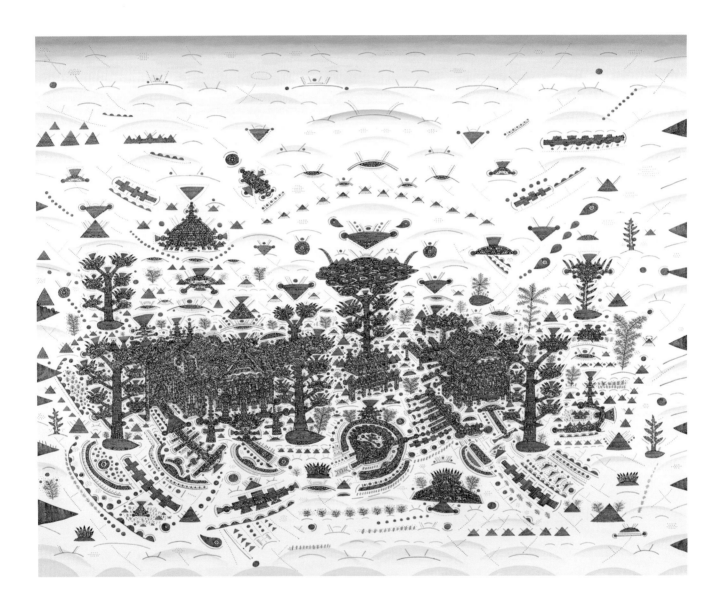

南陽路　Nanyang Road
2016｜壓克力塊、木料 Transparent acrylic block, wood blocks｜依展出空間而定 Variable dimension

林文藻 Lin, Wen-Tsao

南陽路　Nanyang Road
2018｜壓克力塊、木料 Transparent acrylic block, wood blocks
依展出空間而定 Variable dimension

人類簡史　Sapiens: A Brief History of Human Beings
2018│複合媒材 Mixed media│60×340cm

劉子平 Liu, Zi-Ping

棲居　Inhabitant
2018｜複合媒材、畫布 Mixed Media, Canvas
150×150cm

棲居　Inhabitant
2018｜複合媒材、畫布 Mixed Media, Canvas
150×150cm

劉子平 Liu, Zi-Ping

劉子平 Liu, Zi-Ping

石城　Stone City
2018｜複合媒材、畫布 Mixed Media, Canvas
150×150cm

周東彥 Chou, Tung-yen

睡與醒之間　Between Being Asleep and Awake
2013｜錄像14分58秒 Video 14' 58"
依展出空間而定 Variable dimension

睡與醒之間　Between Being Asleep and Awake
2013｜錄像14分58秒 Video 14' 58"
依展出空間而定 Variable dimension

張永達 Chang, Yung-Ta |

hyper. data-N°3 [9ch. ver.]
2014｜電腦、50吋LED螢幕（FullHD）、客製化電腦程式
50inch LED displays, computers
H400×W900×D600cm

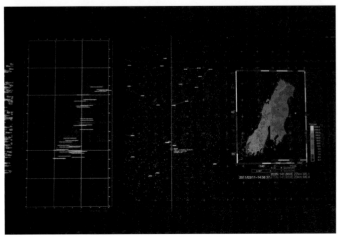

城市美學——府城藝術史話

潘安儀／策展人（康乃爾大學藝術史與視覺研究系教授）

　　城市之興因人類聚集、共居，產生了有組織、系統的城市結構與意識、風範。在此陳跡中，美術與建築最能反映城市美學歷程。因不同人、族群之居住與統理，城市美學也不斷變異；因之、城市空間蘊藏著時間軸所層疊的文化精華。透過對大臺南地區美術發展史之梳理，吾輩可了解府城美學之更替、演進。

　　臺灣最早由原住民占領，至17世紀已經有大肚王國（臺中）、瑪家王國（屏東）及大龜文王國（屏東）等，臺南還不是一個重要的據點。直至1624年，荷蘭東印度公司在上鯤鯓建立了貿易據點（臺南安平區）熱蘭遮城（Zeelandia），後又建普羅民遮城（Provintia）（臺南中西區），開啟了臺南的城市歷史。

　　1661年4月鄭成功於禾寮港（臺南開元寺附近）登陸，取得了普羅民遮城，隔年取得了熱蘭遮城，當年12月荷蘭同意退出臺灣，臺灣自此成為漢人治權所及之地。1683年康熙將領施琅在澎湖海域與鄭軍大戰，鄭軍最終投降，而清朝正式占領臺灣。隔年設臺廈道，下設一府三縣：臺灣府（臺南）、臺灣（臺南市南部）、鳳山、諸羅三縣；此為臺南為臺灣首府名稱之由來。

　　明鄭之後，強於與中原溝通的水路決定了城市經濟發展的要素，臺灣因之有「一府、貳鹿、三艋舺」盛況，其中尤以臺南總覽政、經之要。當時來臺的官宦若非堪書擅畫，亦為沾濡風雅之文人墨客。而其時名宦、巨賈聘請內陸文儒講學、教導子女乃天經地義之事，寓居臺灣的雅士與本地人士交流，延續了明鄭奠基的漢人美學脈絡，其中林朝英、林覺、莊敬夫三家獲「閩習三家」雅稱。較林朝英、莊敬夫稍晚，活耀於道光年間的林覺為民間畫師，善用禿筆、蔗粕作畫，其〈四季山水〉四屏散發出野逸疏遠之氣。

　　提到傳統繪畫，不得不重視清代高奇佩所崇尚的「指頭畫」，而臺南早期樂於此道者就有甘國寶、葉文舟、陳邦選三家。甘國寶栩栩如生的〈虎〉可看出明顯的指畫痕跡，然其指、甲與拳並用產生的意趣卻不下於用筆之畫家。葉文舟之〈指畫松〉則呈現出幾乎無法辨識為指畫的高超技法。

　　直至日本於1895年甲午戰爭後統治臺灣，臺南的城市美學沁濡在中原文化傳統之中，其中無論是官宦或其佐幕都為臺南地區留下相當可觀的文化遺產。其中擊退法軍的臺灣首任巡撫劉銘傳的〈般若波羅密多心經〉四屏，可以看出這位武將有其溫文儒雅與修行佛法的一面。《馬關條約》後，臺人與大陸聯繫漸漸受阻，皇民政策與日本教育意味府城美學進入新的階段。日人引進洋式教育，改變了以漢人為主的文化生態，並在學校傳授「圖畫」一類課程。1898年公學校及1899年的臺南師範學校進一步推動圖畫、美勞、等西式、重實用與寫生的美術課程。

　　而與傳統繪畫相關的書畫，則由所謂「南畫」及「東洋畫」等名稱及風格所取代；而

「書法」則成為「書道」。漢文化雖然沒有被完全消滅，只能依附在日本文化下的新名稱以「改良」的風貌延續，如連橫的〈弧悅雙映竹城〉及楊鵬摶的〈柳宗元詩〉。以傳統繪畫言，初期的題材與畫風似乎沒有太大改變，如林紓的〈風暖行舟〉及潘春源的〈叱石成羊〉。然如呂壁松的〈虎溪三笑〉、陳玉峰〈達摩渡江〉雖都為中國古典題材，然因日人喜好，已儼然成為日本藝術特殊性題材。

府城美學因為新式教育效應，產生全然不同面貌，以下以當時的「東洋」、「西洋」分類論之：

▎西洋

明治維新的國際化隨著其統領臺灣而帶來新的風氣，在臺灣施行工業化與建立現代教育體系，都對臺灣學子影響深遠。日本藝術家開始進駐臺灣，親授水彩與油畫之技巧，奠定了20世紀初臺灣美學轉向的基礎，其中大臺南地區又為一個重鎮，許多戰後的臺灣前輩畫家都與臺南有深厚的淵源。

當時到臺灣的日本藝術家包括了石川欽一郎、三宅克己、鄉原古統等，他們所學的歐洲現代主義對萌芽時期的臺灣藝術家擔當啟蒙的重任，往後臺籍藝術家嚮往西畫的，多循先赴日留學，若有機會再往巴黎古都的路徑。當時到日本的包括了黃土水、王白淵、張秋海、陳澄波、廖繼春、楊三郎等名家；以下則簡述大臺南地區藝術家。

堪稱「帝展第一人」的陳澄波生於1895年，即《馬關條約》簽署那年，逝於1947年，成為二二八事件中臺籍犧牲人士之一。

1907年陳澄波進入嘉義第一公學校，後來考取臺北國語學校公學師範部，時石川欽一郎在該校授課，陳澄波與之結下師生之緣。[1]1923年陳遠赴東京，進入東京美術學校，受到日本外光派名師岡田三郎助、久米桂一郎、藤島武二、山卜新太郎、田邊至等的指導，[2]對其一生的畫風影響甚鉅。這種結合後期印象派、加上藝術家主觀意識的自然主義，成為陳澄波往後最為人知的風格。

1926年陳以〈嘉義街外〉入選第七屆帝展。[3]1929年畢業後，即往上海新華藝專及昌明藝專任教，直至1933年因局勢變化而辭去教職返臺，接著即與同好組成後來在臺灣相當重要的臺陽美術協會。

與其說陳澄波受到雷諾瓦與梵谷的綜合影響（如其自述），不如說梵谷的影響更多些。[4]其〈自畫像〉（1927）濃郁的色彩反應了梵谷早年室內繪畫風格的啟發，與梵谷同樣有對生命濃烈的執著與熱情，陳澄波自畫像的背景被視為是「自創的連續花朵」，[5]其實仔細看還更像「鳳梨乾」，畫家特意強調了均等的厚度，這或許是他在日本時期對家鄉認同的一種暗示性表述。

受到外光派及梵谷影響的陳澄波勢必要走向自然，歌頌自然。他所到之處，無論是臺灣或大陸各地，都成為他寫生的對象。在風格上，陳澄波超越了外光派與後期印象派的格調而邁向更自我的表現主義風格。〈嘉義公園〉（1937）的狂逸筆法非常接近蘇丁（Chaim Soutine）的風格。畫面雖取景家鄉公園，然整幅畫完全依照藝術家心靈的韻律，頗具交響樂的節奏感與音樂性。

1941年返臺期間，陳澄波造訪了老同學廖繼春，[6]被長榮中學女子學校的西式建築所吸引，而畫了許多長榮女中校園之油畫，〈新樓風景〉即其一。畫以校園為前景，新樓為主體，左側還可看到中式傳統建築的特色。陳澄波善用濃郁的油彩在畫布上混色，形成濃稠交織的情感表現，這是他得自梵谷的啟發。

陳澄波的女婿蒲添生於1926年出生在文風鼎盛的嘉義美街（米街）。祖父為畫家兼佛像雕刻師，父親為裱畫師傅。[7]所以蒲添生對平面與立體創作都很熟悉，也是他得天獨厚之處。十幾歲就參與了「春萌畫會」，成員包括了林玉山、潘春源等後來的名家，[8]更以日本風的〈鬥雞〉一作獲得新竹美展首獎。[9]

1931年蒲添生前往日本，先在東京川端畫學校學習素描，隔年考進東京帝國美術學校日本畫科。[10]然而蒲添生嚮往雕塑一途，經友人介紹進入朝倉文夫的私塾。[11]朝倉文夫也是楊英風在日本時期的恩師，有趣的是兩位藝術家在戰後臺灣皆以雕塑著稱。朝倉文夫強調細微觀察，而創作時從記憶中展現處理肌理能力。[12]在日本時，蒲添生已是日本雕塑家聯盟之會員，且入選過「紀元二千六年聖德太子奉祝美術展覽會」。

1945年二戰結束，臺灣重回中國領土，新政府意欲去除日本殖民影響與建立臺灣與中華民國的關係，遂在積極拆除日本豎立銅像的同時，又常在其基座上重塑中華民國的偉人，蒲添生因之得到了許多委託製作。臺北中山堂前的〈國父銅像〉就是蒲添生所塑，其如〈蔣主席戎裝銅像〉、〈鄭成功像〉、〈吳稚暉像〉、〈蔣公騎馬銅像〉、〈吳鳳騎馬銅像〉等大型雕塑，可說戰後挑起塑造新政府形象的蒲添生就是其中一人。

在個人藝術創作上，蒲添生鍾愛人體，在造型、質感、動態上特別受到Aristide Maillol及Gaston Lachaise的影響，但較接近前者的自然主義風格，而孜孜不倦專研人體造型：「〔人體雕塑〕是一門藝術、一門學問，要走正確、走的澈底才可以。」[13]人體是1980年代以後蒲添生創作的重心。1981年〈亭亭玉立〉入選法國冬季沙龍，隔年〈懷念〉入選「法國獨立沙龍」百年紀念展，[14]代表了蒲添生最成熟的作品。

而蒲添生一生中兩件重要的具有東方意涵的作品是1940年的〈海民〉與47年的〈靜思〉（後於1983年重新命名為〈詩人〉。1947年的〈靜思〉雖在造型上沿用了羅丹的〈沉思者〉，其主題則是20世紀中國的一大文豪，對20世紀中國歷史影響至鉅的魯迅。戰後從1945年至50年左右臺灣掀起了魯迅熱，臺籍左翼人士與陸籍左翼人士當時營造了臺灣戰後左翼的輝煌時期。蒲添生一方面接受政府的委託製作政治人物銅像，一方面在私領域中塑造他所欽佩的文豪、一個20世紀偉大的人道主義者。

顏水龍是個在臺南出生，也在臺南奉獻最久的藝術家之一。1903年出生於紅厝村，由於父母早亡，他的童年相當艱辛。1916年顏水龍考上了臺南州立教員養成所，兩年後畢業被分發到下營公學校。[15]在校期間受到同事澤田武雄鼓勵，更堅定了他成為藝術家的意志。1920年顏水龍到了日本，經過兩年半工讀努力，進入了東京美術學校，受到藤田武二與岡田三郎助的影響較深。1927年畢業後瞬即考上該校研究所，與十三位臺籍留日藝術家共組「赤島社」畫會，其中包括與大臺南地區淵源深厚的陳澄波、郭柏川、廖繼春等。

1929年學成歸國，在臺中與臺南舉行畫展籌措旅歐經費。在歐期間，顏水龍廣泛吸收巴黎多元的現代主義風貌，又不忘古典美學的厚度，特別心儀安格爾畫風。[16]這對他日後擔綱重製小早川篤四郎臺灣歷史畫中的〈最後的離別〉，打下了很好的歐洲史詩般大幅人物群像畫的基礎。

1932年顏水龍回到臺灣，大部分時間在臺南地區奉獻於美術與工藝之發展，如1940年在臺南州學甲鄉創立「南亞工藝社」，次年組織「臺南州藺草產品產銷合作社」。又隔年在關廟鄉成立「竹細工業產銷合作社」。1945年是一個大轉變，顏水龍進入了公領域，在臺南工業學校建築工程學科擔任講師，光復後先後在臺南工學院、臺南家專任教，也曾遠赴臺北在國立藝專及實踐家專任職。[17]

　　臺灣藝術家中有兩位同時對純美術、工藝、臺灣農村、原住民關懷的是楊英風及顏水龍。前者雖非臺南人，但也參與了臺南戰後的許多公共藝術建設，諸如〈鄭成功像〉及〈古時士農工商〉等雕塑，而顏水龍則是生於斯長於斯的臺南藝術家。關於以原住民為主題，顏水龍畫過諸如「魯凱小姐」般的肖像，以簡約有力的筆法與最鮮麗活躍的色度與藝術語彙表達出樂觀的畫面。他的蘭嶼系列作品經常以蘭嶼獨木舟為對象，寫出臺灣原住民中特殊的海洋性生活之一面。〈蘭嶼風景〉簡化、近半抽象的形式，以平行、垂直的線性構圖尋求畫面的安定感，而波浪與原住民的三角形圖騰融為一體，添增了某種「工藝性」，正是顏水龍的特色。遠方的夕陽增添了整幅畫浪漫的情懷，調和了畫面幾何結構的現象。

　　前國美館館長黃才郎在記述郭柏川時提到：「府城臺南是郭柏川的出生地，是戰後他回歸的家園，更是他持續藝術創作的沃土，也是他與畫友共同發起臺南美術研究會繁花滋榮的根據地。懷抱鳳凰城的溫熱熾情，郭柏川有著深刻的情愫，畫寫臺南留給我們無盡的豐藏。」[18]

　　郭柏川1901年生於一個與藝術無關的家庭，父親在他三歲時即去逝。郭柏川跟著母親長大，臺南第二公學校（現立人國小）畢業後曾當過商行店員，後來進取入臺北國語學校師範本部就讀。[19]原來1926年到日本意圖攻讀法律，卻被藝術吸引而終生投入，1928年進入東京美術學校西洋畫科，1933年畢業。1937年郭柏川羈旅大陸，在東北各省寫生，一年後到了國立北平師範大學及國立北平藝專任教，後來也在京華藝專兼職。[20]在北平與梅原龍三郎的邂逅對郭柏川一生畫風的轉變至關重要，梅原在北平寫生多半由郭柏川嚮導。綜合梅原的野獸派色彩、黃賓虹變形主義風格、塞尚的短筆觸及用宣紙油彩作畫，成了郭柏川日後繪畫故都古城的獨特風格。1947年一場大病後，郭柏川於隔年回到臺灣療養，也正因此免於淪陷大陸。

　　回臺後，郭即環島寫生，關注臺灣風景。1950年開始，郭柏川在成大建築系任教，同時開創了「臺南美術研究會」，對南臺灣美術貢獻卓著。[21]

　　20世紀初期，日本殖民政府將總督府設在臺北意味著臺灣政、經重心的轉移，府展與後來的省展、國展都在臺北。1952年郭柏川邀集同好在臺南成立了「臺南美術研究會」並擔任會長，就是要讓臺南古都與文化重鎮地位的重要性不會在歷史趨勢中被沖淡、遺忘。郭柏川對臺南的願景不僅止於此，他還孜孜不倦地籌組臺南市美術館。雖然在他有生之年美術館未能實現，然經後輩繼續的堅持與努力，臺南市美術館成為臺灣第一所以法人為基礎的市級美術館，郭柏川的宏願終於得以實現。

　　郭柏川的〈故宮鐘鼓樓大街〉可以看到初期結合野獸派鮮豔色彩與塞尚斜角短筆法的探視，而〈赤崁樓（一）〉則看得出他奔放自在的無牽絆的成熟風格。無論在故都或是回到家鄉，郭柏川鍾情於人文遺跡的寫生，因此他留下相當數量以臺南家鄉為題材的畫作。除此之外，郭柏川對親人與家中的景致也不時描繪，其〈黃刺梅〉（1946）及〈四女為節〉則是這一面向的寫照。

　　1902年出生於臺中的貧苦農家，么兒廖繼春在家裡還是受到母親疼惜。及長，得到兄長的支持，廖繼春得以到臺北國語學校就學。此時的廖繼春靠著打工延續他對繪畫的熱忱，利用賺來的錢購買材料與書籍來自學。[22]畢業後廖繼春回鄉服務一年，旋即北上進入田村壽美畫室學習。老師回日本後，廖繼春靠著函授方式的「通信教育」繼續學習。1924年廖繼春負笈日本，考取了東京美術學校圖畫師範科，與陳澄波同班。[23]1927年3月學成歸臺後，廖繼春到臺南私立長老教中學（39年改為長榮中學校）任教。當年5月與同好共組屬於南臺灣的「赤陽會」，旋即與北部的「七星畫壇」合而為一，成為「赤島社」；成員包括楊三郎、郭柏川、陳澄波、陳植棋、顏水龍、倪蔣懷等十三人，同年又入選第一屆臺展。隔年又以兩張油畫獲得臺展免審查展出，可謂成績斐然。[24]1932年起，廖繼春連續三年擔任臺展的審查委員。1948年廖繼春離開了臺南，在臺中短居教學一年後，到臺北的臺灣省立師範學院（今之師範大學）美勞圖畫專修科任講師。

　　1948年到韓戰結束前，臺灣的局勢風雨飄搖；從廖繼春的畫作中，可以隱約察覺時局左右了他的風格。1948年的〈百合花〉屬於寫實的作品，廖繼春採用了畢卡索「藍色時期」的憂鬱氛圍。儘管如此，強烈光線打在綻開的白色花朵上，象徵了強烈求生意念。而1950年以後的作品，如〈基隆港〉則回到色彩奔放的外光、野獸風格。

　　從此以後，廖繼春走向艷麗奔放的風格，色彩逐漸取代了具象寫生，最終到達半抽象或類抽象的野獸派風格。綜觀廖繼春一生風格，〈有香蕉的院子〉及〈花園〉可作為指標。前者是他在臺南居住時的傑作，描繪自家前方庭園一景，根據潘籓對照現在景觀照片，可看出廖繼春在忠實於景物與發揮藝術家自由創作精神間取得平衡。[25]而畫家特別以香蕉點綴「南國」風情，正符合了官展所強調的「地方色彩」，因此1928年入選第九屆帝展。〈花園〉成於1962年，廖繼春已經能夠完全掌握形與色，而更加自如的遊走於半具象與抽象之間，這張畫超越了對形的執著，而成為禮讚花園中色彩艷麗奔放協奏曲，至此廖繼春已經成為一個名符其實的大師。與〈花園〉同年完成的〈風景〉（順益博物館藏），取材於臺灣有名的淡水眺望觀音山風景，同樣地顯現出藝術家的自信與用色獨特之處，外在世界只是畫家藉以移情做自我表現的媒介。

　　劉啟祥1910年生於臺南柳營，雖家族之功業可推至鄭成功時代，其曾祖父在臺灣的糖業經營才是直接奠基、影響到劉啟祥日後優渥的生活。[26]幼年時家裡有御用肖像畫家，對劉啟祥藝術萌芽階段產生相當的影響。[27]十三歲時，劉啟祥就到日本讀中學，在留美老師的指導下，扎下素描的根基。[28]1928年他進入文化學院洋畫科，其師資多屬「二科會」的元老。[29]「二科會」在日本當時屬於最前衛的洋畫藝術團體，別於早先引進的印象派，而著重於之後的野獸派、立體派、表現主義、超現實主義等新潮。所以當劉啟祥1931年返臺時，他所帶回的是嶄新的畫風。從當年他參展臺展的作品〈持曼陀林的青年〉與〈札幌風景〉[30]可看出他還在嘗試階段，呈現不同派別的影響。

　　以其優渥的經濟條件，劉啟祥啟程浪漫的藝術之都是可預期的，1932年，他偕同楊三郎到了巴黎，與已經在那的顏水龍會合。[31]由於時局變化，1935年劉啟祥返臺，短暫停留後即置產於東京木黑區，立志成為專業畫家；終於在1943年獲得「二科賞」並獲推薦為二科會會友。[32]

　　然因戰後局勢變化，臺灣歸屬中華民國，劉啟祥於1946年舉家遷回臺灣。由於他在日本的成就與地位，回臺後就擔任首屆省展的審查委員。也許個性使然，1948年劉啟祥便搬離都會區的臺南，而到當時還是鄉下的高雄。1954年更搬到小坪頂，建立起他的世外桃源。[33]雖喜離群索居，劉啟祥對推動南部美術不遺餘力，他結合了高雄、臺南、嘉義畫友，輪流舉辦展覽，成為後來的「臺灣南部美術協會」。[34]

以小坪頂作基地，劉啟祥不斷關注臺灣的自然景觀，他回臺南、到花蓮、玉山、阿里山等地寫生。1965年的〈臺南孔廟〉以紅色為基調，透過敞開的紅門為框，作了特殊的取景，孔廟的大成殿被推至遠景，且僅部分呈現，產生意趣多變的透視構圖。1969年〈玉山雪景〉的粗獷筆觸加上熟練的畫刀技巧，展現了他藝術造詣成熟的階段。信手幾筆，已準確表達出玉山寒冬冷冽風雪的氣勢；這似乎也是劉啟祥一生豪邁不羈的個性之寫照。

臺南府城美學之建構若也包括在外的臺南子弟，則更為豐富與多元。近年來沈昭良在攝影界漸居領導地位，他以關注底層常民生活著稱，尤其對電子花車如此特殊的臺灣常民美學多所著墨。2005至2014年間，沈昭良分別以當代和古典語法拍攝了〈舞臺車〉，以及〈歌手與舞臺車〉以及〈臺灣綜藝團〉三系列作品，成為大規模臺灣本土娛樂文化的視覺彙編。總量一百一十八件作品以細緻的黑白、彩色照片，從魔幻與寫實、靜謐與騷動的對照中顯現出臺灣常民與民俗文化、美學之精華。本展特選〈Stage # 20〉，是對建醮慶典的紀錄。

▎東洋

林玉山1907年生於嘉義文風薈萃的米街，與蒲添生背景一樣，家裡經營裱畫業，並聘有畫師。[35]林玉山就在家裡畫師蔡禎祥、蔣才的指導下，啟蒙了他的藝術生涯。[36]1926年林玉山十八歲，當時臺灣赴日留學的畫家已不在少數，林也順應潮流到了日本，在川端繪畫學校上學。時川端玉章已過世，其生徒岡村葵園、結城素明、平福百穗等繼續主持。[37]在日期間，林玉山便積極參與臺展，1929年返臺後依然努力不懈，終於1930年以〈蓮池〉獲得臺展特選第一席之殊榮，奠定了他在臺灣美術史上的地位。1935年林玉山二度留日，進入堂本印象的東丘社學習。[38]林玉山後來回憶東丘社對他的影響在於色彩：「在他那裡，我才真正的了解色彩應該怎樣用，過去我只知道要什麼顏色就塗什麼顏色，對於色彩的效果，色彩的生命，色的層次等等，沒有絲毫認識。」[39]也就是說，從事膠彩畫而不懂特殊色彩美學與運用幾乎等於是色盲，林玉山在堂本印象門下終於理解了色彩的奧妙。

戰爭期間，林玉山為了生活曾經以畫漫畫維生，甚或在醬油公司工作過。戰後，林玉山也歷經了二二八的驚恐，後於1950年得到靜修女中的美術主任工作而定居臺北。1951年應黃君璧之聘，林玉山到了師大，直到1977年退休為止。

戰後臺北有許多從大陸來的畫家，省展與國展中「國畫」之爭如火如荼，林玉山雖然捍衛膠彩畫，但時勢所趨，他日後的創作也漸漸轉以水墨居多。但即便是水墨，林玉山還是以寫生為主，幾乎不用皴法，而以眼睛直觀為重，可以看出日式現代美術教育對他的深厚影響。同時，他不忘色彩的奧祕，所以他畫中的色彩依然豐富，堪稱為「彩墨」，這是戰後臺灣水墨發展中的另一條蹊徑。〈雲深伐木聲〉作於1980年，表面上有傅狷夫的影子，但實際上林玉山的筆法並非公式化的皴擦，而是細心觀察自然後力求塊面結構的處理，整幅畫具有立體的量感與空氣感。同時，在墨上加以濃厚的石綠也是延續日本「琳派」技法的痕跡。總之，林玉山的彩墨是綜合了日本畫與寫生自然的結晶，為臺灣水墨樹立了新的典範。其〈農村秋晴〉

（1951）與〈高山猿啼〉（1964）更加專注在臺灣農村與名勝為寫生主題。前者描繪麻雀在稻穗上覓食情境，後者則以阿里山神木為主結構，勾劃出高山森林，幽啼鳴空的效果。

生於1911年的薛萬棟有著與其他畫家不同的養成路徑，他沒有學院的訓練，也沒有到過日本；在那個年代像這樣的業餘畫家想出頭的可能性是微乎其微，而薛萬棟得以脫穎而出為一特例。

十九歲時，薛萬棟跟著臺籍畫家蔡媽達學習東洋畫達三年之久。[40]從此他將目標設定在臺展、甚或帝展，希望透過展覽得名而一舉成名，前後入選過第六屆及第八屆臺展，於1938年更以〈遊戲〉一作榮獲「府展」最高特選「總督賞」。[41]得獎後，媒體大肆報導暨分析得獎原因與評論這張畫。當時輿論認為臺展廢除推薦制，得以讓毫無師承系譜光環的薛萬棟出線。

對於科班出身的藝術家來説，薛萬棟對膠彩畫嚴格的上色技巧尚未能完全掌握。林玉山就提到：「人家都説他不是畫畫的人，居然也得一個大獎，……那幅畫掛在『府展』裡，近看時，畫面有塗塗改改畫出來的，説髒也是有點髒。但稍微遠一點看，整個的調子非常和諧，的確別具一番風味。」[42]林玉山很厚道，卻也一語道破了從學院的角度看到這張畫的優、缺點。無論如何，薛萬棟的驚人之舉為他贏得短暫的光彩。

戰後的時局影響了薛萬棟的前途，膠彩畫（東洋畫、日本畫）在光復後被排日情緒推擠到「國畫」之外，邊緣化的困境迫使只有小學教育又不懂中文的薛萬棟另尋謀生方向，他因此成立了「萬棟畫室」專為往生者畫肖像。[43]另外，順應時代潮流，薛萬棟再拜賴敬程為師學習水墨。

開始專注在水墨畫後，薛萬棟最喜歡的題材之一就是火雞。根據潘青林的查訪，薛萬棟常去觀察寫生的地方是孔廟，以他熟練的素描技巧，描繪出火雞的特徵與細節。[44]而潘元石則回憶薛萬棟速寫火雞時，是不斷跟著火雞轉的苦差事。[45]〈全家福〉描繪火雞「夫婦」與小火雞在鐵樹旁覓食的景象。就筆墨的掌握來看，薛萬棟仰賴素描的技巧頗為明顯，因此未能發揮墨的特性與可能性，而使得畫面稍顯生硬。

前述府城美學的建構著眼於藝術家，他們個別的努力與合作形成的網絡與發展成為府城美學的基礎。但美學之建構並不只單一從微觀的藝術家個人著手，也可由主政者操控，形成宏觀大環境之趨勢、風格，甚至主題。前面的分類依據東、西兩大陣營就是日本殖民之影響，殖民時期的日本也利用藝術試圖鞏固其在臺灣治權的正當性。[46]

縱觀府城美學之沿革與變遷，宏觀的歷史因素決定了大方向與基調，明鄭時期起中原文化作為府城美學的基本元素，塑造了美術方面的特色，其中以雜糅了文人與民間水墨的書畫為主。日本殖民介紹新式教育改變了府城美學生態，大多數的學子嚮往東京為東方藝術之都，少數藉此為跳板跨足巴黎，西方古典與現代主義於焉亦成為府城美學的重要元素。而殖民者強調東洋畫取代水墨也塑造了新的東、西對壘之態勢，東洋畫遂成為府城新東方藝術主軸。

戰後國民政府在清理殖民餘孽過程中，犧牲了諸多重要的創作，從而又藉用在地藝術家幫忙塑造與圖繪新的統治階級群像；同時、藝術家為自己理想的努力也開創了府城美學的新章。

府城美學或可尊為重要的在地非物質文化遺產，但它並非是一層不變的概念。隨著物換星移，府城美學已經蛻變多次，今後還是會循著同樣的軌跡，在宏觀與微觀歷史因素的影響下，繼續豐富其內涵。

註：

1. 王秀雄，《陳澄波〈長榮女中校園〉》，臺北：藝術家出版社，2012，頁14-15。
2. 王秀雄，《陳澄波〈長榮女中校園〉》，臺北：藝術家出版社，2012，頁10。
3. 王秀雄，《陳澄波〈長榮女中校園〉》，臺北：藝術家出版社，2012，頁17。
4. 陳澄波在一九三是年發表的文章中提到：「……迄今以來的嘗試方針是雷諾瓦的線性動感、加上梵谷的擦筆與筆勢，再以富濃厚東方色彩來表現，這種畫風一直持續到現在。」轉引自工秀雄，《陳澄波〈長榮女中校園〉》，台北：藝術家出版社，2012，頁11。
5. 王秀雄，《陳澄波〈長榮女中校園〉》，臺北：藝術家出版社，2012，頁29。
6. 王秀雄，《陳澄波〈長榮女中校園〉》，臺北：藝術家出版社，2012，頁7-8。
7. 蒲宜君，《蒲添生〈詩人局部〉》，臺北：藝術家出版社，2012，頁15。
8. 蒲宜君，《蒲添生〈詩人局部〉》，臺北：藝術家出版社，2012，頁15。
9. 蒲宜君，《蒲添生〈詩人局部〉》，臺北：藝術家出版社，2012，頁15。
10. 蒲宜君，《蒲添生〈詩人局部〉》，臺北：藝術家出版社，2012，頁16。
11. 蒲宜君，《蒲添生〈詩人局部〉》，臺北：藝術家出版社，2012，頁17。
12. 蒲宜君，《蒲添生〈詩人局部〉》，臺北：藝術家出版社，2012，頁18。
13. 引自 蒲宜君，《蒲添生〈詩人局部〉》，臺北：藝術家出版社，2012，頁29。
14. 圖片請參 蒲宜君，《蒲添生〈詩人局部〉》，臺北：藝術家出版社，2012，頁51-52。
15. 黃光男，《顏水龍〈熱蘭遮城古堡〉》，臺北：藝術家出版社，2012，頁14。
16. 黃光男，《顏水龍〈熱蘭遮城古堡〉》，臺北：藝術家出版社，2012，頁17。
17. 黃光男，《顏水龍〈熱蘭遮城古堡〉》，臺北：藝術家出版社，2012，頁18。
18. 黃才郎，《郭柏川〈鳳凰城－台南一景〉》，臺北：藝術家出版社，2012，頁6。
19. 黃才郎，《郭柏川〈鳳凰城－台南一景〉》，臺北：藝術家出版社，2012，頁13。
20. 黃才郎，《郭柏川〈鳳凰城－台南一景〉》，臺北：藝術家出版社，2012，頁15-16。
21. 黃才郎，《郭柏川〈鳳凰城－台南一景〉》，臺北：藝術家出版社，2012，頁19-20。
22. 潘　褔，《廖繼春〈有香蕉的院子〉》，臺北：藝術家出版社，2012，頁13-14。
23. 潘　褔，《廖繼春〈有香蕉的院子〉》，臺北：藝術家出版社，2012，頁15。
24. 潘　褔，《廖繼春〈有香蕉的院子〉》，臺北：藝術家出版社，2012，頁17。
25. 潘　褔，《廖繼春〈有香蕉的院子〉》，臺北：藝術家出版社，2012，頁9。
26. 曾媚珍，《劉啟祥〈成熟〉》，臺北：藝術家出版社，2012，頁15。
27. 曾媚珍，《劉啟祥〈成熟〉》，臺北：藝術家出版社，2012，頁16。
28. 曾媚珍，《劉啟祥〈成熟〉》，臺北：藝術家出版社，2012，頁16-17。
29. 曾媚珍，《劉啟祥〈成熟〉》，臺北：藝術家出版社，2012，頁17。
30. 曾媚珍，《劉啟祥〈成熟〉》，臺北：藝術家出版社，2012，頁17-18。
31. 曾媚珍，《劉啟祥〈成熟〉》，臺北：藝術家山版社，2012，頁18-19。
32. 曾媚珍，《劉啟祥〈成熟〉》，臺北：藝術家出版社，2012，頁21。
33. 曾媚珍，《劉啟祥〈成熟〉》，臺北：藝術家出版社，2012，頁26。
34. 曾媚珍，《劉啟祥〈成熟〉》，臺北：藝術家出版社，2012，頁26。
35. 潘　褔，《林玉山〈蓮池〉》，臺北：藝術家出版社，2012，頁18。
36. 潘　褔，《林玉山〈蓮池〉》，臺北：藝術家出版社，2012，頁19。
37. 潘　褔，《林玉山〈蓮池〉》，臺北：藝術家出版社，2012，頁21。
38. 潘　褔，《林玉山〈蓮池〉》，臺北：藝術家出版社，2012，頁23。
39. 轉引自潘褔，《林玉山〈蓮池〉》，臺北：藝術家出版社，2012，頁24。
40. 潘青林，《薛萬棟〈遊戲〉》，臺北：藝術家出版社，2012，頁15。
41. 潘青林，《薛萬棟〈遊戲〉》，臺北：藝術家出版社，2012，頁16。
42. 謝里法，《日劇時代台灣美術運動史》，臺北：藝術家出版社，1992，頁188-189。
43. 潘青林，《薛萬棟〈遊戲〉》，臺北：藝術家出版社，2012，頁16-17。
44. 潘青林，《薛萬棟〈遊戲〉》，臺北：藝術家出版社，2012，頁26。
45. 潘青林，《薛萬棟〈遊戲〉》，臺北：藝術家出版社，2012，頁26。
46. 可從小早川篤四郎的台灣歷史畫系列中看出。

Urban Aesthetics — Art Stories from Tainan

Pan, An-Yi/Curator, Professor of the Department of the History of Art & Visual Studies, Cornell University

Convergence and cohabitation in human behavior led to the rise of cities, resulting in the organization and systematization of urban structure, consciousness and spirit. Under this trajectory, art and architecture best reflect the course of urban aesthetics. Urban aesthetics is under constant change due to the residential and unification differences in diverse people and ethnic groups; therefore urban space encapsulates the cultural essence that is accumulated through time. Through an examination of art history and its development in the Tainan area, we are able to better understand the progression and performance of Tainan aesthetics.

Taiwan was first inhabited by aboriginal tribes, and by the 17th century, the island was ruled by the Kingdom of Middag (Taichung), the Makazayazaya Kingdom (Pintung) and the Tjaquvuquvulj Kingdom (Pintung). Tainan had yet to become an important stronghold. In 1624, the Dutch East India Company established the Zeelandia trade base in Shankuhnsin (Anping District, Tainan), followed by the establishment of Provintia (Central and Western District of Tainan), marking the beginning of Tainan's urban history.

In April, 1661, Zheng Cheng-gong (Koxinga) landed at Heliao Port (near Tainan's Kaiyuan Temple) and took Provintia from the Dutch. Zheng's army took Zeelandia in the following year, forcing the Dutch to withdraw from Taiwan in December, starting an era of Han colonization in Taiwan. In 1683, Emperor Kangxi sent General Shi Lang to wage war against the Zheng army in the surrounding waters of Penghu. Zheng eventually surrendered, and the Qing Dynasty officially occupied Taiwan. In the following year Taixia Governance was established, with one central government and three counties: Taiwan Prefecture (Tainan), Taiwan County (Southern Tainan), Fengshan County and Zhuluo County; thus the origin of Tainan's being known as the capital of Taiwan.

After Ming Zheng's occupation, the waterway became crucial in communicating with the Central Plains of China and determined urban economic development. Taiwan entered a period of urbanization under the establishment of "first Tainan, second Lukang, and third Monga," with Tainan becoming the center of political economic growth. At the time, bureaucrats who came to Taiwan were either trained in painting, or well versed in the ways of the literati. High ranking officials and wealthy merchants would hire inland literary scholars to teach their children. Exchanges between local literati in Taiwan and traveling literati induced a continuation of Ming Zheng's Han aesthetics. Among the literati, Lin, Chao-ying, Lin, Chueh, and Zhuang, Jing-fu were awarded the title of "the Three Masters of Minan-pratice." Lin, Chueh, who lived in the Daoguang period and was active in a later period compared to Lin, Chao-ying and Zhuang, Jing-fu, was a folk painter and skilled in the use of bald pens and sugar canes. His four paintings in "Four Seasons Landscape" exudes a wild and alienated beauty.

When referring to traditional paintings, the "finger paintings" created by Gao, Qi-pei in the Qing Dynasty must be emphasized. Early enthusiasts in Tainan are Kan, Guo-bao, Ye, Wen-zhou and Chen, Bang-xuan. We see obvious traces of finger painting in Kan's life-like "Tiger," with the skill in his finger, nail and fist equal to painters who used brushes, whereas Ye's "Finger-painted Pines" presents superb techniques that renders his work almost indistinguishable as a finger painting.

When Japan took over Taiwan after the Sino-Japanese War in 1895, Tainan's urban aesthetics were deeply immersed in Central China's cultural traditions, with bureaucrats and their literati staff leaving a considerable cultural heritage for the Tainan region. Among them, the four screen work depicting the "Heart Sutra (Prajñāpāramitā Hrdaya sutra)" created by Taiwan's first governor Liu, Ming-chuan, who defeated the French army, illustrates the military commander's gentle and refined manner as well as his dedication to the practice of Dharma. After the Treaty of Shimonoseki, the connection between Taiwan and the mainland was gradually blocked, ushering in a new era of Tainan aesthetics with the implementation of imperial government policies and Japanese education. The Japanese introduced Western-style education, changing the cultural ecology of the Han ideology, and taught "picture" classes in school. The public school in 1898 and the Tainan Normal School in 1899 further promoted westernized art courses in painting, art and crafts, with an emphasis on practicality and sketching.

Paintings and calligraphy related to traditional arts are replaced by names and styles such as "Nanga" and "Toyoga/Dongyang Paintings;" whereas "Calligraphy" became "Shodō." Although the Chinese(Han) culture was not completely eliminated, it was only continued under the flag of "improvement" with new names attached to the Japanese culture, such as Lian Heng's "Arcs and Double Reflections on Bamboo City" and Yang, Peng-tuan's "Liu, Zong-yuan's Poems." In traditional painting, themes and styles showed no significant change in the early stages of colonialism, such as Lin Shu's "Warm Winds and Floating Boats" and Pan, Chun-yuan's "Stones into Sheep." However, Lu, Bi-song's "Three Laughs on Tiger Creek" and Chen, Yu-feng's "Dharma Crossing," though all classical themes in Chinese painting, became the subject of Japanese art due to Japanese preferences.

Tainan aesthetics entered a completely different stylistic stage as a result of new educational effects. The following is a separate analysis of "Toyo" (Japanese) and "Western" categories at the time:

Western

The internationalization of the Japanese Meiji Restoration period brought new ethos to its Taiwanese colony. Industrialization and the establishment of a modern education system had a profound impact on Taiwanese students. Japanese artists began to establish creative bases in Taiwan to teach watercolors and oil painting techniques, laying the foundation for Taiwan's aesthetic turn in the early 20th century. The Tainan area was central to this movement, as many post-war creative predecessors in Taiwan had deep connections with Tainan.

Japanese artists who came to Taiwan at that time included Ishikawa Kinichiro, Miyake Katsumi, and Gobara Koto. The European modernism they represent caused the enlightenment of Taiwanese artists in the early stages of modernism, leading artists drawn to Western paintings techniques to study abroad in Japan before making their way to the ancient capital of Paris should the opportunity arise. Japanese trained artists at the time include famous masters such as Huang, Tu-sui, Wang, Bai-yuan, Zhang, Qiu-hai, Chen, Cheng-po, Liao, Chi-chun, and Yang, San-lang. The following is a brief description of renowned artists in the Tainan area.

Chen, Cheng-po, known as the first to enter the Emperor's Exhibition, was born in 1895, the year the Treaty of Shimonoseki was signed. He died in 1947 as one of the victims of the Taiwanese 228 Incident. In 1907, Chen entered the first public school in Chiayi. Later, he was admitted to the Department of Public Administration at the Taipei Mandarin School, where Ishikawa Ichiro also taught at the time, allowing Chen to become his student[1]. In 1923, Chen enrolled at the Tokyo Fine Arts School in Tokyo, Japan, and was instructed by Japanese Pleinairism masters Okada Saburōsuke, Kume Keiichiro, Fujishima Takeji, Yamashita Shintarō, and Tanabe Itaru[2]. Their instruction had a profound influence on Chen's creative style, and a combination of post-impressionism with the artist's subjective perception in naturalism became the most renowned style of Chen's works.

In 1926, Chen's "Beyond Chiayi Streets" was selected as an entry to the 7th Emperor Exhibition[3]. After graduating in 1929, Chen went to teach in Shanghai's Xinhua Academy of Art and Changming Art School until 1933, when he resigned from the Faculty to return to Taiwan due to changes in the political climate. He then formed the Taiyang Art Association with a group of passionate artists that became quite important in Taiwan.

Chen stated an influence by the combined effects of Renoir and Van Gogh in his autobiography, though later studies show Van Gogh as the more influential[4]. His "self-portrait" (1927) and its rich color reflect inspiration taken from Van Gogh's early indoor paintings, and display the same strong dedication and enthusiasm for life. The background in Chen's self-portrait is regarded as "a continuous blossoming of self-creation,"[5] though more like "dried pineapples" upon close review. Chen deliberately emphasized thickness in his strokes, and is suggestive of an expression of his Taiwanese identity during the Japanese rule.

With Pleinairism and Van Gough's influence, Chen's work showed a gravitation toward Naturalism as well as praise to nature itself. Wherever he was, whether in Taiwan or across the mainland, natural beauty became the object of his sketches. In terms of style, Chen passed the boundaries of Pleinairism and post-impressionism, moving towards a more self-expressive style. The spontaneous brushwork of "Chiayi Park" (1937) is very close to the style of Chaim Soutine. Although the scenes are taken from a local park in his hometown, the completed work is completely synchronized with the music of the artist's spirit, with the rhythm and musical beauty of a symphony.

During his return to Taiwan in 1941, Chen visited his old classmate Liao, Ji-chun[6] and was attracted by the Western-style architecture of Evergreen Girls' Middle School, where he painted many oil paintings on the campus of Evergreen Girls. "The New Building Landscape" is one of these works, using the campus as the foreground, the new building as the main body, and traditional Chinese architectural characteristics to the left. Chen is expert at using rich oil paint to mix colors on the canvas to form a thick and intertwined emotional expression, taking his inspiration from Van Gogh.

Chen's son-in-law, Pu, Tian-sheng, was born in 1926 in the cultural center of Chiayi: Mei Street (Mi Street). Pu's grandfather was a painter and a Buddha statue engraver, and his father was a frame master[7]. Pu is therefore familiar with both one and three-dimensional creations, a unique skillset at the time. In his teens, Pu participated in the "Spring Blossom Painting Society," members of which include famous artists such as Lin, Yu-shan and Pan, Chun-yuan[8]. Pu's Japanese influenced painting "The Cockfight" — won first prize in the Hsinchu Art Exhibition[9].

In 1931, Pu went to Japan to study sketching at the Kawabata School in Tokyo. He was admitted to the Japanese Painting Department of the Imperial Academy of Fine Arts in Tokyo in the following year[10]. However, Pu found his true passion was in sculpture, and a friend introduced him to Fumio Asakura's private tutelage[11]. Asakura was also the mentor of Yang, Ying-feng, and interestingly, both artists became famous for their sculptures in Taiwan after the war. Asakura emphasizes subtle observations, while his creations demonstrate the ability to deal with textures[12]. In Japan, Pu became a member of the Japan Sculptors' Union and his work was selected for the "Japanese Imperial Year Kōki 2600 Art Exhibition for Prince Shōtoku" in 1940.

After the end of World War II in 1945, Taiwan returned to Chinese territory. The new government strived to remove all Japanese colonial influence and rebuild relations between Taiwan and the Republic of China; thus actively replacing Japanese bronze statues with those of the the

Republic of China public figures on the emptied pedestals. Pu received many commissioned projects in this period. The statue of the "Founding Father" in front of the Zhongshan Hall in Taipei is a bronze sculpture created by Pu. Others such as "President Jiang's Bronze Statue in Uniform," "Zheng, Cheng-gong Statue," "Wu, Zhi-hui Statue," "President Jiang Riding a Horse Statue" and "Wu Feng Riding a Horse Statue," and so on. Pu was one of the many artists who helped establish a public image for the new government.

In personal artistic creations, Pu loved to sculpt the human body. His work was influenced by Aristide Maillol and Gaston Lachaise in terms of shape, texture and dynamics, though closer to the naturalistic style of the former. Pu tirelessly studied the shape of the human body: "[Human sculpture] is an Art, a science, and necessary to be correct and be through[13]." The human body is the main focus of Pu's work after the 1980s. In 1981, "Slim" was selected for the French Winter Salon. In the following year, "Nostalgia" was selected for the "French Independence Salon" Centennial Exhibition[14] and represents the most mature work of Pu's career.

Pu's two most important works in oriental representation was the 1940 "People of the Sea" and 1947 "Meditation" (later renamed "Poet" in 1983). Although "Meditation" in 1947 borrowed Rodin's "The Thinker" in style, its main theme is the great 20th century Chinese writer Lu Xun, who was greatly influential in Chinese history. After the war, between 1945 to 1950, Taiwan was greatly influenced by Lu Xun's works with left-wing activists building a brilliant period of Taiwanese post-war left activism. Publicly, Pu was entrusted by the government to produce bronze statues of politicians, though privately he created the likeness of the writer he most admired, a great humanitarian in 20th century Chinese literature.

Yan, Shui-long is one of the artists who was born in Tainan and also dedicated most of his life to Tainan. Born in Hung Tsu Village in 1903, Yan's childhood was very difficult due to his parents' early death. In 1916, Yan was admitted to the Tainan State Faculty Development Institute and after two years assigned to Xiaying Public School[15]. At the school, his colleague Sawada Takeo's encouragement strengthened Yen's will to become an artist. Yan arrived in Japan in 1920 and entered the Tokyo School of Fine Arts after two and a half years of hard work. Yan was deeply influenced by Okada Saburōsuke and Fujishima Takeji and after graduating in 1927, entered the school's graduate program. He led a painting group called "Red Island Society" with 13 Taiwanese artists, including Chen, Cheng-po, Kuo, Po-chuan and Liao, Ji-chun, all of whom are deeply connected to the Tainan area.

In 1929, Yan returned to Taiwan after graduation and held a painting exhibition in Taichung and Tainan to raise funds to travel to Europe. During his stay in Europe, Yan absorbed the extensive and diverse modernist style of Paris, without forgetting the thick texture of classical aesthetics, and was especially enamored with the neo-classical style of Jean Auguste Dominique Ingres[16]. This laid the foundation for the European epic large group portrait in his later re-production of the "Last Parting" in Kobayakawa Tokushirō's painting of Taiwanese history.

In 1932, Yan returned to Taiwan and devoted most of his time to the art and crafts development in Tainan. In 1940, he established the "Southern Asia Crafts Society" in Hsuehjia Township, and the "Tainan Prefecture Soft Rush Product Production and Marketing Cooperative" in the following year. In 1942, the "Bamboo Industry Production and Marketing Cooperative" was established in Guanmiao Township. Yan experienced a major change in 1945 by entering the public domain and working as a lecturer in the architectural engineering department of Tainan Industrial School. After the Chinese regained rule over Taiwan, he taught successively at the Tainan Institute of Technology (later becoming National Cheng Kung University) and the Tainan Woman's College of Arts and Technology (later becoming Tainan University of Technology). He also went to Taipei to work in the National Taiwan University of Arts and Shih Chien University[17].

Yang, Ying-feng and Yan, Shui-long are two representatives of Taiwanese artists who heavily emphasize pure art, crafts, rural Taiwan and indigenous people in their works. Though the former was not born in Tainan, Yang participated in many public art constructions in postwar Tainan, such as the creation of "Zheng, Cheng-gong Statue," and the "Statue of Scholars, Farmers, Artisans and Merchants of Yore." Yan, Shui-long was born in Tainan, and painted aboriginal themed portraits such as "Miss Lu Kai," expressing optimism with simple and powerful brushwork in addition to vividly active color and artistic vocabulary. His Lanyu series often uses Lanyu canoes as a subject depicting the unique maritime lifestyle of Taiwanese aborigines. The simplified and nearly semi-abstract form of Lanyu Landscape seeks to stabilize the image with parallel and vertical linear composition. Waves and the aboriginal triangle totem are integrated to add a "craftsmanship" and is unique to the characteristics of Yan's artistic creations. Distant sunset glow adds a romantic feeling to the image, and reconciles as well as softens the geometric structure of the painting.

Huang, Cai-lang, former director of the National Taiwan Museum of Fine Arts, mentioned in his account of Kuo, Po-chuan: "Tainan is the birthplace of Kuo, Po-chuan and his homeland after returning from the war. It also provided a fertile ground for his continuous artistic creativity and a creative base for the Tainan Fine Art Association co-sponsored with his artist friends, allowing the association to thrive and blossom. Tainan is known as the Phoenix City, for which Kuo, Po-chuan has a deep love that is evident in his many illustrations and artistic depictions, leaving us with endless wealth in his creations[18]."

Kuo, Po-chuan was born in 1901 to a family without any background in art. Kuo's father passed away when he was three years old and Kuo grew up under his mother's care. After graduating from Tainan Second Public School (now Municipal Liren Elementary School), he worked as a store clerk and later entered the Taipei Mandarin Normal School[19].

Kuo travelled to Japan in 1926 under the intention of studying Law, but he was attracted by art and devoted his life to the arts instead. In 1928, he entered the Western Painting department of the Tokyo University of the Arts and graduated in 1933. In 1937, Kuo traveled to mainland China where he sketched in the northeastern provinces, and a year later went to teach at National Beijing Normal University and the National Beijing Art Institute, and later also worked part-time in Jinghua Art Institute[20]. Encountering Ryūzaburō Umehara in Beijing led to a crucial transformation of Kuo's artistic style. The scenes of Umehara's sketches in Beijing was mostly guided by Kuo. The combination of Umehara's Fauvism color, Huang, Bin-hong's supra-realism, Cézanne's short strokes and use of oil paint on rice paper became the unique style of Kuo's paintings of the ancient city in his hometown. After becoming seriously ill in 1947, Kuo returned to Taiwan for recuperation in the following year, and was thus spared from the communist overtake of China. After returning to Taiwan, Kuo travelled around the island to sketch, paying special attention to the natural scenery of Taiwan. Beginning in 1950, Kuo taught at the Department of Architecture at National Cheng Kung University and at the same time, created the "Tainan Fine Art Association," contributing to artistic development in Southern Taiwan[21].

In the early 20th century, the Japanese colonial government's establishment of the Governor's Office in Taipei solidified the transfer of Taiwan's political and economic core. Governmental exhibitions and later, provincial exhibitions as well as national exhibitions were held in Taipei. In 1952, Kuo, Po-chuan invited his contemporaries in the establishment of the "Tainan Fine Art Association" and served as its president, stressing the importance of Tainan's status as ancient capital and cultural center while keeping it from being diluted and forgotten under shifting political and historical trends. Kuo's vision for Tainan goes beyond the research association, as he also tirelessly advocated the establishment of Tainan City Art Museum. Although the art museum was not actualized in his lifetime, under the efforts of those who follow, the Tainan Art Museum became the first city-level art museum that is found by legal persons, finally realizing Kuo's ambitions.

Kuo's "The Palace Museum's Bell and Drum Tower Street" is an example of his early combinations of the bright colors of Fauvism and Cezanne's oblique short strokes, and the "Red House (1)" is a prime example of his unrestrained and mature style. Whether in transit or returning to his hometown, Kuo loved to paint documentations of humanity, thus leaving a considerable number of paintings under the theme of life in his hometown, Tainan. Kuo also illustrates the daily lives of his family and relatives in their homes from time to time. His "Yellow Euphorbia Milii" (1946) and "The Forth Child Wei-Chieh" are portrayals following this aspect.

Born in Taichung in 1902 to poor farmers, Liao, Ji-chun was cherished by his mother as the youngest son. After he came of age, Liao was able to attend the Taipei Mandarin School under the support of his older brother. At the time, Liao relied on working part-time to continue his enthusiasm for painting, using the money he earned to buy materials and books for self-study[22]. After graduation, Liao returned to his township to teach for one year, and immediately went north to study under the tutelage of Tamura Toshimi. After his teacher returned to Japan, Liao continued to study by means of correspondence. In 1924 Liao travelled to Japan and was admitted to the Tokyo Academy of Fine Arts, where he was in the same class as Chen, Cheng-po[23]. After returning to Taiwan in March, 1927, Liao went to teach at the Tainan Private Presbyterian High School (which became Evergreen Middle School in 1939). In May, 1927, Liao established "the Red Sun Club" in southern Taiwan with his peers, and was immediately integrated with the "Seven Stars Painting Forum" in the north to become the "Red Island Society." The society welcomed members including Yang, San-lang, Kuo, Po-chuan, Chen, Cheng-po, Chen, Zhi-qi, Yan, Shui-long, Ni, Jiang-huai and the addition of 13 other members. Liao's work was selected for the first Taiwan Fine Art Exhibition in the same year, and in the following year, two oil paintings entered the Taiwan Fine Art exhibition without critical examination[24]. From 1932, Liao served as a reviewer for the Taiwan Fine Art Exhibition for three consecutive years. In 1948, Liao left Tainan and after a year of short-term teaching in Taichung, he went to Taiwan Normal College in Taipei (now National Taiwan Normal University) to work as a lecturer in the Art and Crafts Department.

From 1948 to the end of the Korean War, Taiwan was faltered under uncertain politics and this uncertainty was reflected in Liao's paintings and influenced his style. His 1948 "Lily" is a work of realism, with Liao using melancholy effects reminiscent of Picasso's "Blue Period." Despite the melancholy touches, strong light hits the blooming white flowers, symbolizing a strong desire for life. Liao's works from 50 years later, such as "Keelung Port," return to the vivid colors of Pleinairism and Fauvism.

From then on, Liao returned to flamboyant styles, and color gradually replaced figurative sketches, eventually becoming a semi-abstract or abstract Fauvism style. The trajectory of Liao's style can be seen in "The Courtyard with Bananas" and "Garden:" the former is a masterpiece during his residence in Tainan, depicting a scene in his front garden. According to Pan Pan's comparison with current landscape photos, Liao's balance between being faithful to the scenery and exercising free artistic and creative spirit is evident[25]. The artist's special emphasis on "tropical charm" using bananas was in line with the "local color" theme emphasized by exhibition officials, and therefore selected as a participant in 1928's 9th Emperor Exhibition. "Garden" was finished in 1962, where Liao demonstrated his ability to fully grasp shape and color, and move freely between semi-figuration and abstraction. This painting transcends the boundaries of shape and completes a colorful and unrestrained concerto praising vivid colors in the garden. At this point, Liao has become a true master. "Scenery" (Shung Ye Museum of Formosan Aborigines Collection), completed in the same year as "Garden" is inspired by the famous sight in

Taiwan overlooking Guanyin Mountain from Tamsui and also shows the artist's self-confidence and unique use of color. The external world is just a medium for self-expression and empathic extension of the painter's pathos.

Liu, Chi-Hsiang was born in Liuying, Tainan in 1910. Although the family's roots can be traced back to Zheng, Cheng-gong's army, his great-grandfather's sugar business in Taiwan was the direct foundation and affluent influence in Liu's life[26]. In the beginning of his childhood, portrait painters were invited to his home and had a considerable influence on Liu's early education[27]. At the age of 13, Liu attended middle school in Japan, where the foundations for his sketch work was laid under the guidance of his American educated instructor[28]. In 1928, Liu entered the Cultural Institute's Department of Western Painting (Bunka Gakuin), where his instructors were mostly founders of the "Second Branch" art group, a prestigious, avant-garde art group in Japan at that time[29]. Their works differed from the Impressionists introduced earlier, and focused on the later trends of Fauvism, Cubism, Expressionism, and Surrealism. When Liu returned to Taiwan in 1931, he introduced a brand new style of painting to the country. From past works he exhibited at the Taiwan Fine Art Exhibition "Man with Mandolin" and "Sapporo Landscape"[30], traces of experimentation and the influence of different artistic factions remain obvious.

With his superb economic conditions, Liu's pilgrimage to the city of light was inevitable. In 1932, he went to Paris with Yang, San-lang and met with Yan, Shui-long who was already there[31]. Due to changes in the political climate, Liu returned to Taiwan in 1935. After a short stay, Liu purchased property in Meguro, Tokyo and decided to become a professional painter. He finally won the "Second Branch Award" in 1943 and was recommended as a member of the Second Branch art group[32].

Due to post-war changes, Taiwan was returned to the Republic of China, and Liu moved to Taiwan in 1946. Due to his achievements and status in Japan, he returned to Taiwan as a reviewing committee member of the first provincial exhibition. Liu moved from the metropolitan area of Tainan in 1948 under personal reasons, and moved to the still rural Kaohsiung. In 1954, he moved to Xiaoping Peak to establish a secluded paradise[33]. Although he prefers isolation, Liu spared no effort in promoting the art of southern Taiwan, combining his peers in Kaohsiung, Tainan, and Chiayi to hold consecutive exhibitions and later becoming the "Southern Taiwan Art Association.[34]"

With Xiaoping Peak as his base, Liu paid diligent attention to the Taiwanese natural landscape. He constantly returned to Tainan and went to Hualien, Yushan and Alishan to sketch. In 1965, his "Tainan Confucius Temple" was based on the color red and framed by an open red door that created special composition. The Confucius Temple's Dacheng Hall was set as a distant view and only partially presented, resulting in a versatile perspective and transparent composition. In 1969, the rough brushstrokes of "Yushan Views of Snow" and the skillful use of palette knifes in the painting show the maturity of his artistic growth. With few strokes, Liu accurately expressed the momentum of the cold winter snow in Yushan and seems an accurate portrayal of Liu's unrestrained personality.

The construction of Tainan aesthetics are even richer and more diverse when including the accomplishments of Tainan artists who live elsewhere. In recent years, Shen, Chao-liang has gradually gained a leading position in the photography industry. Shen is famous for focusing on the lives of the mundane and the working masses; especially emphasizing Taiwanese folk aesthetics such as electronic floats. Between 2005 and 2014, Shen photographed three series of works, namely, "Stage Car," "Singer on Stage Cars" and "Taiwanese Folk Arts Group" in contemporary and classical composition, becoming a large-scale visual compilation of the Taiwanese entertainment culture. A total of 118 works in meticulous black and white, color photos, form Shen's contrast between magic and realism, tranquility and turmoil that show the essence of Taiwan's ordinary people and folk culture aesthetics. Our special exhibition "Stage # 20" is a record of the Jianjiao Ceremonial Festival.

▎ Toyo (Japanese)

Lin, Yu-shan was born in 1907 in Mi Street, Chiayi's cultural center, and shares the same background with Pu, Tian-sheng. Lin's family is in the framing industry with painters under their employment[35]. Lin's artistic career started under the guidance of painters Cai, Zhen-xiang and Jiang Cai, both of employed by his family[36]. In 1926, Lin turned 18 and at the time, Taiwanese painters studying in Japan were no longer a minority. Lin also followed the trend to study in Japan and went to study at Kawabata Painting School. Gyokushō Kawabata had passed away, though his students, Okamura Kien, Yuuki Somei, and Hirafuku Hiyakusui continue to teach[37]. During his stay in Japan, Lin actively participated in Taiwanese exhibitions. After returning to Taiwan in 1929, he continued his endeavors and in 1930, won the first place in the Taiwan Fine Art exhibition with "Lily Pond" and established his position in the history of Taiwanese art. In 1935, Lin went to Japan for a second time and entered Inshō Dōmoto's Higashigaoka Society[38]. Lin later recalled Higashigaoka Society's influence as color: "There I really understood how color should be used. In the past, I only knew what color to apply and had no understanding of the effect of color, the life of color, levels of color, and so on.[39]" That is to say, engaging in Nihonga without understanding its special color aesthetics and application is almost equal to being color blind; therefore Lin finally understood the subtlety of color under Higashigaoka Society's tutelage.

During the war, Lin drew comics as a living, and even worked in soy sauce companies. After the war, Lin also experienced the horror of the 228 Incident. In 1950, he worked as an art director in Blessed Imelda's School and settled in Taipei. In 1951, Huang, Chun-pi invited Lin to teach at the National Taiwan Normal University until his retirement in 1977.

After the war, there were many painters from the mainland came to Taipei and caused constant friction in provincial and national exhibitions in "Chinese paintings" categories. Although Lin defended Nihonga, popular trends led his future creations to gradually turn to ink and Chinese watercolor. Even when painting with ink, Lin focused on sketches, almost never using wrinkle methods, but using his initial perception: illustrating the profound influence of Japanese modern art education. At the same time, he did not forget the mystery of color, so his paintings were still rich in color and can be called "color ink," another direction in the development of Taiwanese ink painting after the war. "Sounds of the Woodcutter Deep in the Clouds" was created in 1980, and though there is a shadow of Fu, Juan-fu on the surface, Lin's brushwork refrained from systematic wrinkling, but demonstrated a careful observation of nature and strived to deal with block structures, lending the painting a three-dimensional sense of volume and air. At the same time, the thick stone green on the ink is also continuation of the Japanese "Rinpa School" technique. In short, Lin color ink is a combination of Japanese painting and natural sketches, setting a new model for Taiwanese watercolor and ink. His "Autumn Day in A Rual Village" (1951) and "Monkeys in the Mountains" (1964) are more focused on rural and scenic spots in Taiwan. The former depicts sparrows feeding on ears of rice, while the latter uses the scared tree in Alishan as its main structure, outlining the effects of isolated mountains and echoing sound.

Born in 1911, Hsueh, Wan-tung tread a different path from other painters. He did not have institutional training nor has he been to Japan. In that period, the possibility of success in an amateur painter was almost non-existent, yet Hsueh was able to stand out as a unique case.

At the age of 19, Hsueh studied Japanese painting with Taiwanese painter Tsai, Ma-da for 3 years[40]. Since then, his goal was to become famous by entering the Taiwan Fine Art Exhibition, or even the Emperor Exhibition. He was selected for the 6th and 8th Taiwan Fine Art Exhibitions, and in 1938, won the "Governor Award," the highest choice in the "Taiwan Fine Art Exhibition[41]." After the awards, the media reported and analyzed the reasons for his victory, whereas public opinion believed that abolishing the recommendation system in Taiwan Fine Art Exhibitions allowed Hsueh, with no educational pedigree, to qualify.

To artists with institutional training, Hsueh had not fully grasped the strict Nihonga coloring techniques. Lin, Yu-shan mentioned: "Everyone said that he is not a painter, but he's won a big prize,... The painting that is hung in the Taiwan Fine Art Exhibition' has traces of mistakes and amendments upon close inspection and is a bit dirty honestly. But from a distance, the complete effect is harmonious, and shows different flavor.[42]" Lin was conservative, but spoke of the advantages and shortcomings of this painting from the college's perspective. In any case,

Hsueh amazing achievement gave him a short period of glory.

The post-war situation affected Hsueh's future. Eastern Gouache (Toyoga / Dongyang Painting, Japanese Painting) was pushed out of the "Chinese painting" category after the war, marginalizing the primary school educated, non-Mandarin speaking Hsueh to change directions in order to survive. He established the "Wantung Studio" to paint portraits for the deceased[43]. Furthermore, to keep with current trends, Hsueh went on to study ink and water-color with Lai, Ching-cheng.

After focusing on ink, one of Hsueh's favorite subjects are turkeys. According to Pan, Qing-lin's interview, Hsueh often went to the Confucius Temple to create sketches. He used his skillful sketching techniques to draw the characteristics and details of the turkey[44], whereas Pan, Yuan-shih recalled that when Hsueh sketched turkeys, he followed the turkey around tirelessly[45]. "Family" depicts the scene of a turkey "couple" and a small turkey foraging by the iron tree. Judging from the mastery of ink and brush, Hsueh's reliance on sketching is quite obvious, failing to exercise the characteristics and possibilities of ink, making the painting slightly stiff.

The construction of the aforementioned Tainan aesthetics focuses on artists, and the network and development formed by their individual efforts and cooperation has become the foundation of Tainan aesthetics. However, the construction of aesthetics is not only an individual effort from the artist's microscopic perspective, but is also controlled by the government to form trend, style and even themes in the macro environment. The previous classification was based on Japanese and Western influence during Japanese colonialization. Colonial Japan also used art to consolidate its legitimacy in Taiwan[46].

Throughout the evolution and changes in Tainan aesthetics, macroscopic historical factors determine its general direction and tone. From the Ming Zheng era, the Central Plains culture formed the basis of Tainan aesthetics, shaping the characteristics of art which includes the ink and watercolor works of both literati and folk painters. The Japanese colonial rule introduced new education that changed Tainan aesthetics, with most students yearning for Tokyo as the capital of oriental art and a select few using Tokyo as a springboard to Paris. Western classical and modern influence became an important element of Tainan aesthetics, whereas the colonists emphasized the replacement of ink painting with Nihonga paintings shaped a new east-west confrontation, and Nihonga painting became the main axis of Tainan's New Oriental Art.

After the war, the National Government sacrificed many important works in the process of cleaning up colonial residues, and then used local artists to help sculpt and paint new ruling class groups. At the same time, these artists created a new chapter in Tainan aesthetics to fit their ideals.

Tainan aesthetics is seen as an important, intangible cultural heritage, but it is not a constant concept. In a constant, temporal flux, Tainan aesthetics has been transformed many times. In the future, it will follow the same trajectory and continue its enrichment under the influence of macro and micro historical factors.

1. Wang, Xiu-xiong. "Chen, Cheng-po, 'Evergreen Girls' Middle School'." Taipei: Artists Publishing Co., 2012, p. 14-15.
2. Wang, Xiu-xiong. "Chen, Cheng-po, 'Evergreen Girls' Middle School'." Taipei: Artists Publishing Co., 2012, p. 10.
3. Wang, Xiu-xiong. "Chen, Cheng-po, 'Evergreen Girls' Middle School'." Taipei: Artists Publishing Co., 2012, p. 17.
4. "Chen, Cheng-po mentioned in an article published in the year of 1993: '...my attempts so far has been the linear motion of Renoir, together with Van Gogh's brush and gesture, expressed in rich oriental colors. The trend has continued until now." Quoted from Wang, Xiu-xiong. "Chen, Cheng-po, 'Evergreen Girls' Middle School'." Taipei: Artists Publishing Co., 2012, p. 11.
5. Wang, Xiu-xiong. "Chen, Cheng-po, 'Evergreen Girls' Middle School'." Taipei: Artists Publishing Co., 2012, p. 29.
6. Wang, Xiu-xiong. "Chen, Cheng-po, 'Evergreen Girls' Middle School'." Taipei: Artists Publishing Co., 2012, p. 7-8.
7. Pu, Yi-jun. "Pu, Tian-sheng, 'Parts of the Poet'." Taipei: Artists Publishing Co., 2012, p. 15.
8. Pu, Yi-jun. "Pu, Tian-sheng, 'Parts of the Poet'." Taipei: Artists Publishing Co., 2012, p. 15.
9. Pu, Yi-jun. "Pu, Tian-sheng, 'Parts of the Poet'." Taipei: Artists Publishing Co., 2012, p. 15.
10. Pu, Yi-jun. "Pu, Tian-sheng, 'Parts of the Poet'." Taipei: Artists Publishing Co., 2012, p. 16.
11. Pu, Yi-jun. "Pu, Tian-sheng, 'Parts of the Poet'." Taipei: Artists Publishing Co., 2012, p. 17.
12. Pu, Yi-jun. "Pu, Tian-sheng, 'Parts of the Poet'." Taipei: Artists Publishing Co., 2012, p. 18.
13. Pu, Yi-jun. "Pu, Tian-sheng, 'Parts of the Poet'." Taipei: Artists Publishing Co., 2012, p. 29.
14. Image from Pu, Yi-jun. "Pu, Tian-sheng, 'Parts of the Poet'." Taipei: Artists Publishing Co., 2012, p. 51-52.
15. Huang, Guang-nan. "Yan, Shui-long, 'Zeelandia Castle.'" Taipei: Artists Publishing Co., 2012, p. 14.
16. Huang, Guang-nan. "Yan, Shui-long, 'Zeelandia Castle.'" Taipei: Artists Publishing Co., 2012, p. 17.
17. Huang, Guang-nan. "Yan, Shui-long, 'Zeelandia Castle.'" Taipei: Artists Publishing Co., 2012, p. 18.
18. Huang, Cai-lang. "Kuo, Po-chuan, 'Phoenix City - Tainan Scenery'." Taipei: Artists Publishing Co., 2012, p. 6.
19. Huang, Cai-lang. "Kuo, Po-chuan, 'Phoenix City - Tainan Scenery'." Taipei: Artists Publishing Co., 2012, p. 13.
20. Huang, Cai-lang. "Kuo, Po-chuan, 'Phoenix City - Tainan Scenery'." Taipei: Artists Publishing Co., 2012, p. 15-16.
21. Huang, Cai-lang. "Kuo, Po-chuan, 'Phoenix City - Tainan Scenery'." Taipei: Artists Publishing Co., 2012, p. 19-20.
22. Pan, Fan. "Liao, Ji-chun. 'Courtyard with Bananas.'" Taipei: Artists Publishing Co., 2012, p. 13-14.
23. Pan, Fan. "Liao, Ji-chun. 'Courtyard with Bananas.'" Taipei: Artists Publishing Co., 2012, p. 15.
24. Pan, Fan. "Liao, Ji-chun. 'Courtyard with Bananas.'" Taipei: Artists Publishing Co., 2012, p. 17.
25. Pan, Fan. "Liao, Ji-chun. 'Courtyard with Bananas.'" Taipei: Artists Publishing Co., 2012, p. 9.
26. Zeng, Mei-zhen. "Liu, Chi-hsiang. 'Mature'." Taipei: Artists Publishing Co., 2012, p. 15.
27. Zeng, Mei-zhen. "Liu, Chi-hsiang. 'Mature'." Taipei: Artists Publishing Co., 2012, p. 16.
28. Zeng, Mei-zhen. "Liu, Chi-hsiang. 'Mature'." Taipei: Artists Publishing Co., 2012, p. 16-17.
29. Zeng, Mei-zhen. "Liu, Chi-hsiang. 'Mature'." Taipei: Artists Publishing Co., 2012, p. 17.
30. Zeng, Mei-zhen. "Liu, Chi-hsiang. 'Mature'." Taipei: Artists Publishing Co., 2012, p. 17-18.
31. Zeng, Mei-zhen. "Liu, Chi-hsiang. 'Mature'." Taipei: Artists Publishing Co., 2012, p. 18-19.
32. Zeng, Mei-zhen. "Liu, Chi-hsiang. 'Mature'." Taipei: Artists Publishing Co., 2012, p. 21.
33. Zeng, Mei-zhen. "Liu, Chi-hsiang. 'Mature'." Taipei: Artists Publishing Co., 2012, p. 26.
34. Zeng, Mei-zhen. "Liu, Chi-hsiang. 'Mature'." Taipei: Artists Publishing Co., 2012, p. 26.
35. Pan, Fan. "Lin, Yu-shan 'Lily Pond'." Taipei: Artists Publishing Co., 2012, p. 18.
36. Pan, Fan. "Lin, Yu-shan 'Lily Pond'." Taipei: Artists Publishing Co., 2012, p. 19.
37. Pan, Fan. "Lin, Yu-shan 'Lily Pond'." Taipei: Artists Publishing Co., 2012, p. 21.
38. Pan, Fan. "Lin, Yu-shan 'Lily Pond'." Taipei: Artists Publishing Co., 2012, p. 23.
39. Cited from Pan, Fan. "Lin, Yu-shan 'Lily Pond'." Taipei: Artists Publishing Co., 2012, p. 24.
40. Pan, Qing-lin. "Hsueh, Wan-tung 'Game'." Taipei: Artists Publishing Co., 2012, p. 15.
41. Pan, Qing-lin. "Hsueh, Wan-tung 'Game'." Taipei: Artists Publishing Co., 2012, p. 16.
4.2 Shaih, Li-fa. "The History of Taiwanese Art Movement in Japanese Colonial Times." Taipei: Artists Publishing Co., 1992, pp. 188-189.
43. Pan, Qing-lin. "Hsueh, Wan-tung 'Game'." Taipei: Artists Publishing Co., 2012, p. 16-17.
44. Pan, Qing-lin. "Hsueh, Wan-tung 'Game'." Taipei: Artists Publishing Co., 2012, p. 26.
45. Pan, Qing-lin. "Hsueh, Wan-tung 'Game'." Taipei: Artists Publishing Co., 2012, p. 26.
46. As seen in Kobayakawa Tokushirō's Taiwanese Historical Series.

四季山水（四屏）　Four Seasons Landscape
年代待考 Date Unknown｜水墨、紙本
Ink on paper｜97×23.5cm×4
臺南市美術館典藏（楊文富家族捐贈）
Collection of Tainan Art Museum (donate from Yang, Wen-fu family)

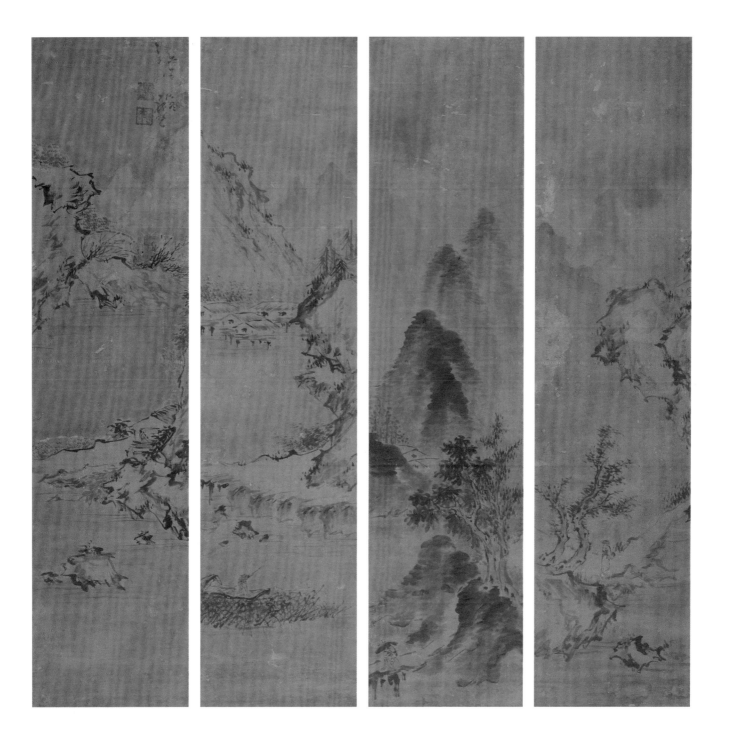

甘國寶 Kan, Guo-Bao

虎　Tiger
年代待考 Date Unknown
水墨、紙本 Ink on paper｜140×44cm
財團法人大牛兒童城文化推廣基金會藏
Collection of Louitech Children's Culture
Progressive Foundation

東崗天鏡兩煥然 千尺蟠虬
墜悉濺 六十餘年桀骜漥
知我更老於松
歲辰喜倣青藤居士筆意
藕香葉文舟摭畫

指畫松條幅　Finger-painted Pines
年代待考 Date Unknown｜水墨、紙本
Ink on paper｜136×36cm
財團法人大牛兒童城文化推廣基金會藏
Collection of Louitech Children's Culture Progressive
Foundation

陸鼎 Lu, Ding

左腕書條幅　Calligraphy by Left Hand
年代待考 Date Unknown｜墨、紙本
Ink on paper｜177×38cm×2
臺南市美術館典藏（楊文富家族捐贈）
Collection of Tainan Art Museum
(donate from Yang, Wen-fu family)

倪湜 Ni, Shih

左腕書條幅　Calligraphy by Left Hand
年代待考 Date Unknown｜墨、紙本 Ink on paper｜209×45cm
臺南市美術館典藏（楊文富家族捐贈）
Collection of Tainan Art Museum (donate from Yang, Wen-fu family)

103

蕭聯魁 Hsiao, Lian-Kuei

行書斗方　Calligraphy in Semi-cursive Script
年代待考 Date Unknown｜墨、紙本 Ink on paper｜39×42cm
臺南市美術館典藏　Collection of Tainan Art Museum

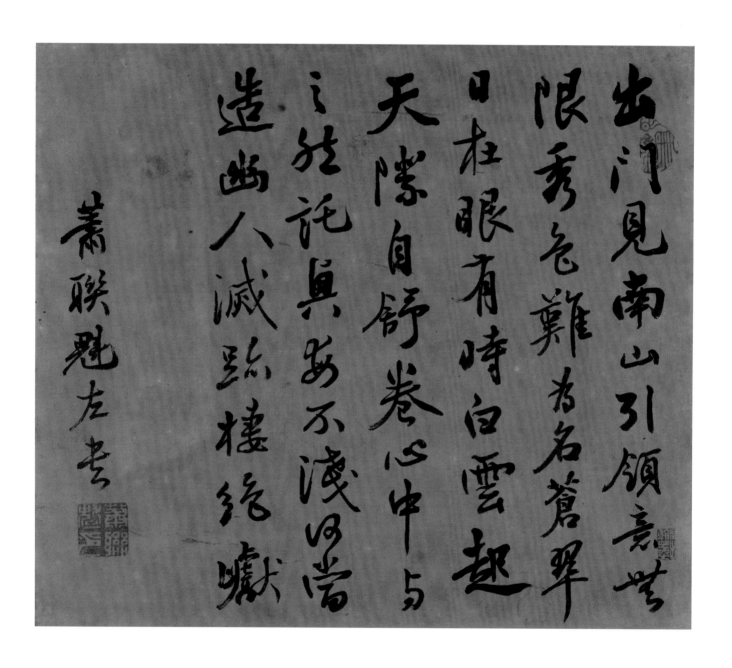

行書橫軸　Calligraphy in Semi-cursive Script
年代待考 Date Unknown｜墨、紙本
Ink on paper｜59×85cm
臺南市美術館典藏（楊文富家族捐贈）
Collection of Tainan Art Museum
（donate from Yang, Wen-fu family）

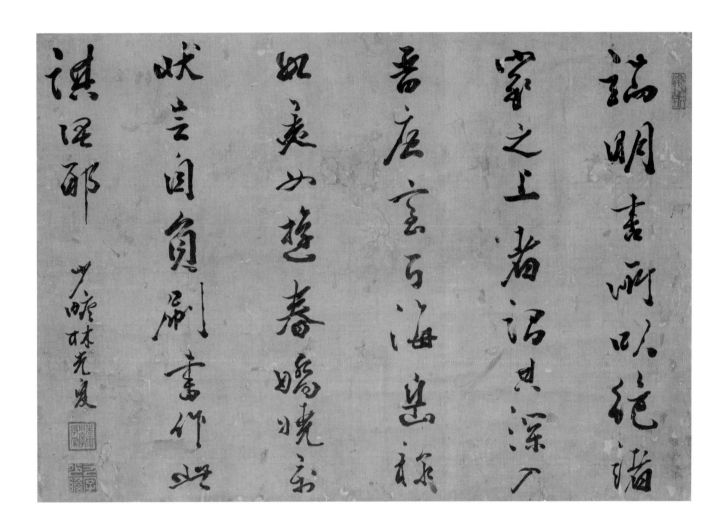

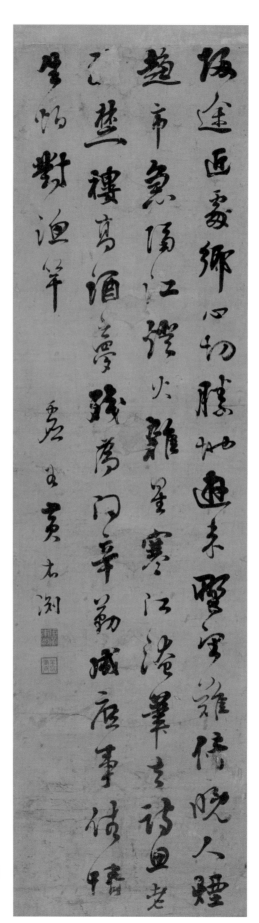

行書　Calligraphy in Semi-cursive Script
年代待考 Date Unknown
墨、紙本 Ink on paper｜196×50cm
臺南市美術館典藏（楊文富家族捐贈）
Collection of Tainan Art Museum
(donate from Yang, Wen-fu family)

般若波羅密多心經（四屏）
Heart Sutra (Prajñāpāramitā Hrdaya sutra)
年代待考 Date Unknown
水墨、宣紙 Ink on paper｜172×47cm×4
財團法人何創時書法藝術基金會藏
Collection of HCS Calligraphy Arts Foundation

般若波羅蜜多心經觀自在菩薩行深般若波
羅蜜多時照見五蘊皆空度一切苦厄舍利子
色不異空空不異色色即是空空即是色受想
行識亦復如是舍利子是諸法空相不生不滅不

垢不淨不增不減是故空中無色無受想行識
無眼耳鼻身意無色聲香味觸法無眼界乃至
無意識界無無明亦無無明盡乃至無老死亦無
老死盡無苦集滅道無智亦無得以無所得

故菩提薩埵依般若波羅蜜多故心無罣礙無罣
礙故無有恐怖遠離顛倒夢想究竟涅槃三世
諸佛依般若波羅蜜多故得阿耨多羅三藐三菩
提故知般若波羅蜜多是大神咒是大明咒無上咒

是無等等咒能除一切苦真實不虛故說般若波
羅蜜多咒即說咒曰揭諦揭諦波羅揭諦波羅僧
揭諦菩提薩婆訶揭諦揭諦波羅揭諦波羅僧
揭諦菩提薩婆訶空

兩孫仁兄大人雅屬
省三劉銘傳書

東寧女子陳氏 Tong-lêng Lady, Chen

盧雁圖　橫軸　The Painting of Flying Gooses (TBC)
年代待考 Date Unknown｜水墨設色、紙本
Ink and color on paper｜34×96cm
財團法人大牛兒童城文化推廣基金會藏
Collection of Louitech Children's Culture Progressive Foundation

曾茂西 Tseng, Mao-Hsi

河鴨圖橫幅　A Duck Swimming Among The Lotus
年代待考 Date Unknown
水墨、紙本 Ink on paper｜130×190cm
臺南市美術館典藏（楊文富家族捐贈）
Collection of Tainan Art Museum
(donate from Yang, Wen-fu family)

林紓 Lin, Shu

風暖行舟　Warm Winds and Floating Boats
年代待考 Date Unknown
水墨、紙本 Ink on paper｜124×46cm
財團法人大牛兒童城文化推廣基金會藏
Collection of Louitech Children's Culture
Progressive Foundation

虎溪三笑　Three Laughs on Tiger Creek
年代待考 Date Unknown
水墨設色、紙本
Ink on paper｜128×54cm
財團法人大牛兒童城文化推廣基金會藏
Collection of Louitech Children's Culture
Progressive Foundation

王爇琛 Wang, Hsian-Chen

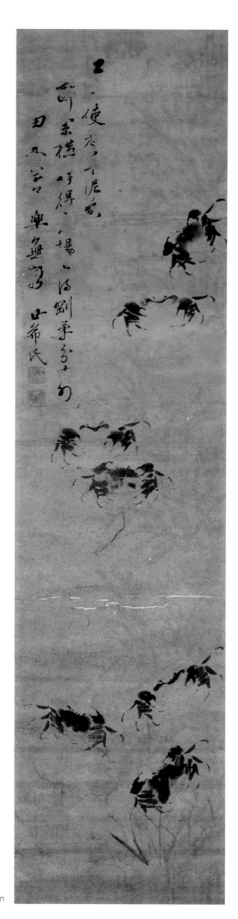

墨蟹條幅　Inked Crabs

年代待考 Date Unknown

水墨、紙本 Ink on paper｜120×30cm

財團法人大牛兒童城文化推廣基金會藏

Collection of Louitech Children's Culture Progressive Foundation

叱石成羊中堂
Stones into Sheep
年代待考 Date Unknown
水墨、紙本
Ink on paper｜135×67cm
財團法人大牛兒童城文化推廣基
金會藏
Collection of Louitech Children's
Culture Progressive Foundation

陳玉峰 Chen, Yu-Feng

達摩渡江　Dharma Crossing

年代待考 Date Unknown

水墨、紙本 │ Ink on paper │ 136×54cm

財團法人大牛兒童城文化推廣基金會藏

Collection of Louitech Children's Culture

Progressive Foundation

連橫 Lian, Heng

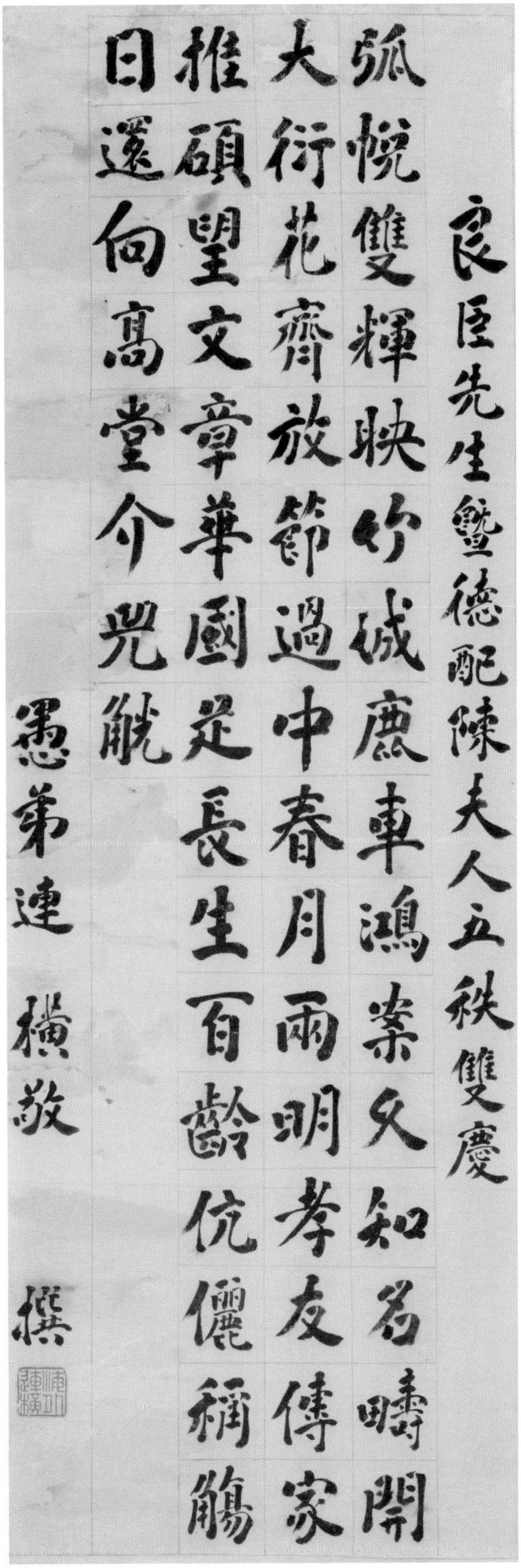

弧悅雙輝映竹城

良匠先生鑒德配陳夫人五秩雙慶

弧悅雙輝映竹城廳車鴻案攵知苦疇開
大衍花齋放節過中春月雨明孝友傳家
推頏望文章華國延長生百齡伉儷稱鶼
日還向高堂介覘骹

愚弟連橫敬 撰

弧悅雙輝映竹城
Arcs and Double Reflections on Bamboo City
年代待考 Date Unknown｜墨、紙本
Ink on paper｜96×32.5cm
財團法人何創時書法藝術基金會藏
Collection of HCS Calligraphy Arts Foundation

楊鵬摶 Yang, Peng-Tuan

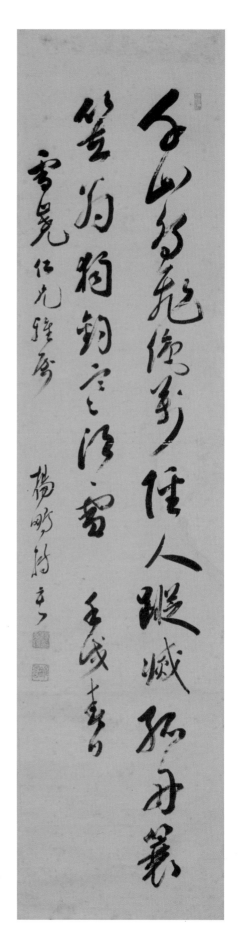

柳宗元詩　Liu, Zong-yuan's Poems

年代待考 Date Unknown

墨、紙本 Ink on paper｜184.5×44.5cm

臺南市美術館典藏（楊文富家族捐贈）

Collection of Tainan Art Museum

(donate from Yang, Wen-fu family)

自畫像　Self-portrait
1928｜油彩、畫布 Oil on Canvas｜41×31.5cm
陳澄波文化基金會藏
Collection of Chen Cheng-po Cultural Foundation

蔡草如 Tsai, Cao-Ju

赤坎朝旭　Sunrise at Chih-Kan Tower
1958｜膠彩　Gouache on Silk｜70×86cm
臺南市美術館典藏　Collection of Tainan Art Museum

蔡草如 Tsai, Cao-Ju

行書對聯

Calligraphy in Semi-cursive Script

1989｜墨、紙本

Ink on paper｜136×32cm×2

臺南市美術館典藏

Collection of Tainan Art Museum

薛萬棟 Hsueh, Wan-Tung

全家福　Family
1980｜重彩、紙本 Ink and color on Paper｜75.5×102cm
臺南市美術館典藏　Collection of Tainan Art Museum

蒲添生 Pu, Tian-Sheng |

詩人　The Poet
1947｜青銅 Bronze｜H72×W38×D28cm
蒲添生雕塑紀念館藏
Collection of P.T.S. Sculpture Memorial Museum

林玉山 Lin, Yu-Shan

農村秋晴　Autumn Day in A Rural Village
1951｜水墨、淡彩、紙本
Ink and color on Paper｜69.7×80.4cm
林柏亭提供　Lin, Po-Ting provide

高山猿啼
Monkeys in the Mountains
1964｜水墨、紙本
Ink on paper｜136×66cm

廖繼春 Liao, Ji-Chun

風景 Landscape
1962｜油彩、畫布Oil on Canvas｜43.5×51cm
順益台灣原住民博物館典藏
Collection of Shung Ye Museum of Formosan Aborigines

黃刺梅　Yellow Euphorbia Milii
1946｜油彩、宣紙 Oil on Paper｜40×31cm
家屬收藏　Artist's family collection

郭柏川 Kuo, Po-Chuan

四女為節　The forth child, Wei-Chieh
1946｜油彩、宣紙 Oil on Paper｜32×25cm
家屬收藏　Artist's family collection

玉山雪景　Yushan Views of Snow
1969｜油彩、畫布 Oil on Canvas｜76×86cm
私人收藏　Private collection

金潤作 Chin, Jun-Tso

觀音落日 II Sunset at Mountain Kuan Yin II
1974｜油彩、畫布 Oil on Canvas｜73×91cm
臺南市美術館典藏 Collection of Tainan Art Museum

鳳凰小姐　Lady Fong Huang
1982｜油彩、畫布 Oil on Canvas｜108×80.8cm
臺南市美術館典藏　Collection of Tainan Art Museum

張炳堂 Chang, Ping-Tang

南鯤鯓廟宇　Nan Kun Shen Temple
待考 unknown｜油彩、畫布
Oil on Canvas｜72.5×91cm
臺南市美術館典藏 Collection of Tainan Art Museum
Collection of Tainan Art Museum

籬畔　Turkeys Beside the Fence
2003｜水墨、重彩、宣紙
Ink and color on Paper｜231×186cm
臺南市美術館典藏　Collection of Tainan Art Museum

陳永森 Chen, Yung-Sen

玫瑰花籃　Rose Basket
1934｜膠彩 Gouache on Silk｜29.5×41cm
臺南市美術館典藏　Collection of Tainan Art Museum

農村清晨
The Morning of Farming Villag
2009｜水墨設色、紙本
Ink and color on Paper｜
144×80cm
臺南市美術館典藏
Collection of Tainan Art Museum

潘元石 Pan, Yuan-Shih

臺南寧南門　Grand South Gate
2003｜木刻水印 Watermark Woodcut｜40×30cm
臺南市美術館典藏　Collection of Tainan Art Museum

3/50　　　寧南門　　　潘元石 '03

安平民房　Houses in Anping
1985｜水彩、紙本 Watercolor on Paper｜38×53cm
臺南市美術館典藏　Collection of Tainan Art Museum

陳英傑 Chen, Ying-Chieh

迎春　Greet Spring
1953｜銅 Copper｜H37×W15×D12cm
臺南市美術館典藏　Collection of Tainan Art Museum

爽秋　Cool Autumn
1983｜版畫膠版 Offset-printing｜80×64cm
臺南市美術館典藏　Collection of Tainan Art Museum

林智信 Lin, Chih-Hsin

阿嬤飼雞　Grandma Feeding Chicken
2004｜版畫膠版 Offset-printing｜75×65cm
臺南市美術館典藏　Collection of Tainan Art Museum

風雲際會（一） Gathering of the Great 1
1993｜壓克力、麻布 Acrylic on Canvas｜91×116.8cm
臺南市美術館典藏 Collection of Tainan Art Museum

蔡茂松 Tsai, Mao-Sung

安平古堡燈塔　The Lighthouse of Anping Fort
1985｜水墨、紙本 Ink on paper｜69×137 cm
臺南市美術館典藏　Collection of Tainan Art Museum

STAGE-20
2009｜數位影像輸出 Inkjet C Print｜120×150 cm

1990年代臺南當代藝術發軔小史

——「起南風」的策展姿態與立場講述

李思賢／策展人（東海大學美術系所 副教授）

▌一、緣起：南風驟起

在臺灣美術史上，上世紀90年代無疑是個思想蓬勃發展、社會風氣開放、藝術思潮躍進的爆發年代，其主要原因來自於1987年的解除戒嚴。「解嚴」之後，因社會丕變、民心思變，過去所禁錮的一切頓時間解放開來，臺灣社會就像股市的跌深反彈，形成一股猶如洪水猛獸般反撲的力道，不僅僅是在政治，在美術上也出現了一波被稱為「後解嚴美術」的特殊時代現象。這是臺灣邁向民主的里程碑，同時也是臺灣美術被明確標註的年代。

臺灣美術中所有當代藝術的發生幾乎都是以1990年代為濫觴，臺南當地的美術發展自不外於這個整體環境的基礎之上。是以，在臺南市美術館開館的當下，為了連結近代、現代與當代，也為了認證地方藝術脈絡對南美館未來館務開展的有效性，除了要有過去前清、日治以降的美術脈絡爬梳外，自當有銜接傳統美術畫科到當代藝術多元表現的轉折，而此一時代轉換的關鍵期便是上世紀末的90年代。因此，筆者以單刀直入的《起南風》為策展主題，提要式地將1990年代臺南當代藝術發軔當時的作品蒐攏而來，通過探討臺南地區當代藝術起源階段的藝術風格、藝術家和空間特性，除了在為臺南當代藝術的初起做梳理，同時也在為南美館預見未來當代藝術的開展，表達出一種開闊的姿態與具歷史縱深和多元並陳的格局。

▌二、時代氛圍：開新・立異

猶記在2003至2005年之間，臺北市立美術館規劃了一個以「○○年代臺灣美術發展」為題的系列展覽，從50到90年代總共五檔，分別以兩個字作為該時代的精神象徵：50年代「長流」、60年代「前衛」、70年代「反思」、80年代「開新」和90年代「立異」。從這些展覽命題便能清楚地發現，80至90年代的「開新」和「立異」是個承先而啟後、從開展新局到大鳴大放的階段，以今日當代藝術多元表現的位置往回看，那無疑是臺灣美術發展史上一個非常重要的翻轉年代，是一個銜接舊和新的關鍵轉折期。80年代中末期至千禧年之前，臺灣歷經了政治的解嚴，因社會的開化而形成對整體臺灣人文社會的衝擊，引發的諸多關於本土認同、身分辯證的反省，也是對過去既有規範下的體制、制度和模式，開始有了深刻的內省與反動的時期。

1987年的解嚴，為反省威權、本土論述和新的國家認同提供了有利的發展條件。從過去「黨外」人士在政治體制上的抗爭、「野百合」學生運動到藝文界對藝術內涵所形成的討論，在在都指向了一個新時代的即將出現。撇開政治問題不談，對臺灣文化最大的影響，莫過於對本土文化的重新認識和挖掘、深耕；由於這種本土的自我認識，讓大中國思想猶如夢幻泡影般地不切實際，也讓「三民主義統一中國」逐漸變成一種遙不可及的夢想。自1971年中華民國政府退出聯合國之後，從沒有一個時刻像政治桎梏解放之後有這麼大規模的鳴放、抗爭、重組和討論。李登輝總統執政時期所喊出的「中華民國在臺灣」，從今日看來像是兩個時代交替時的過度，是策略也是一時的權宜之計；明白的來說，「臺灣」二字自此正式浮上檯面，它所代表的不僅僅是取代了包含中國大陸的一個政體的認知，更重要的是針對關於臺灣這個海島的文明與文化建構的內涵間所形成的整體認識和思考。藝術家的敏銳嗅覺，促使他們用各自的藝術手法表現了對政治、社會、文化等種種層面問題上的思考，而這些也都成為今日我們談論「後解嚴藝術」最重要的具體內容。

作為臺灣文化、政經主流中心的臺北，其藝術表現始終引領著風潮，任何風格時代的出現始終都是以臺北為標竿。1983年，臺灣首座官方美術館「臺北市立美術館」正式開館，自此之後就出現了「官方」和「民間」、「朝」與「野」兩個相互對峙但實際也互為補充的藝文空間狀態，當時的藝術家們或不滿足、或無法進入官方的展覽機制，因此激發了因藝術家自力救濟、相互集結的所謂「替代空間」（alternative space）的興起。這種引進自西方的空間規劃設置，成了當時社會開放以後極為重要的一種藝術現象。

1988年臺北的「伊通公園」、1989年高雄「阿普畫廊」和臺北「二號公寓」的出現，都以一種前所未見的特殊型態，引領了臺灣美術家們在空間營運和藝術創作上出現與過去全然不同的辯證與思考。而全臺各地的藝術領域，也在這股以大城市為中心所帶動的文化氣氛之下蔓延開來，且在多年後而為成了一種時代的風格象徵，當然也包括臺南在內。近年深耕於臺南藝術界的青年文字與藝術工作者楊佳璇便曾著述道：「臺南的『替代空間』，則是跟隨著臺北的腳步，於1992年開始有所謂不同於商業及官方體制之外的展覽空間。」[1] 這「跟隨著臺北的腳步」足以說明，臺南藝術作為「臺灣美術」一環的綿密依存關聯的現實與深刻。

▎三、地域狀態：複合・替代

臺北文化氛圍的吹拂罩染到全臺，比對現有可考的資料，均顯示臺南的當代藝術發展和早年北部「替代空間」概念的推進有著密切的聯繫。除了某幾位今日已成為臺南地區重量級的當代藝術家，於當年所共同組成的畫會和畫廊之外（如許自貴的「高高畫廊」），最重要的不外乎是：1992年成立的「邊陲文化」（~1995）、「新生態藝術環境」（~1999），以及1998年的「原型藝術」（~2005），它們是臺南當代藝術最原初的起點，而參與其中的藝術家們，如今也多已成為臺南地區頗具代表性的藝術典型。

1990年代其實也是大批海歸派學者回到臺灣的主要年代，當今矗立在各大公、私立博物館、美術館和大專院校擔任館長或院長以上行政職務者，多為當時返回臺灣任教的青年學者、藝術家。他們跨出了早年僅能通過《雄獅美術》和《藝術家》雜誌的海外特派，如謝里法等前輩所書寫的報導，方能接收國外藝術訊息的侷限。他們將在海外生活與學習時所看到的藝術取向、風格、創作形式與思惟，甚或是藝術空間的謀畫、運作等悉數帶回家鄉，作為仿照或參照地在臺灣各地實現開來。就如在臺南的黃步青（1948-）、方惠光（1952-）、李錦繡（1953-2003）、曾英棟（1953-）、許自貴（1956-），以及高雄的盧明德（1950-）、李俊賢（1957-）等人，加上較早自西班牙返國（1977）的葉竹盛（1946-），和雖未留洋但藝術面向新穎、質地極佳、創作思考亦十分深刻的在地藝術家黃宏德（1956-）、顏頂生（1960-）、林鴻文（1961-）等人，他們的留學經驗、藝術認知和文化思考將新的空間精神和當代藝術的思辯內涵直接呈現在國人面前。新的視野、新的表現、新的思惟，催生了一個新的美術時代的誕生，一個姿態昂揚、不可一世的90年代蛻變風潮。

臺灣美術自此擺脫了過去前清、日治時期以來傳統畫科的分類方法，儘管這些當時被稱為「新一代藝術家」創作的手法和媒材依然延用油畫、雕塑、水墨，但他們的創作內涵和藝術觀念已全然不是傳統視覺美學和媒材質地的探討所能夠予以概括的，就像古典繪畫和現代繪畫（modern painting）完全不同一樣。複合式的空間表現、複合媒材的材質實驗，以及空間屬性掌握的多層次展演方式，除了在他們自身的作品創作以外，也同時置放到替代空間屬性的展覽中。有趣的是，臺南早年的替代空間屬性不同於臺北那種純粹展覽空間的規劃，臺南的藝術家以一種畫會式群體戰的「合作畫廊」模式出擊（如「邊陲文化」），不僅如此，畫廊經營者的巧思將空間規劃為兼具圖書、展覽、表演、電影和餐飲的複合式空間（如杜昭賢的「新生態藝術環境」），這種多層次的空間營運在今日雖早已蔚為風潮，但在當時的臺灣卻是前所未見的。前輩經驗、後世之師，「邊陲」與「新生態」的空間經驗，成為後來臺南地區真正以「替代空間」屬性成立的「原型藝術」和「文賢油漆行」（2000-2018）的珍貴參考範例。

替代（alternative）的意涵，如前所述，其實是另外一種相對於主流、官方或固定體制、機制的對照，是一個提供當代藝術家有更為多元表現的空間平臺；空間的多重可能性應著藝術家創作型態的多元需求而生，而藝術家在這些替代空間中的展覽和創作，將這些空間屬性帶入更為深刻的文化翻轉，成為1990年代的一種鮮明標誌。這些雖不是臺南藝術家或藝文空間的特權或專屬，但臺南的案例在這波臺灣美術風潮中卻顯得極為特殊，也是使得它作為一種研究切片時成為一種非典型的經典案例。

▎四、藝術取向：異象‧紛呈

世界藝術史走到1990年代，除了現今的數位、新媒體藝術之外，其他藝術類型基本都已經達到完備的程度；也就是說，在各種視覺形態、媒材掌握和藝術觀念上，90年代的臺灣美術表現和其全新的樣貌，都已然有了今日當代藝術的雛型。臺灣的藝術家在直接經歷紐約、巴黎、舊金山、柏林、馬德里、東京等世界主流藝術場域的洗禮之後，在藝術語言和形態的開拓上，功底愈發深厚、作品相對成熟、視野也更為開闊，當他們在80、90年代回到臺灣後迅速成為臺灣美術一股不容小覷的重要中堅力量，在解嚴時勢的推波助瀾下，多數成為了書寫臺灣美術史、標誌臺灣文化的英雄。

解嚴後的社會風氣對於許多過去舊有思想和環境都有極大的顛覆性和可能性，人們在面對如此全新思潮的社會狀態時，心理上其實是有某種程度的不安和焦慮的，而這些動搖人心的狀態卻恰恰成為藝術家探討社會和當時整體文化現象的主軸。此外，沿襲了這60、

70年代以降的抽象風潮，90年代的畫家們也因為在視覺解放的同時複合了媒材實驗的開拓，因而有著較為大膽的創新與突破。因此即便我們不難在他們的作品中看到抽象風格的延續、書寫意象的表達，但卻也有很多新奇的媒材探索和現成物拼合在他們的創作之中出現。

　　林鴻文的抒情抽象、黃宏德的書寫抽象、李錦繡的生活隨筆，以及黃步青的心靈抽屜、許自貴的紙漿雜糅，乃至於新一輩的黃金福（1969-）面對時代糾結和對環境遭破壞的控訴，和方偉文（1970-）空間性、心性遊走的自語喃喃，在在都顯現了1990年代的臺南當代藝術家深刻的藝術質地，他們在特定的藝術氛圍下完成了自己，也用他們自己的藝術顯現了90年代的臺灣和臺南。

▍五、結語：南方美術

　　綜上所述，「起南風」展所欲以探討的問題，就是依循著這個時代的氛圍和藝術主軸進行。筆者羅列了90年代相對重要的臺南藝術家當時的作品來作為探討的引子，不可諱言地，他們不是臺南當代藝術的一切，但從今日的角度來看，臺南當代藝術的發生與他們之間卻有著相應的臍帶相連的關係。本展將於臺南南市美術館1館的展廳內，以意象化手法還原當時替代空間的現場，除將1990年代的作品一併展陳之外，並置入當年相關藝術空間的視覺場景元素，以室內設計的手法回溯那一段臺南美術的歷史情境。為了不過於放大臺南，並兼及早期高雄當代藝術在臺灣美術中所扮演的至關重要的「南方」角色，「起南風」中除了邀集1990年代活躍於臺南美術界藝術家的創作之外，同時也將輔以幾位或是臺南本地出身、或也活動於臺南和高雄之間藝術家的作品。通過他們作品的展陳，演繹展覽本身所欲為臺南市美術館開館而賦予的地方性、藝術性、前衛性的本土連結與開闊面向。作為南美館開館主題策展的策展人之一，筆者期望用「起南風」為南美館的開館做文化鋪墊，同時也成為南美館未來面向當代開展的輻射起點。

註：

1. 參見楊佳璇文：〈主流之外的集結場域——「替代空間」在臺灣的早期發展〉，收錄於《在微光下，從南方出發：臺南藝文空間回訪1980-2012》，臺南市：佐佐目藝文工作室，2012，頁13。

The 1990s: A Brief History of Embarkment of Contemporary Art in Tainan — 'A Southern Wind' Exhibition Concept and Position

Li, Szu-Hsien/Curator , Associate Professor of the Department of Fine Arts, Tunghai University

I. Introduction：A Southern Tempest

In the history of Taiwanese art, the 1990s was undoubtedly a time of flourishing ideals, open social atmosphere, and progressive artistic thought. The main reason for this outburst of social development was the end of the martial law era in 1987. After the end of the martial law era, all thought and expression that had been banned in the past was liberated due to social changes and progressive advocacy of the Taiwanese people. The Taiwanese society rebounded like its stock market, formulating a force of reformation that was as powerful as flood and beasts that was not only seen in politics, but in artistic expression as well. There was also a periodical wave called "post-martial laws fine art," which marks a milestone in the Taiwanese march towards democracy, and a definitive era in Taiwanese art.

The origin of most contemporary art in Taiwan almost always refers to the 1990s. Tainan local art development is also founded in this period; therefore, in the current opening of the Tainan Art Museum, we attempt to connect the early modern, modern, and contemporary in order to certify the validity of this contextual thread in local art and future developments in our museum. In addition to reviewing past influences from the Qing Dynasty and Japanese colonial rule, we identify a turning point from traditional art and painting to multi-expressional contemporary art in the 1990s, marking a pivotal period of transformation. Therefore this author evokes a direct curatorial theme in "A Southern Wind" to summarize Tainan contemporary art works in the 1990s, exploring artistic style, artist and spatial characteristics in the originating stage of Tainan contemporary art. In addition to tracing the origins of Tainan's contemporary art, our museum will also demonstrate future developments in contemporary art, exhibiting both open attitude as well as historical depth and diversity in our exhibition.

II. Periodical Background：Break New Ground ・ Branch Out

Between 2003 and 2005, the Taipei Fine Arts Museum planned a series of exhibitions titled "Taiwanese Fine Arts Development in the 1900s." From the 50s to the 90s, with a total of five exhibitions, each with two words to symbolize of the period's ideology: the "from the ground up" of the 50s, "avant-garde" in the 60s, "reflections" in the 70s, "break new ground" in the 80s, and "branch out" in the 1990s. These exhibition themes clearly indicate that "break new ground" and "branch out" the 1980s and 1990s are a pivotal point in Taiwanese art and represents a period in art history that is both continuation and innovation. Looking back at the period from the perspective of diverse expressions we enjoy today, the 80s and 90s were undoubtedly crucial to the history of Taiwan's fine arts development and marks a key turning point which connects the old to the new. From the mid 80s to the millennium, Taiwan experienced the end of political martial law and its impact on Taiwanese social humanities which inspired many of the introspective discourse on local identity and dialectical identity that interrogates the existing norms of past institutions, structures, and social models; ushering in a era of introspective thought and reaction.

The 1987 stipulation provided favorable developmental conditions for reflection in authoritarianism, local discourse and constructing new national identity. From the past struggles of "non-party" activists in the political system, to the "wild lily" student movement and the discussion of artistic connotations in the art world, all point to the dawn of a new era. Regardless of political issues, the end of martial law's biggest influence on Taiwanese culture is the development of a new understanding of identity that led to self-excavation and in-depth cultivation of local culture. Due to this local self-awareness, past political goals in uniting Great China was revealed to be a grand illusion, whereas the unification of China through democratic ideology gradually became a distant dream. Apart from the Taiwanese government's withdrawal from the United Nations in 1971, the country has never seen such a large-scale denouncement, struggle, reorganization and discussion like the period of post-martial law political liberation. President Lee Teng-hui's administration's main focus was to recognize "the Republic of China in Taiwan," now seemingly an excessive transition between the two eras, yet at the time it was a strategic move as well as temporary expediency. Frankly, "Taiwan" only became a common and formal phrase during Li's administration, not only displacing the recognition of a political system that includes the Chinese mainland, but more importantly, this recognition is aimed to inspire a comprehensive understanding and deliberation on the connotations of civil and cultural construct of the Taiwanese island culture. Artist's keen sensibilities prompted them to express their thoughts on political, social and cultural issues through their respective artistic methods, leading to key contents pertinent to our discussion of "post-martial law art."

Taipei is at the center of Taiwanese culture and politics, its artistic performance always set the trend whereas the appearance of periodical style has always originated in Taipei. In 1983, Taiwan's first official art museum, "Taipei Fine Art Museum" officially opened. Since then, there has always been polarizing forces in art forms between "official" and "civil," "administrative" and "opposition;" dual conflicts that actually complement each other through their struggles. Artists at the time were either unsatisfied or unable to enter official exhibition systems, thus stimulating a rise of the "alternative space" movement that relied on the artist's self-reliance and mutual collaboration. This introduction of Western spatial design became an extremely important artistic phenomenon after social liberation.

The appearance of "Yi-tong Park" in Taipei in 1988, "Apu Gallery" in Kaohsiung, and "Apartment No. 2" in Taipei in 1989 was a mode of exhibition the country had never seen before, leading Taiwanese artists to consider space operations and art creation from new perspectives and form new dialectic. Artistic spaces around Taiwan spread under the cultural ambiance originating from major cities, and after many years becoming a symbol of an era's contemporary style, Tainan included as well. In recent years, Yang, Jia-hsuan, a young writer and deeply involved in Tainan's art scene, once wrote: "'alternative spaces' in Tainan follows the footsteps of Taipei. In 1992, we began to see exhibition spaces that differ from commercial and official systems"[1]. This "following the footsteps of Taipei" is enough to illustrate the reality of Tainan art as a profound and integral link in "Taiwanese art."

III. Geographical State：Complex · Replacement

Research materials of Taipei's cultural atmosphere's influential spread throughout Taiwan show that the development of contemporary art in Tainan is closely related to the north's promotional concept of "alternative space" in the early years. In addition to some contemporary artists who are now heavily influential in Tainan, painting societies and galleries that were formed in the same era (such as Hsu, Tzu-kuey's "Kao Kao Gallery") were highly important. Among those were "Border Culture" established in 1992 (~1995), "New Phase Art Space" (~1999), and "Prototype Art Space" (~2005) established in 1998, all regarded as the original starting point of Tainan contemporary art, with the participating artists each representatives of their respective fields in Tainan.

The 1990s was also the main era where a large number of scholars trained overseas returned to Taiwan. Today, they work in public or private museums, art galleries, colleges and universities as administrative curators or directors. These were mostly young scholars and artists who returned to teach in Taiwan at the time. They overcame difficulties in receiving information on foreign art only through limited reports written by critics such as Xie Li-fa and published in the overseas specials of "Lion Art: and "Artist" magazines. They brought artistic orientation, style, creative format and innovative thought to their homeland, and even the planning and operation of the art spaces they experienced abroad. These pioneers were recognized in Taiwan as an innovative model or point of reference. For example, Huang, Buh-ching (1948-), Fang, Huei-kuang (1952-), Li, Jin-sho (1953-2003), Tseng, Ying-tung (1953-), and Hsu, Tzu-kuey (1956-) in Tainan, as well as Lu, Ming-te (1950-) and Li, Chun-shien (1957-) in Kaohsiung. Together with Yeh, Chu-sheng (1946-), who returned from Spain in 1977, in addition to local artists Yen, Ding-sheng (1960-), Lin, Hong-wen (1961-) and Huang, Hung-teh (1956-). The latter three had no overseas experience but revealed a novel approach to art and displayed excellent texture, as well as profound creative thought. Their international experience, artistic perspective and cultural mentality represent the spirit of new spaces and portray to the Taiwanese a contemplative essence of contemporary art. New visions, new performances, and new thought spawned the dawn of a new era of art, leading to a high-profile and incomparable wave of change in the 1990s.

Taiwanese art has since been freed from the classification methods of traditional paintings since Qing Dynasty and Japanese colonial rule. Although the "new generation of artists" still use oil painting, sculpture, and ink as their creative technique and media, the essence of creation and artistic concept was no longer assimilated by the traditional discussion of visual aesthetics and media material, just as classical painting completely differs from modern painting. A complex spatial representation, material experiments that led to multi-media and multi-level performances with spatial attributes are not only seen in the creation of their works, but also inserted in the attributes of alternative space exhibition. Interestingly, alternative spaces in Tainan's early years were different from the pure exhibition spaces of Taipei. Artists in Tainan challenged the conventional with collected works and "cooperative gallery" models (such as "Border Culture"), in addition to the curators adding compound elements to spatial design such as allotting bookstore, exhibition, performance, movie and restaurant sections (such as Du, Zhao-xian's "New Phase Art Space"). This multi-functional space operation has already become an established trend, but at the time unprecedented in Taiwan. The experience of these pioneers educated later generations, thus the spatial experience of "Border" and "New Phase" became precious reference for "Prototype Art" and "Wen-xian PAINT HOUSE fourm & studio" (2000~2018), both established in Tainan as authentic "alternative space."

The meaning of alternative, as mentioned above, is actually an opposition with the mainstream, the official, fixed institutions and mechanisms. It is a spatial platform providing contemporary artists with the opportunity to display diverse performances; the multiple possibilities of space reflect the diverse needs of an artist's creative form, whereas the artist's exhibition and creation in these alternative spaces integrate spatial characteristics to produce a profound cultural subversion, becoming a distinctive symbol of the 1990s. Although these attributes were not the privilege of or exclusive to Tainan artists and artistic spaces, Tainan's example is extremely special in the Taiwanese art wave, making it a classic case of atypical study.

IV. Artistic Direction：Beyond Vision · Occurrence

In the 1990s, the history of world art reached a level of completion in most art forms, with the exception of digital and new media art; at the same time, Taiwanese fine art in its various visual forms, media mastery and artistic concept had matured enough in performance and innovation to become the prototype of today's contemporary art. After experiencing a baptism of mainstream international art in places such as New York, Paris, San Francisco, Berlin, Madrid, and Tokyo, Taiwanese artists have are increasingly profound in the development of artistic language and form, reflecting in their relatively mature works and broadened horizons. When these artists returned to Taiwan in the 1980s and 90s, they quickly became an important intermediate force in Taiwanese arts. Under a wave of liberation after the end of martial laws, most of these artists became heroes who wrote Taiwanese art history and distinguished the Taiwanese culture.

Social trends after the end of martial law brought great subversion and possibilities to old concepts and environments. In the face of new trends, thoughts and social change, people tend to develop a certain degree of anxiety and psychological unease. The various states of unease have become the main axis of an artist's exploration of society and an overall cultural phenomenon of that era. In addition, following the abstract wave of the 1960s and 1970s, painters in the 1990s also produced bold innovations and breakthroughs by combing the development of media experiments at the same time of visual liberation. Therefore, though the continuation of abstract styles and the symbolic expression remain obvious in their works, innovative media explorations and ready-made objects that appear in their creations were also evident.

Lin, Hong-wen's abstract emotion, Huang, Hung-teh's abstract writing, Li, Jin-xi's life essays, Huang, Buh-ching's soul drawer, Hsu, Tzu-kuey's kneaded pulp, the new generation's Huang, Chin-fu's (1969-) interaction with the entanglement of times and accusations toward environmental destruction, and Fang, Wei-wen's (1970-) murmurs of the spatial and spiritual; each shows the profound artistic texture of Tainan contemporary artists in the 1990s. They achieved self completion in the specific artistic atmospheres of the 90s and also defined Tainan as well as Taiwan through their art.

V. Conclusion: Southern Art

In summary, the main issue that "A Southern Winds" exhibition hopes to explore is to follow the periodical artistic atmosphere and the main artistic axis of the 1990s. I list the works of relatively important Tainan artists in the 1990s as an invitation to inspire more dialogue, though indisputably they are not the sole representatives of Tainan contemporary art, yet but from current perspective, they are the origin of the city's contemporary art and artistic development. This exhibition is held in the first Building of the Tainan Art Museum and will endeavor to restore the alternative spaces from the period. In addition to 1990s artistic works, visual elements of relevant art spaces will be reconstructed as an attempt to convey authenticity and the original aura that is part of the Tainan art history through interior design. In order to not emphasize Tainan in the exhibition and recognize the important "Southern" role early Kaohsiung contemporary art plays in Taiwanese art, "A Southern Wind" exhibition invites artists native to Tainan or active in Tainan and Kaohsiung to add their creations to those of artists active in the Tainan artscape in the 90s. Through these works, we share an interpretation of the local, artistic and avant-garde, linking localization to expansive experiences and conveying the exhibition's contribution as the Tainan Art Museum's opening display. As one of the curators of the opening themes of the Tainan Art Museum, I hope to emphasize the museum's cultural lineage through "A Southern Wind," as well as serve as a nucleus for contemporary development.

---

1 Cited from Yang, Jia-hsuan： 〈Assembled Spaces outside of Mainstream—Early Developments of "Alternative Spaces" in Taiwan〉, published in 《Embarking from the South under Dim Light：Tainan Artistic Spaces and Interviews 1980-2012》 page 13, Tainan：Tzuo tzuo mu Arts Studio, 2012.

洪根深 Hung, Ken- Shen

都市空間　City Space
1994｜壓克力、墨、紙、畫布
Acrylic、ink、paper on canvas
130×162cm

人間遊戲　Games People Play
1997｜壓克力、墨、紙、石膏、樹脂、畫布 Acrylic、
ink、paper、plaster、resin、oil on canvas
145×112cm

陳水財 Chen, Shui-Tsai

叔公之一　Granduncle
1999 ｜ 複合媒材 Mixed media
162×162cm

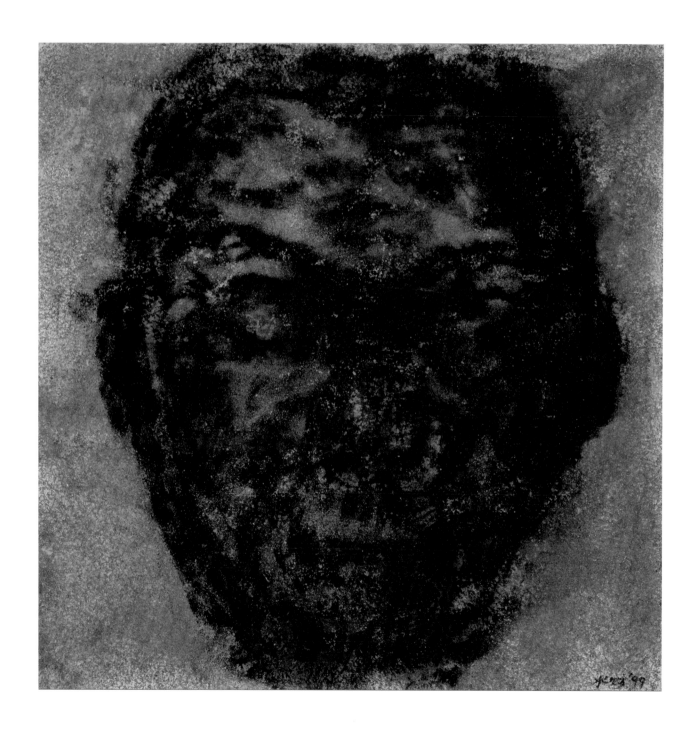

秩序與非秩序　Order and Non-order
1985-87 ┃ 複合媒材 Mixed media
120×210cm

黃步青 Hwang, Buh-Ching

藍色記憶　Blue Memory
1994｜抽屜、瓶子、染料、水
Drawer, bottle, dye, water
H57×W255×D14cm

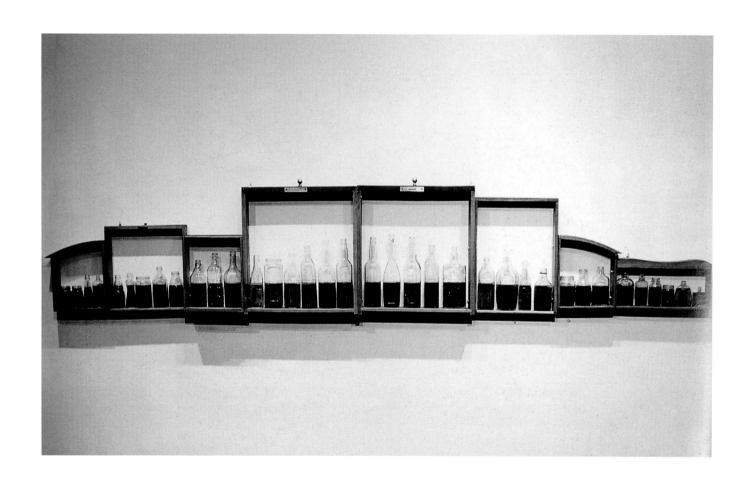

進化 & 啟示系列之二　Evolution & Revelation Series 2
1991-92 | 複合媒材 Mixed media
182×182cm
加力畫廊提供　Licence Inart Space provide

方惠光 Fang, Huei- Kuang

唐吉軻德　Don Quixote
1993｜青銅 Bronze
H30×W15×D50cm
臺南市美術館典藏
Collection of Tainan Art Museum

方惠光 Fang, Huei- Kuang |

憐憫　Mercy
1992｜青銅 Bronze
H73×W20×D20cm

李錦繡 Lii, Jiin-Shiow

林間（黃） Woodland (yellow)
1989｜壓克力顏料、畫布 Acrylic on canvas
91×116cm

四方同聚　Union of All
1993 | 壓克力顏料、畫布 Acrylic on canvas
162×112cm

曾英棟 Tseng, Ying-Tung

海洋系列：海-2　Sea Series-Sea (II)
1997｜複合媒材 Mixed media
162×131cm

曾英棟 Tseng, Ying-Tung

日與月　Sun and Moon
1993｜油畫 Oil on canvas｜97×194cm
吳佳蓉小姐典藏／東門美術館提供
Collection of Wu, Chia-Rong ／ Licence Art Gallery provide

許自貴 Hsu, Tzu-Kuey

海洋文明史　The History of Ocean Civilization
1995｜複合媒材 Mixed media
H55×W150×D6cm
阿貴美術館提供
Akui Art Museum provide

許自貴 Hsu, Tzu-Kuey |

史前柱子　Prehistoric Pillar
1990｜複合媒材 Mixed media
H248×W70×D70cm

李俊賢 Li, Chun-Shien

105榴炮的回憶2　The Memory of 105 Cannon 2
1992｜壓克力顏料、畫布 Acrylic on canvas
51×128cm
加力畫廊提供　Licence Inart Space provide

八方93-2　All Places 93-2
1993｜壓克力顏料、磁土 Acrylic and clay on canvas
97×130cm
泰郁美學堂藏　Collection of Taiyu Beaux Arts Salon

顏頂生 Yen, Ding-Sheng

射入　Incident
1990｜壓克力顏料、磁土 Acrylic and clay on canvas
91×116.5cm

悠悠天堂　The Elegant Heaven
1996｜複合媒材、畫布 Mixed media on canvas
192×260cm

林鴻文 Lin, Hong-Wen

無題　Untitled

1999 | 海漂竹 Bamboos | 85×85×250cm

那件西裝　The Suit
1991 | 油彩、畫布 Oil on canvas | 53×45.5cm
東門美術館提供　Licence Art Gallery provide

李昆霖 Lee, Kuen-Lin

椅子　The Chair
1998 ｜木 Wood ｜ H112×W45×D45cm
東門美術館提供　Licence Art Gallery provide

從綠色→灰色的軌道痕跡
The Trace of Track from Green to Gray
1996 | 複合媒材 Mixed mdeia
H90×W480×D125cm

方偉文 Fang Wei-Wen

野生花園　Wild Garden
1998｜複合媒材　Mixed mdeia
依展出空間而定（現地製作重現）
Variable dimension

重新詮釋中

張清淵／策展人（臺南藝術大學 應用藝術研究所教授）

　　臺灣憑藉著獨特地理環境和多元的歷史背景，70年代開始經由經濟實力的提升，人們開始有機會來重新咀嚼過去數百年來的文化資源。這過程中對於生活裡飲茶的方式開始產生變革。結合中國的潮汕工夫茶文化，與日本的茶道、煎茶道（17世紀中國的隱元隆琦禪師傳入），逐漸發酵形成了極具品飲特色與感觀體驗的「臺灣茶藝」，因此，臺灣的茶文化的演化與積累，建構了趨於完整且全面的論述，由此來看，臺灣的茶文化，是最具特色且具世界競爭力的臺灣文化的代言者。

　　臺灣作為一個文化體，沒有積累數百年，甚至於千年令人稱羨的文化底蘊，但是因為地理位置上的特殊性，加上過去好幾個世紀以來的移民與被殖民的交迭沉澱下，構築出許許多多極耐人尋味的味道（flavor）。

　　在這眾多味道中，以「茶」為載體的生活工藝、美術、服飾與建築等，都強烈的顯現臺灣對於接納外來文化與重新詮釋的能力。

　　本展覽的策展核心概念與展出作品，不是在學術上探討臺灣、日本、中國三地「茶道」與「茶藝」的異同，而是企圖透過此次集結來自於臺、日、中的當代工藝品來驗證過去近半世紀的茶文化歷程，聚焦在臺灣如何面對來自中國和日本後殖民的深度影響而顯現的重新詮釋狀態。

　　人類文明發展的進程中，生活器物是人類文化的重要歷史證物，工藝具有的承傳歷史與寶貴的文化資產以外，還具有重要的象徵意義與作用。例如，精緻生活品質的指標，有助於建立集體記憶與感情，提昇國家或族群共同意識等文化認同的因素。

　　「後殖民主義」理論關注的是殖民宗主國與殖民地的文化控制方式與衝突。「後殖民主義」循著文化研究中種族與地域的層面切入，探討殖民經驗對於各地文化衝突的現象。「舊殖民主義」與「新殖民主義」的操控來自軍事政經的強壓，而「後殖民主義」所批判的權力化身則以文化政策為主，如殖民國挾其強勢的語言或教育機制，以媒體視覺符號進行對於其他國家，或特定族群的思想控制。也就是說，「後殖民主義」理論主要著重以文化為核心，來分析權力與知識的構成，以殖民經驗來詮釋當代文化混雜，被殖民者認同錯亂的現象。

　　臺灣就是一個經歷如以上所述的殖民三階段的例子。當代臺灣社會所呈現的是一個文化認同混雜的局面，其所經歷的複雜政治勢力，而顯示於文化的表象，包括了中、日、美交相雜的洗禮。臺灣這個南島住民居住地域，曾是中國南方移民的落腳地，是中、日政治衝突下的犧牲品，也是中、美政治牽引較勁的觀測站。日本挾其西化成果在亞洲擴展殖民帝國野心，使得臺灣經歷了日本以軍事政治及教育文化的殖民手段統治，喪失了自主的權力以及認同感。在日本統治的五十年發展至今，展現在臺灣的社會現實就如陶東風所分析的殖民三階段，由「舊殖民主義」佔領期間土地資源的佔據與控制，「新殖民主義」政治經濟的部分主導權，以及「後殖民主義」理論所談，藉由佔領期間所推展的教育文化制度，對於當今臺灣人民的價值判斷與生活方式依然擁有強勢霸權的優勢。日本統治臺灣，以臺灣為其在亞洲擴展殖民帝國的供應站與誇耀帝國成就的實驗地，為臺灣引進西方現代化的基礎。日本對臺灣的殖民過程是西方殖民帝國在亞洲的翻版，而臺灣與日本之間的殖民經驗，使得臺灣也成為西方後殖民主義理論者所討論的對象。

（林媛婉，〈臺灣工藝研究的議題——一個後殖民文化論述的觀點〉）

　　檢視茶文化在臺灣，就好比西方後殖民主義理論者所討論的對象，追溯臺灣茶藝之由來，其實最早應發源自中國廣東潮洲的「功夫茶」小壺泡。「功夫茶」小壺泡傳至臺灣後，自70年代後期開始，經由無數臺灣茶人、茶會、茶館的專注鑽研傳習延展，文人雅士們結合中國文人文化中的美學、哲學、佛教禪宗，更將日本茶道的思惟融入，再現臺灣現代生活氛圍；到現在，已然轉化並重新詮釋成與本來源頭全然互異的一套包容極廣的飲茶與生活態度。

　　臺灣人在喝茶的過程中，對於茶葉種類、水的特質、煮水方式、茶具的形式以至於喝茶的環境、時機、主客，都有十分專注但不嚴格且貼近自然的關懷，藉由這種關懷去探索不只可以自得其樂，更能引人入勝的精神意境，體現「道藝一體」的真義，與茶相關事物的關注，以及用茶氛圍的營造。欣賞茶葉的色與香及外形，是茶藝中不可缺少的環節；沖泡過程的藝術化與技藝的高超，使泡茶不只是一種美的享受；更是體現個人對生活的一種態度。

　　此次展覽中來自於中國的吳光榮，出生於安徽淮南，畢業於南京藝術學院工藝美術系，目前任教於杭州中國美術學院，同時擔任美院民藝博物館館長。吳光榮的創作，以中國宜興泥板成形技術為核心，但在構築過程中熟練且具巧思的讓材料顯現柔軟的延展性特質。大大的顛覆了中國宜興製壺的極致與高度精準的傳統。

　　陸斌作為中國當代最具有國際影響力的陶藝家，擅長運用陶藝本身的材料屬性與技藝特點，來表達當代的文化觀念與個體思考。陸斌的藝術借「陶」這一物件，深刻理解了藝術媒材的物質屬性與材料屬性，並從中發掘出隱含的文化屬性。他匪夷所思的技術手段並不是為了取悅眼睛或者他人，而是個體思考的一種表達方式。他的創作內核一直涉及有關「緣起與緣滅」、「此在與虛無」、「輪迴與消逝」這些本質性的命題。藝術家希望表達出他對當下紫砂文化現狀的反思態度，在價值觀幻滅的文化背景下，用破碎傳統經典作品的手段，將紫砂壺抽離出原有的文化情境，重新編碼成為了一個新的形象符號，同時釋放出對於當代文化與現實的幻滅感。

吳昊以陶藝特有的材料語言及空間構成方式，將這種精神狀態物化，藉此傳遞屬於自己的、真實的、對於品味人生的愉悅感悟，是一種借物漸修的體驗，從「借物詠懷，托物言志」上再去看器物，在其發生發展過程中，積蘊了龐大的歷史資訊，所謂功用，不過是其中的一個屬性。然而，恰恰這個功用的屬性，卻是核心的要素。沒有「用」，就沒有故事的依託。這就是吳昊器用的思辨價值。

　　李海霖在中國的實用陶藝創作者中，受到南北宋時期文人在生活品味上簡樸的影響，李海霖是少數幾位具有南方文人品味的新世代。

　　黃永星在中國美術學院陶藝系畢業後，目前任教於福建省德化的泉州工藝美術職業學院，正統嚴謹的美術教育訓練下，來到傳統製瓷的德化，黃永星把傳統中製作觀音佛像的瓷土來製作茶壺，藉由極簡的形式來凸顯當地瓷土材料的極致透光與滑潤感。

　　支炳勝創辦的浮雲堂，做為中國當代推展茶道文化的主要推手之一，支炳勝除了主導了茶服的演化之外，同時也在茶具設計上跳脫了宜興的主流思惟，適度地把景德鎮的千年製瓷工藝帶入符合中國當代新古典的美感茶道用具。

　　優家傢俱沈寶宏以「中國基因」為靈感源泉，將傳統明式傢俱中的簡潔美感和複雜的榫卯結構帶入現代的家具設計中。多年來一直致力於中國當代家具的原創設計生產，多次獲得國際獎項與年度設計師獎等。他形容自己是「穿梭在時間隧道裡的旅人。」

　　日本人間國寶中川衛（Nakagawa Mamoru）教授融合傳統與現代技法，並加入了許多自然與人文的微妙表現，其作品皆是從過去的歷史創造當代的價值，擁有令人感動的療癒性元素。其中，最為人所知的「雕鏨鑲嵌」技法，利用鏨刀在金屬上刻畫圖形後，再將合金金屬敲打至器型面上的技法，為其技術高度純熟之展現。

　　十一代大樋長左衛門（Ohi Chozaemon XI），加賀藩三代藩主前田利常推行文化獎勵政策，請來京都千家四代宗室仙叟於藩領普及茶道。1666年（寬文6年）應五代藩主綱紀之邀，樂燒四代傳人之徒土師長左衛門亦隨千仙叟同往，在金澤市郊大樋村開樂燒分窯「大樋燒」。長左衛門後來定居金澤並改姓大樋，至今十一代，傳承三百五十餘年，可謂金澤茶道文化的開創者之一。十一代大樋長左衛門不僅是茶陶藝家，亦身兼畫家、空間與工業設計和創意總監。對大樋年雄而言，這些領域的共通基礎都是工藝，並沒有傳統和當代之分。

　　山村慎哉（Yamamura Shinya）現在擔任金澤美術工藝大學教授，專注漆工藝、蒔繪等加飾技法（螺鈿、蛋殼），以及當代珠寶等方面從事研究創作。長期著迷於創作小而精緻的物件。結合迷人的抽象珍珠貝圖案，極其精緻的漆器製作技術配合簡約的設計。所有這些都使得如手掌大的永恆的抽象維度很現代。

　　桑田卓郎（Kuwata Takuro）解構了茶道中茶碗或水指（壺）的形象，並添加了普普風格的豐富色彩。傳統技法的使用：長石釉（志野釉）的「梅華皮」（在燒成時產生釉藥的崩裂）、「石爆」（在陶土中混合的石塊在燒成時爆裂出表層），和當代態度的介入，破除一般人對陶藝的高雅距離，又同時保留住日本文化的崇高性，是真正開花自日本傳統美學的突破性嘗試。

　　竹村友里（Takemura Yuri）愛知縣立美術大學藝術系設計／工藝研究生陶瓷專業，在傳統茶碗的表象上融入了現代簡約且具女性纖細陰柔的獨特風格，是目前在日本受到高度矚目的新世代女性陶藝家。

松永圭太（Matsunaga Keita）畢業於名城大學建築學院，習慣拉坯後來彎曲土壤並塑造它，接合痕跡一直保留到燒成。同時也嘗試和一位漆藝藝術家Yukimasa Takahashi配合，完成表面的色彩塗裝，這是一種新的嘗試，它以生動的色彩反映了生產痕跡作為骨架的新茶碗。

石山哲也（Ishiyama Tetsuya）非陶藝本科出身的創作者，因為對古陶瓷的迷戀而進入陶藝創作領域，他的創作風格豐富，專業的陶藝雜誌《炎藝術》將列為當代最受矚目與期待的五十位陶藝家之一。

久米圭子（Kume Keiko）金澤美術工藝大學大學院畢業。專門從事金屬精緻細膩的創作。有機的造型結合柔軟的質感是她最擅長的表現手法。

坂井直樹（Sakai Naoki）取得東京藝術大學博士後，對於鐵器茶壺設計，已經建立了明確的個人風格。他希望重拾日本人傳統文化的根，在器皿的實用性之外，更追求美的境界，完美融合鐵的溫度和輕鬆的感覺，藝術感豐厚，亦貼近現代人的生活。

木瀨浩詞（Kise Hiroshi）結合金屬與漆器的器物創作是他慣有的手法。

山岸紗綾（Yamagishi Saya）、池田晃將（Ikeda Terumasa）、村本真吾（Muramoto Shingo）等三位則是剛從金澤市卯辰山工坊駐村完畢的年輕且深具潛力的漆藝創作者，作品都深具實驗精神。

奈良祐希（Nara Yuki）生長於傳統陶藝家族，同時畢業於國立東京藝術大學的建築研究所。此特別邀請他來設計茶室，表達日本80後新世代的茶空間的新品味。

臺灣在當代茶道文化的演化推展中，不管是在器物的形式美感或是使用的準則，皆高度的受到中國和日本的影響。建立在這樣的基礎上，臺灣的當代陶藝從80年代後的突飛猛進中找到與飲茶文化連結的管道。做陶者對於泡茶知識的養成密切的關係到茶道器物的製作細節與新茶器的開發。或者應該是說，本土意識高漲的氛圍下，臺灣本土的茶人為了建立自我文化上的認同，結合當代陶藝或是工藝創作者來共同重新詮釋與建構出新茶道文化。從品茶的環境到茶席的構思不斷的快速演化，茶具的選擇與搭配態度與廣度被越推越廣。所有能創造出極致茶味道的感官過程都伴隨著茶人與藝匠的實驗精神，茶的世界裡看不到疆界，看到的是不斷推陳出新的新價值，這重新詮釋的價值建構出臺灣當代的茶藝系譜和最具話語權的文化體。

▌材質與形式的重新詮釋

本次參展的臺灣藝術家中，蘇保在是目前在海峽二岸介紹中高度矚目的一位創作者，他把過去十多年來對傳統汝窯青瓷釉的研究成果展現在茶具上，整體作品對再現中國宋代文人精神性的特質提出了絕佳的示範。

方柏欽和鍾雯婷則是在臺灣本地修完藝術創作碩士後，各從澳洲墨爾本皇家藝術學院和日本國立東京藝術大學獲得博士學位，這二位創作者分別從自己在異地的學習經驗中提煉出令人玩味的異國風味的茶器。方柏欽從早期柴燒自然落灰的粗獷中與雕塑語彙建構出的群組，到目前更純粹的以器物表面質感來顯現陶瓷材質的美感；鍾雯婷則是延續其女性纖細婉約若有似無的筆觸，在茶具的表現上令人憐惜。臺灣在鶯歌陶瓷博物館開館後，與國際陶藝的接軌建立了一個完整的平臺，除了每兩年的國際陶藝雙年展外，吸引了很多知名的陶藝家來臺駐村創作和交流，在這多樣化的國際交流氛圍中逐漸地刺激了臺灣本土的陶藝創作新世代。這其中如曾獲臺灣金壺獎首獎的卓銘順、羅濟明，關注從傳統茶器物群體中做為核心的茶壺做載體來拓展出個人的雕塑性語彙；劉榮輝則是在大氣度的茶承的表現上在臺灣沒有人能出其右。

▌異材質介入後的機能性重新詮釋

劉世平透過陶瓷材料結合異材質的實驗性探索中啟發了許多新世代的創作者。

吳偉丞和趙丹綺則是在茶器群組的駕馭上更多樣化。吳偉丞以他極現代的造型茶器經營出深具建築語彙的喝茶場域；趙丹綺更從一位金工創作者的角色，鍛造出有別於傳統的茶器，作品中將製作過程中的勞動紀錄轉化為美感的話語，令人玩味。

▌金屬材質茶器的拓展

陳逸在研究所畢業後進入茶具製作的領域，在鍛造技術上結合個人對茶具的詮釋，是目前最令人期待的新世代創作者。黃天來的成就來自於他充分地展現出對鑄造技術的完美掌控，在實用性器物與非實用雕塑間取得令人驚嘆的平衡。

任大賢是臺灣當代金屬媒材雕塑創作者中的佼佼者，此次茶空間的規劃與創作，深具實驗性，也提供了當代茶人來重新檢視飲茶空間的侷促性。

日本茶道起初是貴族的活動，是嚴謹且規範的，但臺灣茶道發展至今仍是常民的文化，任何人隨時隨地都可以泡茶。日本茶道講究的是一種氛圍，一種精神性的狀態，但臺灣人泡茶是為了能把茶葉的特質顯現，達到最味美的狀態。因此，近三十年來，臺灣的茶人經由與茶農和茶具創作者的不斷對話過程中，重新詮釋出嚴謹但不離群、多樣但不複雜的新茶道。

因為日本殖民時期在常民文化上的鋪陳，進而影響臺灣人面對喝茶的態度不純粹的只是來自於中原文化的思惟。把日本人生活中對於喝茶的哲學及美學，以及器物使用的規範，導入根植於中國文化發展的進程來檢視，這是臺灣從常民生活中對飲茶的態度提升下的內在轉化而發展出的一種新品味、新格局的生活藝術形式。

在茶具形式美感和喝茶態度的文化上，當今的中國及亞洲鄰國皆非常明顯地受到臺灣的影響，這已是沒辦法去辯駁的事實，重新詮釋仍在進行中。

A Process of New Interpretations

Chang, Ching-Yuan/Curator, Professor: Graduate Institute of Applied Arts Tainan National University of the Arts

With its unique geographical environment and diverse historical background, Taiwan began to have an opportunity to re-think its cultural resources over the past few centuries through a boost in economic strength in the 1970s. In the process, the Taiwanese way of drinking tea began to change. A combination of Chinese Cha-oshan Gongfu tea culture, the Japanese tea ceremony and traditional Jianchao ceremonies (introduced by the 17th century Chinese Zen Master Enyuan Longqi), tea in Taiwan gradually grew into the "Taiwanese tea art" of great taste and sensory experiences. Taiwan's tea culture has evolved and accumulated experience, constructing a comprehensive and encompassing dialogue. From this perspective, the Taiwanese tea culture is a most distinctive and world-competitive spokesperson of Taiwanese culture.

As a cultural entity, Taiwan does not have the historical experience accumulated over centuries, nor a millennium of cultural heritage, but due to its unique geographical location and the combination of immigration and colonization in the last few centuries, the Taiwanese culture is a construction of many intriguing flavors. Among these many flavors, life crafts, art, costumes and architecture that share a common inspiration in "tea" as a subject strongly demonstrate the Taiwanese ability to accept and reinterpret foreign culture.

The core concept of this exhibition and the works exhibited is not to dwell on an academic discussion of the similarities and differences between "tea ceremonies" and "tea art" in Taiwan, Japan and China, but attempt to gather contemporary works of craftsmanship from Taiwan, Japan and China to examine the historical trajectory of tea culture over the last fifty years. We focus on the representation of Taiwanese post-colonial interpretations of deep cultural influences from China and Japan.

In the process of development in human civilization, material tools are important historical evidences of human culture. In addition its role of precious cultural asset and creating a historical legacy, craftsmanship also has an important symbolic significance and functionality. For example, indicators of a refined quality of life can help establish collective memory and feeling, enhancing the cultural identity of national or ethnic groups.

"Postcolonialism" theory focuses on the cultural control and conflict between the colonial sovereign state and its colonies. "Postcolonialism" follows the racial and regional dimensions of cultural studies and explores the phenomenon of colonial experience leading to cultural conflict around the world. The manipulations of "old colonialism" and "neo-colonialism" comes from of military, political, and economical suppression, while the manifestation of power that has been long criticized by "postcolonialism" exemplifies cultural policies, such as the dominant language or educational mechanisms employed by colonial powers that use visual symbols in the media to control thought in other countries, or specific ethnic groups. That is to say, "postcolonialism" theories mainly focuses on culture as a core analysis of the composition of power and knowledge, interpreting the mixture of contemporary culture through colonial experience and identity confusion caused by colonial rule.

Taiwan is a prime example of the afore-mentioned three-steps of colonial experience. Contemporary Taiwan society represents the post-colonial scenario of mixed cultural identity, and the complex political forces it experienced are evident in cultural signifiers, including a mixture of Chinese, Japanese and American cultural baptisms. Taiwan, once a habitat for Austronesian People, became the home of southern Chinese immigrants and then a victim of political conflict between China and Japan, further becoming a reflective indicator for Chinese and American politics in modern times. Japan's successful efforts in Westernization led to its ambitious expansion of the Japanese colonial empire, leading to the Taiwanese experience of Japanese colonial rule in military, politics and educational culture, losing our independent power and sense of identity. In the 50 years of Japanese rule, the Taiwanese social reality reflects the three colonial stages illustrated by Tao, Dong-feng. As "postcolonialism" illustrates, from the occupation and control of land resources during "old colonialism" to the partial political economy dominance of "neo-colonialism," the educational and cultural systems implemented during colonial occupation still has a hegemonic advantage in the judgment of values and lifestyle seen in Taiwanese citizens. Japan used Taiwan as an experimental station to expand its Asian colonial empire, and as an experimental site to demonstrate the achievements of the Japanese Empire; introducing the foundations of Western modernization to the Taiwanese people as a result. Japan's colonial process against Taiwan is seen as a replica of the Western colonial empire in Asia, therefore marking the colonial experience between Taiwan and Japan a subject of avid discussion by Western postcolonialism theorists.

Patricia Yuen-Wan Lin, "Issues in Taiwanese Craft Studies– A Perspective of Postcolonial Culture discourse."

Examining tea culture in Taiwan is much like a discussion among Western postcolonialism theorists. The origin of Taiwanese tea art can be traced back to the "Kung-fu Tea" small pot brews originating from the Chaozhou region of Guangdong province in China. After the "Kung-fu Tea" small pot was introduced to Taiwan, an intensive study led by countless Taiwanese tea enthusiasts, tea societies and teahouses became popular in the late 1970s. Scholars and enthusiasts combined aesthetics, philosophy, and Buddhist Zen in the Chinese literay culture, also blending the Japanese tea ceremonial concept into modern Taiwanese lifestyle. Contemporary Taiwanese tea culture has been transformed and reinterpreted as a set of inclusive tea drinking and life attitude that completely differs from its source.

In the process of drinking tea, the Taiwanese people follow a focused yet relaxed procedure. The characteristics of water, the way of boiling water, the form of tea sets, the environment, the time of day, and the relationship between host and guest are all areas of concern that the Taiwanese follows naturally. This naturalistic care to explore each aspect of tea and relationships leads to enjoyment in all its participants, but also represents a fascinating spiritual state; demonstrating the true meaning of "Tao and art as One" as well as focus on tea-related details, and the creation of atmosphere. Appreciating the color, fragrance and shape of tea is an indispensable part of tea art; the art of brewing and brewing skills make tea not only an enjoyment of beauty, but also a reflection of the individual's attitude towards life.

Wu, Guang-rong was born in Huainan of the Anhui Province in China. He graduated from the Arts and Crafts Department in Nanjing Academy of Art and is currently teaching at the Hangzhou China Academy of Art and is the director of its Folk Art Museum. Wu's creation is based on the Chinese Yixing mudboard formation technology, adding skillful and ingenious construction procedures to make the material demonstrate softness and malleability; greatly subverting the extreme and highly precise traditions of Yixing pots in China.

As the most internationally influential Chinese ceramic artist, Lu, Bin is expert at employing natural attributes in his material and the technical characteristics of ceramic art to express contemporary cultural concepts and individual thought. Lu's art uses the object of "ceramic" to form an in-depth understanding of the materiality and material properties of art and media and discover hidden cultural attributes. His incredible technique is not to please the observers or others, but an expression of individual thought. His creative nucleus has always been essential propositions in 'arising and ending,' 'present and nihility,' and 'reincarnation and entrophy.' The artist hopes to express his reflective attitude towards the current status of Zisha culture under the cultural background of value disillusions, crushing traditional classics to remove the teapot from its original cultural context and re-encode it into a new symbolic image while releasing the disillusionment of contemporary culture and reality.

Wu, Hao uses the unique material language and spatial composition of pottery to materialize the spiritual state and conveying his own true, and pleasant feelings for the taste of life. It is an experience of understanding the spiritual through the material, viewing materiality by "exalting life through objects, expressing thought in objects." The process of this development conveys a huge amount of historical information, making utility but one of its attributes. Yet utility is key: without "use," there is no medium for "story." Wu, Hao's creations convey this speculative value of materiality.

Li, Hai-lin is a practical ceramics artist in China. He was influenced by the minimalistic ways of life in the Southern and Northern Song dynasties, and is one of the very few with Southern literati tastes in a new generation of artists.

After graduating from the Department of Ceramics at the China Academy of Art, Huang, Yong-xing is currently teaching at the Guangzhou Arts and Crafts Vocational College in Dehua, Fujian Province. Under rigorous education and training in art, Huang arrived in Dehua, known for its traditional manufacturing of Chinese porcelain. Huang used porcelain clay traditionally used to shape the Guanyin Buddha to make teapots, emphasizing the transmission of light and smooth warmth of local porcelain materials in minimalistic design.

Clouds Tea Lifestyle Company, founded by Zhi, Bing-sheng, is one of the main advocates of tea culture in China. In addition to leading the evolution of tea services, Zhi, Bing-sheng also out of the mainstream thought of Yixing pottery in his tea set designs, appropriating the town of Jingde's historical porcelain craftsmanship into tea ceremony tools that demonstrate contemporary Chinese neo-classical aesthetics. With the

"Chinese Gene" as his inspirational source, U+ Furniture's Shen, Bao-hong incorporates the simple beauty and complex structure of traditional Ming furniture to modern furniture design. For many years, he has been committed to the original design and production of contemporary Chinese furniture, and has won many international and annual designer awards. He describes himself as a "traveler shuttling through the tunnels of time."

Japanese national treasure Professor Nakagawa Mamoru combines traditional and modern techniques and adds many subtle expressions of nature and humanity to his work. His creations express contemporary values from past history and have a healing affect that touched the spirits of many. Among his works is the most well-known "carving and inlaid" technique using a chisel to draw patterns on metal, and then tapping metal alloy onto the utensil's surface, a true demonstration of skill.

11th Ōhi Chōzaemon (Ōhi Toshio). Kaga Domain's 3rd hereditary chieftain Maeda Toshitsune implemented a cultural reward policy during his rule, inviting the 4th generation Kyoto Senno Sensou Tea Master to visit his domain and popularize the tea ceremony practice. In the year 1666 (Kanbun 6th year), Tashi Chōzaemon, the apprentice of Raku ceramics' 4th generation pottery master, accompanied Senno Sensou on another trip by invitation of 5th hereditary chieftain Maeda Tsunanori. Tashi Chōzaemon began a branch of Raku ceramics in Ōhi, Kanazawa, changing his name to Ōhi Chōzaemon after settling down in Kanazawa. His legacy spans over 350 years and is now passed on to the 11th, a representation of Kanazawa's tea ceremonial heritage. 11th Toshio Ōhi is not only a tea potter, but also a painter, director of space and industrial design and creative director. He sees craftsmanship as the common foundation in these fields, with no differentiation between traditional and contemporary.

Yamamura Shinya is currently a professor at Kanazawa College of Art, with a focus of lacquer crafts, enamel painting and other decorative techniques (snails, eggshells) in addition to the research and development of contemporary jewellery. Yamamura has a long-term fascination with the creation of small and exquisite objects. He combines intricate abstract pearl shell patterns with ultra-fine lacquer technology in minimalist design. All contributing to the modernized feel and eternal abstract dimension that fits in the palm of your hand.

Kuwata Takuro deconstructed the image of the tea bowl or water finger (pot) in the tea ceremony and added the rich colors of Pop design. His use of traditional techniques include: feldspar glaze (Shiyo glaze), "Kairagi" (the cracking of glaze in fire), "Sutōnbāsuto" (the stone mixed in clay bursting out when burnt), and an intervention of contemporary attitude bridges the distance between ordinary people and elegant ceramics while retaining the sublimity of Japanese culture, and is considered a break-through attempt blossoming from traditional Japanese aesthetics.

Takemura Yuri graduated from the Major of Ceramics at Aichi Prefectural University of Fine Arts and Music. Her work incorporates a unique blend of modern minimalist and feminine detail in the traditional tea bowl. Takemura is a new generation of female pottery artist currently highly regarded in Japan Pottery artists.

Matsunaga Keita graduated from the Department of Architecture at Meijo University, and is accustomed to using a potter's wheel to build a foundation for his work and then bending the clay to shape it, leaving joining marks remain until the clay is heated. At the same time, he collaborates with lacquer artist Yukimasa Takahashi to work in the coloring of surfaces. This new technique reflects the traces of production with vivid colors in the finished tea bowl.

Ishiyama Tetsuya, is an artist without a background in pottery, yet entered the field of pottery creation because of his passion for ancient ceramics. His style is richly creative, and is listed as one of the fifty most anticipated pottery artists to follow in contemporary times by professional pottery art magazine Honoho Geijutsu.

Kume Keiko graduated from the Kanazawa College of Art. Specializing in delicate and intricate metalwork, she combines organic shape with soft texture into metallic creations. After getting a Ph.D. from Tokyo University of Art, Sakai Naoki established a clear personal style in his design of iron teapots. He hopes to regain the traditional roots of Japanese culture. In addition to the practicality of tools, he pursues beauty; perfectly blending the warmth and relaxed feeling of iron, bringing a rich sense of art and closer to modern lifestyles.

Kise Hiroshi's creation of metal and lacquerware is his signature technique. Yamagishi Saya, Ikeda Terumasa, and Muramoto Shingo are three young and promising lacquer creators who have just completed their training at Utatsuyama Crafts Workshop in Kanazawa, and brings experimental spirit to traditional art.

Nara Yuki grew up in a family deeply immersed in the art of traditional pottery and graduated from the Department of Architecture at Tokyo University of Art. He was specially invited to design a tea room that expresses the new tea space atmosphere of Japan's new generation.

In the evolution of contemporary tea culture, Taiwan was highly influenced by China and Japan both in terms of the aesthetics the function of the objects used. Building on this foundation, Taiwan's contemporary ceramic art found a link to the tea culture through the rapid development of the 1980s. The cultivation of tea art is closely related to the production details of tea ceremony tools and the development of new tea crafts. Or we should say that under the emphasis of an elevated local consciousness, Taiwanese tea enthusiasts re-interpret and construct a culture of new tea ceremonies in order to establish a cultural identity unique to Taiwan through a combination of contemporary ceramic art and craft creators. From the environment of tea appreciation to the rapid evolution of tea living set designs, the choice and breadth of tea sets are becoming increasingly popularized. All sensory processes that contribute to the ultimate taste of tea is accompanied by the experimental spirit of tea enthusiasts and artisans. There are no boundaries in the world of tea, and new values are constantly being introduced. This new interpretation of cultural value constructs the lineage of contemporary tea arts in Taiwan, becoming a most identifiable cultural body.

A New Interpretation of Material and Form

Among the Taiwanese artists participating in the exhibition, Su, Bao-zai is currently a high-profile creator on both sides of the Taiwan Strait. He incorporated research in the traditional kiln celadon glaze over the past ten years into the design of tea sets, providing an excellent demonstration of literati cultural characteristics in the Song Dynasty.

Fang, Po-ching and Chung, Wen-ting both hold master's degrees in artistic creation from Taiwanese institutes. They each received Ph.D. degrees from the Royal College of Art in Melbourne, Australia and the Tokyo University of Art, Japan, respectively. These two creators extracted their experiences in foreign lands and injected these experiences to create exotic and diverse tea sets. Fang built a system from the rough and natural ash of early wood burning to sculptural vocabulary to use in the creation of surface textures, showing the beauty and purity of ceramic materials. Chung's work shows the continuation of female sensitivity in the delicate strokes and inspiring performance of her tea set creations. After the opening of the Yingge Ceramics Museum in Taiwan, the country has established a complete platform aligning with international ceramic art. In addition to the international ceramic biennial exhibitions, Taiwan has attracted many well-known ceramic artists to visit, create and communicate experience. A diversified international exchange gradually inspired a new generation of pottery creation in Taiwan. Amongst the new generation, Cho, Ming-shun and Luo, Ji-ming are artists who have both won first prize of the Taiwan Golden Potter Prize, focusing on teapots as a nucleus of traditional tea tools to expand their individual sculptural vocabulary. Liu, Jung-hui's performance of atmospheric tea art is also unparalleled.

Injecting Different Materials and a New Interpretation of Utility

Liu, Shih-pin has inspired many new generation through the experimental exploration of ceramic materials combined with different materials.

Wu, Wei-cheng and Chao, Tan-chi are more diverse in the manipulation of the tea sets. Wu employs his ultra-modern style tea sets to construct an atmospheric environment that deeply reflects architectural signifiers. Chao forges her sets from the perspective of a metalworker, transforming the process of labor into an interesting and aesthetic discourse.

An Expansion of Metal Tea Sets

After graduating with an advanced degree, Chen, Yi entered the field of tea set creation. Chen combines a personal interpretation of tea sets with forging techniques and is the most anticipated creator in the new Taiwanese generation. Huang, Tien-lai's achievements come from the full display of his perfect control of casting, achieving an amazing balance between practical and non-practical sculpture.

Jen, Ta-Hsien is extraordinary amongst contemporary Taiwanese metal media sculpture artists. The planning and creation of this tea space not only experimental but also invites contemporary tea enthusiasts to re-examine the confines of tea space.

The Japanese tea ceremony was originally a noble activity and was rigorous and standardized. However, the development of Taiwanese tea ceremonies is a culture for ordinary people. Anyone can make tea, anytime and anywhere. Japanese tea ceremonies pays attention to atmosphere and spiritual state, but the Taiwanese make tea to emphasize the characteristics of tea and produce its most delicious state. Therefore, in the past 30 years, Taiwanese tea enthusiasts have reinterpreted the rigorous yet engaging, diverse yet uncomplicated new tea ceremony through a continuous dialogue with tea farmers and tea artisans.

The Japanese colonial influence on public culture remains affective on the attitude of Taiwanese tea drinking, causing tea drinking to become more than a continuation of Chinese culture. The introduction of the philosophy and aesthetics of Japanese tea lifestyles and the use of tools is therefore injected into the development of Chinese culture and is an example of the Taiwanese internal transformation from taste to a new form of life and art through tea drinking in the lives of civics. In the cultural appreciation of tea sets and tea drinking attitudes, contemporary China and its Asian neighbors are very obviously affected by Taiwan. This is an indisputable fact, while new interpretations are still in progress.

第十一代　大樋長左衛門 Ohi Chozaemon XI

大樋黑釉窯變茶盌
Firing-Denatured Tea Bowl with Ohi Black, Copper & White Glaze
2018｜陶 Clay｜H 9× Φ13cm

大樋黑釉窯變茶盌
Firing-Denatured Tea Bowl with Ohi Black, Copper & White Glaze
2018｜陶 Clay｜H 9× Φ13cm

蓋置　Futaoki
2016｜銅、黃銅鏤空焊製 Copper, brass openwork, braze
H5.5×W5.5×D5.5cm

久米圭子 Kume Keiko

上圖　蓋置　Futaoki
2018｜黃銅、鏤空焊製 Brass, openwork, braze
H5.5×W5.5×D5.5cm

下圖　蓋置　Futaoki
2018｜黃銅、鏤空焊製 Brass, openwork, braze
H5.5×W5.5×D5.5cm

夜光貝線文中次　Striped Tea Caddy, Turban shell
2018｜螺殼、金粉 Turban shell, gold powder
H6.3 × W6.3 × D7.3cm

山村慎哉 Yamamura Shinya

上圖
金も之字桃形香合　Golden Peach Shaped Incense Case
2018｜鍍金、金粉 Gold plate, golden powder
H6.3×W6.0×D5.7cm

下圖
梅形耀貝茶器　Plum Shaped Tea Ware, Mexican Abalone
2018｜貝殼、金粉 Mexican Abalone, gold powder
H7.8×W7.4×D4.0cm

山岸紗綾 Yamagishi Saya |

植物採集 / ヒメニチリン　Plant Collecting
2017 | 漆、朴、金、銀、夜光貝、木炭
Urushi, Magnolia Obovata, gold, silver, snail, charcoal
H7.5×W3.5×D2.5cm

山岸紗綾 Yamagishi Saya

左圖
植物採集 /ヒトリノドカ　Plant Collecting
2018｜漆、朴、銀 Urushi, Magnolia Obovata, silver
H5×W4.6×D5cm
右圖
植物採集 / カラヒョウシ　Plant Collecting
2018｜漆、朴、卵殻、金、夜光貝
Urushi, Magnolia Obovata, egg-shell, gold, snail
H7.5×W3.5×D2.5cm

多重鑲嵌朧銀花器 Inlaid Vase of the Layer
2018｜鑄造朧銀、金、銀、赤銅、四分一
Cast alloy of copper, silver, and tin with copper, silver, and gold
inlay｜H25×W20cm×D8cm

木瀨浩詞 Kise Hiroshi

銅之割跡　*Crack Traces of Copper*
2018｜銅、黃銅、漆 Copper, brass, urushi
H25×W25.8×D26.3cm

銅之割跡　Crack Traces of Copper
2018｜銅、黃銅、漆 Copper, brass, urushi
H13.9×W21×D21cm

石山哲也 Ishiyama Tetsuya

凹紋茶碗　Dimple Bowl
2018│瓷土 Porcelain
H10.3×W16.8×D12.8cm

石山哲也 Ishiyama Tetsuya |

上圖
凹紋茶碗　Dimple Bowl
2018｜陶土 Stoneware　H10.3×W16.8×D12.8cm

下圖
凹紋茶碗　Dimple Bowl
2018｜陶土、金&鉑金光澤 Stoneware, gold & platinum Lustre
H10.3×W16.8×D12.8cm

池田晃将 Ikeda Terumasa

人造物5　Artifact5
2018 | 漆、木、貝母
Urushi (Japanese lacquer), wood, mother-of-pearl
H62×W12×D6cm

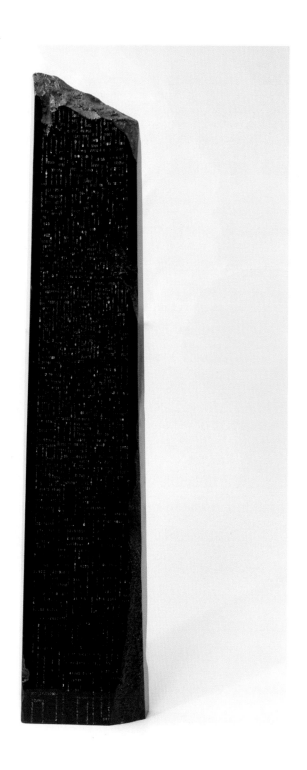

人造物5　Artifact5
2018 | 漆、木、貝母
Urushi (Japanese lacquer), wood, mother-of-pearl
H62×W12×D6cm

盌「現象之際」 Teabowl "Brink of Phenomenon"
2017｜瓷土、銀箔 Glazed porcelain, silver leaf
H10.9×Φ13.6cm

竹村友里 Takemura Yuri

盌「宇宙邊際」　Teabowl "End of Space"
2017｜瓷土、銀箔 Glazed porcelain, silver leaf
H9.6 × Φ12.6cm

盌「鍾馗」　Teabowl "Zhong Kui"
2017｜陶土、銀箔 Glazed stoneware, silver leaf
H9.7 × Φ13.7cm

坂井直樹 Sakai Naoki

鐵壺——湯沸之形　Iron Kettle, Form- Inspiring Water of Steaming
2017｜鐵、漆、鍛造 Iron, lacquer, hammering
H30×W17×D16cm

枝羽——風之軌跡　Wing of a Foliage- The Trajectory of the Wind
2018｜漆、竹、布料、和紙　Lacquer, bamboo, cloth, washi paper
H61×W38×D30cm

松永圭太 Matsunaga Keita

脈脈　Myaku Myaku
2018｜陶土、壓製成形 Stoneware, press molding
H8.5×W14×D13.5cm

左圖
脈脈　Myaku Myaku
2018｜陶土、壓製成形　Stoneware, press molding
H8.5×W13.5×D13.5cm

右圖
2018｜陶土、壓製成形　Stoneware, press molding
H23.5×W17.5×D17.5cm

桑田卓郎 Kuwata Takuro

茶垸　Tea Bowl
2017｜瓷土、釉、顏料 Porcelain, glaze, pigme
H22.5×W22.9×D21.7cm

上圖
茶垸　Tea Bowl
2017｜瓷土、釉、金 Porcelain, glaze, gold｜H15.8×W19.2×D16.0cm

下圖
茶垸　Tea Bowl
2018｜瓷土、釉、顏料、白金 Porcelain, glaze, pigment, platinum
H17×W19.3×D17.7cm

奈良祐希　Nara Yuki

五行茶室

Wu xing / The five elements（in Chinese philosophy: wood, fire, earth, metal and water）Tea Room

2018｜檜木、和紙、玻璃、合板 Hinoki, washi paper, glass, plywood｜H400×W406.5×D406.5cm

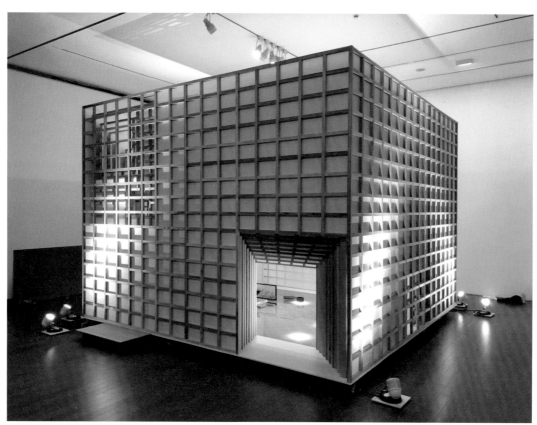

四方軟提梁捏壺之一
Square Kneading Teapot with Handle-1
2007 | 紫砂陶 Yixing clay
H15.2×W12.5×D10.5cm

吳光榮 Wu, Guang-Rong

上圖　四方軟提梁捏壺之二
Square Kneading Teapot with Handle- 2
2007｜紫砂陶 Yixing clay｜H12.5×W12.3×D10.8cm

下圖　捏壺茶具之一　Kneading Teapot Set-1
2002｜紫砂陶 Yixing clay｜H4.2×W13.5×D10.2cm

趨之曲之　Tend and Bend
2008｜宜興陶、描金
Yixing clay, gold tracing
H27×W20×D40cm

吳昊 Wu, Hao

走小僧　The Walking Boy
2016｜宜興陶、描金 Yixing clay, gold tracing
H10×W10×D10cm

白石　White Stone
2014｜瓷 Porcelain｜H9×W11×D14cm

李海霖 Li, Hai-Lin

岩栖No.4　Inhabitable NO.4
2016 ｜ 陶土 Stoneware
H8×W9×D10.5cm

梅花周盤壺（清 邵全章款）
Plum Shaped Zisha Tea Pot
2017｜特拼紫泥 Mixed Yixing clay
H9×W13.2×D21.2cm

陸斌 Lu, Bin

白乳　Bairu
2017｜白瓷 Porcelain｜H6.8×Φ7cm, 120c.c.

黃永星 Huang, Yong-Xing

上圖
龍池　Longchi
2017｜白瓷 Porcelain｜H4.8 × Φ7.8cm, 100c.c

下圖.
大明　Daming
2017｜白瓷 Porcelain｜H7.6 × Φ6.2cm, 120c.c.

浮雲堂 Clouds Tea Lifestyle Company |

上圖
水波紋杯　Tea Cup with ripple pattern

下圖
靈芝杯　Tea Cup with Lingzhi Pattern

浮雲堂 Clouds Tea Lifestyle Company

上圖
扁壺　Flat Tea Pot

右下圖
出川炮口壺　Tea Pot with Straight Spout

左下圖
新彩菊花壺　Tea Pot with chrysanthemum pattern

妙境茶生活空間
"Wonderland" Tea Room
2018｜北美白蠟木 American ash
H260×W300×D300cm

妙境茶生活空間
"Wonderland" Tea Room
2018｜北美白蠟木 American ash
H260×W300×D300cm

方柏欽 Fang, Po-Ching

茶具組　Tea Set
2016｜陶土、瓷土　Stoneware, porcelain
H15×W30×D70cm

器曰　Breaking the Rules
2017｜瓷 Porcelain
H60×W60×D120cm（展示尺寸 Display Size）

吳偉丞 Wu, Wei-Cheng

違秩序　Breaking the Rules
2017｜陶、瓷、不鏽鋼、錫
Clay, porcelain, stainless steel, tin
H60×W60×D120cm（展示尺寸 Display Size）

走獸G　Land Beast G
2018｜陶、瓷 Clay, porcelain｜H8×W18×D20cm

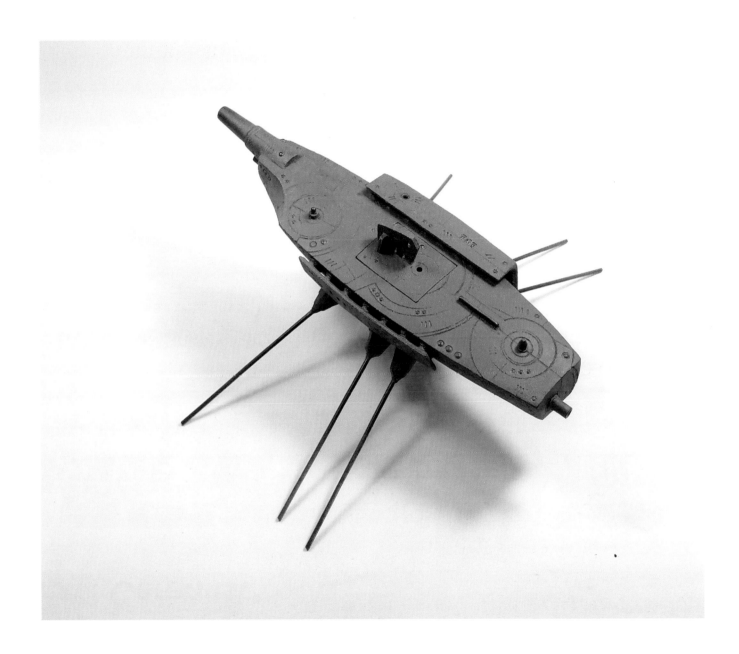

卓銘順 Cho, Ming-Shun

上圖
巡游D　Aquatic Beast D
2018｜陶、瓷 Clay, porcelain｜H10×W11×D17cm

下圖
馴風E　Flying Beast E
2018｜陶、瓷 Clay, porcelain｜H15×W12×D18cm

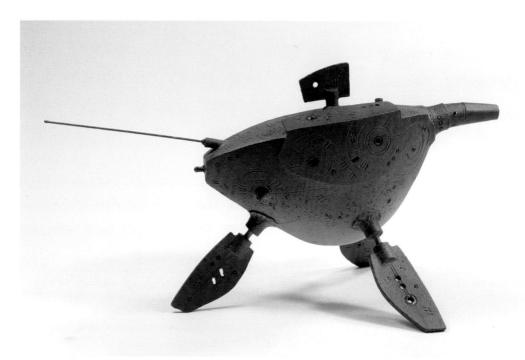

敲痕・茶倉系列 #1~#3
Signs of Raising #1~#3
2018｜Silver, red copper 純銀、紅銅
H10×W15×D15cm each

黃天來 Huang, Tien-Lai

左圖
水舞　Water Feature
1998｜不鏽鋼、銅 Stainless steel, copper｜H47.5×W25.5×D27.8cm

右圖
竹影清風　Bamboo Shadow of Fresh Breeze
1999｜不鏽鋼 Stainless steel｜H52×W28×D30.5cm

趙丹綺 Chao, Tan-Chi

茶席組　Tea Set
2016-2018｜999銀、820銀、錫、紅銅、鑄鐵、硬木、生漆、黑漆、陶土、鐵釉
999 silver; 820 silver; tin, red copper; cast iron, hard wood, raw lacquer; lacquer; clay, iron glaze
L180×H40cm (Display Size)

心經切面壺組　Tea Pots Set with The Heart Sutra
2017｜紫砂、金 Yixing clay, gold
前 Front: H17×W16×D12cm
後 Back: H7.5×W13.5×D7.5cm

劉世平 Liu, Shi-Pin

左圖
獅鈕飾紋壺組──遊　Tea Pots Set with Lion Button and Pattern
2017｜紫砂、金 Yixing clay, gold
前 Front: H14×W25.5×D11cm｜後 Back: H13×W25×D12cm

右圖
黑檀木把飾紋壺組　Tea Pots Set with Red Sanders Handle and Pattern
2017｜紫砂、東非黑黃檀木 Yixing clay, red sanders
前 Front: H15×W27×D11cm｜後 Back: H12.5×W25×D10cm

雲 茶盤　Cloud Shape Tea Tray
2018｜陶、金箔、織布釉　Clay, gold leaf, glaze
H10×W52×D81cm

鍾雯婷 Chung, Wen-Ting

姿　Sugata
2018│瓷 Porcelain
H9×W6×D10cm

烏木金銀彩壺
Red Sanders Tea Pot with Gold and Silver Decoration
2017│陶、金銀彩釉
Clay, glaze│H11×W7×D12cm

羅濟明 Lo, Ji-Ming

上圖
黑石器　Black Stone
2018｜陶、金銀彩釉 Clay, glaze｜H11×W10×D13cm

下圖
黑石器系列　Black Stone
2017｜陶、金銀彩釉 Clay, glaze｜H11×W8×D14cm

秋露　Dew
2018｜配方土、長石釉 Clay, glaze
H20×W45×D85cm（展示尺寸 Display Size）

蘇保在Su, Bao-Zai

上圖
初晴凝香　Just Cleared
2018｜配方土、長石釉 Clay, glaze｜H20×W45×D85cm（整組展示尺寸Display Size）

下圖
碧波清影　The Silhouette of Ripples
2018｜配方土、長石釉 Clay, glaze｜H20×W45×D85cm（整組展示尺寸Display Size）

灰階　Gray Scale
2018｜不鏽鋼 Stainless steel
依展出空間而定 Variable dimension

附錄
Appendix

子題一

「都市・新地景・空間權力」
（以下依筆畫順序排列）

● 周東彥（1981-）

出生於臺北，英國中央聖馬丁藝術暨設計學院劇場與多媒體碩士畢。

重要展覽經歷：2013 年臺北數位藝術中心個展「光流格影」（Lights Flowing Out of Frame）、2015 年首爾 284 文化車站聯展「親密的狂喜」（Intimate Rapture）、臺北國際藝術村個展「暫離練習」（Escape Practice）、2017 年臺北市立美術館聯展「社交場——可交換城市計畫」（ARENA-Interchangeable Cities Project）、政治大學藝文中心個展「一首不小心寫大了的詩」（A Panoramic Poem）。

作品創作理念

〈睡與醒之間〉由世界劇場設計大獎作品〈空的記憶〉延伸發展而成。與舞蹈家周書毅合作，透過環景攝影機拍攝的數個幾乎超現實空間中的舞蹈影像，串連一場睡與醒之間的旅程。

環景鏡頭全面性的拍攝紀錄時，肢體與空間的關係瞬時放大。圓弧與沒有邊際的視界，企圖於空間流轉變化之下，辯證內在流動與外在世界的緊密與疏離並存。

● 林文藻（1977-）

出生於臺中，美國加州州立大學長堤分校畢。

重要展覽經歷：2012 年美國佛蒙特州 Red Mill Gallery 個展「I Must Have Been There」、2015 年菲律賓馬尼拉 First United Building Community Museum 個展「re: tracings - Project」、2016 年臺北 TKG+ 耿畫廊聯展「打開——當代 2016 選」、臺北尊彩藝術中心聯展「2016 大內藝術節——日出的悸動」、2018 年臺北也趣藝廊聯展「2018 Y. E. S TAIWAN VII」。

作品創作理念

延續了「新羅曼史」展覽中的一件作品，再次以「時間」為主軸，表現「微妙改變著，但卻被人們遺忘」的風景。

位於豐原市的「南陽路」是我從老家前往南陽國小的必經之路。「南陽」這個名稱在不同縣市都能見到，因此我對「南陽」的感知，也隨著時間、空間及成長歷程而產生變化。「南陽」已經變成一棟棟高樓大廈——裡面擠滿補習班與年輕學子。我以積木堆疊出屬於我的「南陽路」，積木代表我們小時候玩的各種遊戲。

● 林書楷（1983-）

出生於臺南，國立臺北藝術大學美術系美術創作碩士班畢。

重要展覽經歷：2015 年日本廣島市現代美術館聯展「俯瞰的世界圖」、2016 年國立臺灣美術館聯展「臺灣美術雙年展——一座島嶼的可能性」、2017 年韓國光州國立亞洲文化殿堂聯展「Urban Implosion」、臺南蕭壠文化園區聯展「近未來的交陪：2017 蕭壠國際當代藝術節」、臺南華慶鑄物廠個展「陽台城市文明 × 華慶鑄物廠」。

作品創作理念

「陽台城市文明」系列作品源自於一個都會傳說，是藝術家置身仿效許多人的身體經驗與生活經驗而產生的作品風格。

此系列作品藝術家以深厚的臺南歷史建築與文化脈絡作為基底，發展出藝術家對於臺南新的城市想像。題材採取了從荷治時間到近代的歷史建物以及其歷史故事，以獨特的繪畫風格，天馬行空地轉化成一個具有歷史感卻同時擁有對未來新世界的想像之意向，並以此概念繪製了一系列作品，作品象徵著藝術家生活在這塊土地上所擁有的深厚情感與記憶，也表示對未來的期盼跟再造，更隱喻生活中許多逐漸消逝且再平常不過的人事物，期望能重啟人們的關心以及重視它們的價值。

● 侯淑姿（1962-）

出生於嘉義，美國羅徹斯特理工學院影像藝術碩士畢。

現任國立高雄大學創意設計與建築學系助理教授。

重要展覽經歷：2010 年高雄市立美術館個展「望向彼方——亞洲新娘之歌」、2013 年臺北大趨勢畫廊個展「我們在此相遇」、2015 年臺北 VT 畫廊個展「長日將盡」、2017 年高雄市立美術館個展「鄉關何處——高雄眷村三部曲：侯淑姿個展」、2018 年東京都寫真美術館聯展「I know something about love: Asian Contemporary Photography」。

作品創作理念

民國 98 年，作者踏入了高雄左營的眷村，與高雄眷村結下了不解之緣。隨之而來的是持續長達八年的研究調查、搶救行動與拍攝創作交織的歷程，此「高雄眷村」三部曲的創作始於首部曲「我們在此相遇」（2010-2013 年），關注高雄左營的勵志新村、復興新村、崇實新村與自助新村在眷村改建前與拆遷後的人與景；繼而是以高雄鳳山黃埔新村為題的二部曲「長日將盡」（2015 年），最終是以左營明德新村與建業新村的眷村現況為題的三部曲「鄉關何處」（2010-2017 年），此眷村三部曲為接續先前「亞洲新娘之歌」三部曲（2005-2009 年）後，關注戰後軍眷移民在臺灣高雄面對眷改巨變的女性離散影像敘事曲。

此次展出的四件為首部曲「我們在此相遇」的「崇實新村」系列。崇實新村於 2013 年 8 月從左營地圖上消失。此系列作品譜寫了荒謬的眷改政策下消失眷村的悼念輓歌，最終是為失落的眷村繫上一縷紀念的黃絲帶。

● 張永達（1981-）

出生於南投，國立臺北藝術大學科技藝術研究所畢。

重要展覽經歷：2012 年國立臺北藝術大學關渡美術館個展「Between Seen / Unseen」、2014 年國立臺北藝術大學關渡美術館聯展「識別系統」關渡雙年展、2015 年比利時蒙斯 Maison du Design 聯展「City Sonic 2015」國際聲音藝術節、2017 年法國里昂國立高等藝術學院聯展「瞭望者」、2018 年臺北采泥藝術個展「super penetrating」。

作品創作理念

影像裝置包含九個電腦程式即時運算產生的影像，程式運算資料來自日本 311 強震瞬間觀測站記錄之巨量地震數據，面對冰冷抽象的大量電腦資料編碼一無法理解卻比人造媒體訊息更貼近真實，我們如何感知、接收這些訊息與刺激一儘管這已經超越了人腦所能識別與認知的臨界點；亦或是對看不見的世界產生焦慮與感官的失調？

● 陳飛豪（1985-）

出生於新竹，國立臺北藝術大學藝術跨域研究所。

重要展覽經歷：

曾參與 2016 年臺北雙年展，臺北國際藝術村「銹條通」——2017 街區藝術祭以及 2018 年關渡雙年展。個展經歷為 2015 年東門美術館「臺南新藝獎：記憶另存個展」與 2017 年朝代畫廊「失效的神話」個展。

作品創作理念

本計畫創作背景為臺南市美術館二館前身為日治時期臺南神社的地緣歷史，並以其御祭神北白川宮能久親王的一生為引，帶出大日本帝國在臺灣島上留下的歷史脈絡及其從奮起到崩壞的進程。

● 廖文彬（1986-）

出生於臺北，國立臺灣藝術大學雕塑系畢。

重要展覽經歷：2014 年臺北黑森林藝術空間個展「手的溫度」、2015 年高雄郭木生美術中心聯展「高雄藝術博覽會」、2016 年臺北郭木生美術中心聯展「臺北藝術博覽會」、臺北黑森林藝術空間

個展「自化像」、2017 年臺北黑森林藝術空間個展「遊戲人生」。

作品創作理念

因家庭背景關係，從小就在工地長大的我，看到也體會到，許多處於社會低下階層的勞動族群，感受到他們的辛勞與人情溫度！將工地中，磚與水泥、布手套的記憶，透過藝術的語彙，重現這些材料，並賦予女神維納斯、布手套牛隻等造型呈現，希望能打破觀者對於勞動族群的刻板既定印象！且能從別的角度與思維，重新欣賞社會上那些曾經默默付出的人、事、物！

● 劉子平（1984-）

出生於桃園，國立臺灣師範大學美術研究所創作理論組博士。

重要展覽經歷：2014 年國立台灣美術館聯展「臺灣木版畫現代進行式」、2016 年臺中日月千禧酒店聯展「臺中藝術博覽會」、2017 年桃園中壢藝術館個展「自然的啞劇」、2018 年臺北雅逸藝術中心聯展「寫實新銳展」、臺北松山文創園區聯展「福爾摩沙藝術博覽會」。

作品創作理念

〈棲居〉與〈石城〉兩件作品運用具象繪畫的手法詮釋人類文明的都市地景，都市的空間中交雜了「新與舊」、「動與靜」、「自然與文明」的繁複面貌。另一方面，全球化的地景逐漸消融地域性的建築差異，巨大的水泥叢林建構起了錯綜繁複的空間迷宮。其中，「候鳥」如週期般往來於各異的土地與氣候之間旅行，在如同迷宮般的都市夾縫中棲居、覓食與繁衍，在城市的建構與破壞之間生存，候鳥的形象也作為城市中人類生存狀態的一種指涉。

● 霍凱盛（1990-）

出生於葡屬澳門，澳門理工學院視覺藝術系畢業。

重要展覽經歷：2014 年葡萄牙里斯本 Arte Periférica 畫廊個展「Paraíso」、2016 年西班牙巴塞隆拿 Fira Barcelona 聯展「Swab Barcelona」Art Fair、2017 年香港凱倫偉伯畫廊個展「遠東誌」霍凱盛作品展、2018 年意大利佛羅倫斯 Le Murate 聯展「不可能的黑鬱金香」、臺北日帝藝術藝廊個展「今昔輿。圖」霍凱盛個展。

作品創作理念

數百年前的澳門是怎樣的？那數百年後的澳門又是怎樣的？如果這座城市只有世遺建築，或只有一幢幢高聳入天的博彩娛樂場，或只有堵滿車輛的街道……這情景會是過去？現在？還是未來？一成不變未必能經得起考驗，變幻未必是永恒，中庸也未必長久。歲月流轉，昨日的澳門已不是今天的澳門，今天的澳門也許不會是明日的澳門。

● 羅展鵬（1983-）

出生於嘉義，國立臺灣師範大學美術研究所畢。

重要展覽經歷：2012 年日本大阪 YOSHIAKI INOUE Gallery「亞洲具像——四國聯聯展」、2013 年美國洛杉磯 ESMoA 美術館「EXPERIENCE03. TRUTH」-El Segundo Museum of Arts、2014 年美國康乃爾大學強生美術館「界：臺灣當代藝術展 1995-2013」、2017 年臺北大觀藝術空間個展「墨墨嵐」。

作品創作理念

一個跨越人類歷史四千年的想像，一個文明的綜合體，從信仰到建築，有多采多姿的樣貌，唯一不變的只有人性，以及風化後的遺跡。

子題二

「府城藝術史話」
（以下依筆畫順序排列）

● 王獻琛（1830-1889）

讀書赴試，久不得售，乃為鎮署稿識。能作水墨畫，擅畫蟹，書亦疏放。光緒十五年卒，年六十。（資料出處：《臺灣歷史人物小傳——明清暨日據時期》，臺北：國家圖書館，2003，頁64、《臺南市人物采風》網站）

作品創作理念

款文：（殘損不釋）……氏稀氏
鈐印：王獻琛（白文）、字世希（朱文）

● 甘國寶（1709-1776）

字繼趙，一字和庵，福建古田人。雍正十一年（1733）武進士，由侍衛授廣東遊擊，改湖廣洞庭協副將，擢貴州威寧鎮總兵，乾隆二十五年（1760）任鎮守臺灣掛印總兵官。臺地番漢雜錯，乃教番民明禮義、務耕種。後復權鎮廣東雷瓊，以擒五指山黎酋功，再授臺灣掛印總兵。平王添送覆鼎山之亂。旋以病卒於官，年六十八。雖官武職而切念民瘼。生平樂善好施，雅好文墨，善畫虎，能傳其威鷙之神。在臺灣時，嘗作「紀典」，以補府志所未及。（張子文）
（資料出處：《臺灣歷史人物小傳—明清暨日據時期》，臺北：國家圖書館，2003，頁79。）

作品創作理念

款文：甘國寶指頭生活。
鈐印：甘國寶印（白文印）、私藏（朱文印）

● 朱玖瑩（1898-1996）

晚年曾居於臺南安平而自號安平老人、安平久客，堂號為師掃帚齋，中國湖南人，中華民國政治人物與書法家，曾擔任過湘軍總司令部政務委員兼秘書、內政部土地司司長、衡陽市長、湖南省民政廳長、財政部鹽務總局局長兼臺灣製鹽總廠總經理等職，1968年退休後隱居於臺南安平。其書法啟蒙自其父，後師從譚延闓，以顏體楷書最出色，曾於1990年4月獲得中華民國行政院國家文藝獎書法教育特別貢獻獎。著有《學書淺說》、《臨池三論》等書。（節錄自臺南市美術館數位典藏）

作品創作理念

釋文：一庭花發來知己 萬卷書開見古人
款文：長沙朱玖瑩

● 呂璧松（1872-日治時期）

福建泉州人，清朝時期寓居臺南，擅長南宗書法，無論山水、花鳥、人物、走獸均專精，對臺南畫師有深遠影響，曾指導陳玉峰與潘春源等人。（徐明福、蕭瓊瑞，《雲山麗水：府城傳統畫師潘麗水作品之研究》，宜蘭：國立傳統藝術中心，2001，頁36。）

作品創作理念

款文：虎溪三嘯，畫於台郡竹齋。（待考）
鈐印：呂璧松（朱文圓形印）

● 李錦繡（1953-2003）

南臺灣嘉義人，活躍於70年代後的女性藝術家，作品多為抽象與半抽象形式的平面繪畫，在師大美術系的學院基礎與私人畫室的非學院訓練，以及三位師長席德進、廖修平以及李仲生啟蒙的現代藝術基礎上，持續進行與潛意識交流的心象式創作，展現具個人特色之

形式語彙。早期關心的題材是家族與記憶的再現，1983年留學法國後對透明材質與光影折射產生興趣，回臺後轉向表現樹形的東方人文線性以及日常生活與物件交雜的多層次空間。（節錄自臺南市美術館數位典藏）

作品創作理念

李錦繡的作品不似傳統繪畫中重視空間景深的描繪，她大多不刻意暗示空間，畫面背景多採用平塗方式，甚至有時畫面中會出現疑似空間倒置的感覺，這件作品〈風雲際會（一）〉以室內景象為主，作品的左邊部分被各種雜物推滿，分成上下景，前景被各種不同類型的椅子，有凳、辦公室椅、竹編的椅子等；後面的桌上置放著檯燈、神像、香爐、某者祥瑞形象的擺飾品，桌子前方還有桌帷，而畫面的右半部，前景淺棕色的竹簍，使視覺動線帶出後方的物件，引導出空間的深度，是在其他作品中少見的形式，整個畫面的前後景，以畫面中心的檯燈下半部做為連接，畫作中的所有物件讓大家得知李錦繡的收藏極為多樣。（節錄自臺南市美術館數位典藏）

● 沈哲哉（1926-2017）

出生於臺南。師事廖繼春、郭柏川，未正式進入美術學校，仍致力於藝術創作，曾獲全省美展、教師展、臺陽美術展臺陽獎等獎項，並獲頒臺南市美術功勳獎、臺南市長獎、臺南市榮譽市民獎，為南美會創始會員之一。創作題材主要為風景、人物、花，油畫作品色彩豐富而浪漫，其所創作之裸女、芭蕾舞少女，表現女性溫柔、優雅的體態。（節錄自臺南市美術館數位典藏）

● 沈昭良（1968-）

出生於臺南。

重要展覽經歷：2011年加拿大多倫多湖濱中心攝影藝廊個展「STAGE」、2013年塞爾維亞諾威薩佛伊弗迪納（Vojvodine）當代美術館聯展「凝視自由：臺灣當代藝術展」、2017年美國伊色佳康乃爾大學強生美術館聯展「悚憶：解與紛」、2018年日本東京21_21 Design Sight聯展「新星攝影城市展——威廉克萊恩以及活在22世紀的攝影家們」、2018年西班牙維多利亞Sala Am rica藝廊個展「STAGE」。

作品創作理念

此次展出的STAGE（舞臺車）作品，為目前仍普遍在臺灣各地的綜藝團演出中使用，由大貨車所改裝而成的油壓式舞臺車，於現實環境中開展的姿態。冀望其中獨特的產業類型與豐厚的文化信息，馳騁的發想與炫麗圖案，足以誘發觀者對於這項臺灣特有的娛樂文化，含括時間、空間、橫向、縱向、平面及立體架構的連結與想像。

● 東寧女子 陳氏（生卒年不詳）

作品創作理念

款文：東寧女子陳氏繪
鈐印：漫漶不可識

● 林光夏（約嘉慶年間）

嘉慶年間游宦來臺書家。

作品創作理念

釋文：端明書所以絕諸家之上者，謂其深入晉唐室耳。
海岳稱如美女遊春，嬌嬈萬狀，豈自負刷書，作此譏語耶。
款文：少瞻林光夏
鈐印：光夏小字子常（朱文）、又字少瞻（白文）、讀書沁脾庭（白文）

● 林玉山（1907-2004）

出生於嘉義，本名英貴，號雲樵子、諸羅山人及桃城散人。受到幼時家中聘請的民間畫師影響，自小展露繪畫天分。19歲負笈東瀛，留學東京川端畫學校，一年後參加第一回臺灣美術展覽會即獲入選，

與郭雪湖、陳進同被譽為「臺展三少年」。1935 年赴日深造，建立了個人風格，已是領導嘉義地區的人物。

曾自述創作兩次變化的過程，第一次是川端畫學校回來後，問學於悶紅老人，由寫生派參透文人畫的契機；而京都時期是摹古考古期，摹取的對象是中國宋人的畫作。「寫生」的觀念，始終是林玉山創作的源頭與鼓吹的信念，不僅實踐於畫中，亦常在其文章中提及。（資料取材自文化部「臺灣網路美術館」網站）

● 林紓（1852-1924）

福建人，為同治光緒間客寓旅臺的書畫家。（資料參考：黃華源，〈誌『墨潮──瀛臺先賢書畫展』〉，《墨潮──瀛臺先賢書畫展》，臺南：臺南市政府文化局，2016，頁 13。）

作品創作理念

款文：風暖汀洲吟興生，遠山如畫雨初晴。作於都門，客次，畏廬，林紓。

鈐印：臣林紓印（朱文）、一字畏廬（白文）

● 林智信（1936-）

出生於臺南歸仁，畢業於臺南師範藝師科，曾擔任臺灣省全省美展、全國版畫展評審委員、臺北市立美術館審議委員、國立台灣美術館典藏委員、高雄市立美術館典藏委員、臺南市美術研究會（南美會）會長及獲得第六屆「臺南文化獎」。

其版畫曾至韓國、日本、美國、荷蘭、烏拉圭、西德、澳洲等國家展覽，另外，在水墨、油畫、交趾陶、雕塑等創作領域也都有傑出不凡的成就。著名的作品有版畫〈迎媽祖〉、大型油畫〈芬芳寶島〉等。（節錄自臺南市美術館數位典藏）

作品創作理念

〈爽秋〉林智信四季童玩系列包括〈嬉春〉、〈歡夏〉、〈爽秋〉、〈暖冬〉，作品呈現濃濃的古早味，刻畫農村孩童天真與稚氣模樣，以及早期臺灣農村情景與古早童玩的樂趣。〈爽秋〉畫面以黃褐、棕、磚紅等大地色系構成，背景有一片白色似羽毛的植物，以秋天時節推論為芒草，畫面的中央有一男一女騎著腳踏車，手拿著風車，快速旋轉的風車，以及後方都倒向右邊的芒草，可以看得出畫面中的景象是有風的，帶出動態感，兩位主角的衣服都換成長袖宣示著秋天到來的氛圍。（節錄自臺南市美術館數位典藏）

〈阿嬤飼雞〉

在農業社會的時代裡，臺灣的農村家家戶戶都有養雞，而且讓母雞自孵小雞，一代代繁衍著：有公雞、母雞、小雞，這家族顯得很旺盛，牠們點綴在農村裡增添了幾許的生趣。身著古傳統中國藍衣配黑褲，纏小腳的阿嬤，在徐徐風搖的芭蕉樹下，閒來無事飼雞來作伴：阿嬤喝雞來的叫聲、母雞咯咯叫、小雞覓食聲，這群雞嫣然形成一幅既熱鬧又興旺的畫面。（節錄自臺南市美術館數位典藏）

● 林覺（1796-1850）

字鈴子，號臥雲子、眠月山人。善繪花鳥、人物、山水、走獸等題材，且筆法、墨影之間頗具揚州八怪之一黃慎之風格，尤其所繪線條轉折之間的「飛白」，瀟灑自然以外，更是意趣飛揚。另外，林覺也為廟宇及建築物作壁畫，亦成為備受敬重的一位「頭手師父」。其主要活動的地區域以府城為主，遊蹤也曾到過嘉義、竹塹潛園等處。（節錄自臺南市美術館數位典藏）

作品創作理念

這是林覺存世最完整的山水畫，分別以「春日郊遊」、「夏日遇雨」、「秋江行舟」、「雪窗閒吟」為主題，其中山石的畫法，仍可得見林覺反筆勾勒的習慣，而畫中人物的造型，放大而視，仍是林氏快筆勾勒的作風。四幅中只有最後一幅落款，惟文字已經破損，不易辨識，幸署名「林覺」二字，及鈐印「林覺之印」及「臥雲子」，均仍完整可讀。（節錄自蕭瓊瑞，《林覺〈蘆鴨圖〉美術家傳記叢書歷史・榮光・名作系列》，臺北：藝術家，2012，頁 57。）

● 金潤作（1922-1983）

出生於臺南，原名丙丁，15 歲前往日本，之後進入大阪府立工藝學校（今大阪市立工藝高等學校）就讀；畢業後再入大阪美術學校（今大阪美術學院）圖案設計科，就學期間曾前往私人畫室學習繪畫，期間受小磯良平（Koiso Ryohei）指導最深。金潤作在戰後初期的臺灣畫壇，從首屆全省美展即以〈路傍〉（又名「賣香菸的男孩」）獲得特選，此後連續三年獲得特選，並經歷多次無鑑查出品後，1956 年以 34 歲的年紀榮膺省展評審委員。（節錄自臺南市美術館數位典藏）

作品創作理念

此為 1974 年金潤作的〈觀音落日 II〉，觀音山是臺灣許多畫家熱愛描繪的景緻，1973 年金潤作購屋於臺北近郊的社子，在這裡，可以隔著淡水河遠眺觀音山。畫面中藝術家頗為特殊的以紅色描寫山形，河面的反照和實景，排列成平行的構圖，山下的幾處紫、黑表現夕陽照不到的地方，近景的幾抹藍、綠，一方面增加了畫面色彩對比的動感，一方面也穩定了全幅構圖的重心，整幅作品以溫暖的紅色為主調，尤其大膽地將整座觀音山以紅色來處理，猶如夕陽將整座山都澈底染紅。（節錄自臺南市美術館數位典藏）

● 倪湜（光緒年間）

倪湜，字筱梅，號隱叟，福建同安人。光緒初游幕來臺，入臺防廳袁聞拆幕參與撫番。嗜吟詠，著有《浪遊隨筆及吟稿》。因與陸鼎、蕭聯魁二人之字皆有「梅」字，世人合稱「三梅」。（資料出處：黃華源，〈誌『墨潮─瀛臺先賢書畫展』〉，《墨潮─瀛臺先賢書畫展》，臺南：臺南市政府文化局，2016，頁 12。）

作品創作理念

釋文：擔水夫何也？典史雖小，尚屬朝廷命官；擔水夫雖尊，與他無涉。今之學

● 涂燦琳（1947-）

出生於臺南，字北門邨人。師承傅狷夫、賴敬呈、歐豪年。1985 年獲吳三連文藝創作獎，1989 年獲國家文藝創作獎。因從小生長在臺南北門鄉下，對臺灣鄉村景緻具有深刻的體會與描寫，兼擅山水、花鳥、走獸，其作品融合了寫意與造境，賦予表達對象質感與量感。自許發展詩、書、畫相依相生相映的繪畫創作途徑。（節錄自臺南市美術館數位典藏）

作品創作理念

涂璨琳作畫的題材多取自於庶民生活，〈籬畔〉中背景的茅草與竹籬是早期農村常見的景象，而火雞亦是其童年的記憶。畫面中，成群火雞聚集一起，熱鬧而壯觀，作者表現火雞開屏之姿態形韻兼備，羽翼層次濃淡分明，繪畫手法細緻而富有趣味。詩題：「相呼覔食竹籬西，隨伴村雞到曉啼，每在臨池思舊侶，畫成又作小詩題。」（節錄自臺南市美術館數位典藏）

● 張炳堂（1928-2013）

出生於臺南。1941 年小學六年級即以〈大成坊〉入選第七屆臺陽展，1942 年入選第五屆府展。曾受顏水龍、廖繼春指導，師事郭柏川，1952 年與郭柏川、謝國鏞、沈哲哉、張長華等人創立南美會。張炳堂的油畫創作用色大膽，多以色彩的原色進行畫面構圖，色彩對比強烈，深具野獸派風格，以臺南廟宇與古蹟、鄉土風景為主要創作題材。（節錄自臺南市美術館數位典藏）

作品創作理念

這幅作品描繪的是南鯤鯓代天府的正殿，畫面帶有張炳堂一貫的風格，使用了大量強烈對比、鮮豔的色彩，帶有歐洲野獸派的風格，然而近觀其畫面筆觸，卻又帶有表現主義的豪放風格。

南鯤鯓代天府是一座位於臺南市北門區的廟宇，是全嘉最古老的王爺信仰中心，有「臺灣王爺總廟」之稱，與歸仁保西代天府、佳里

金唐殿並稱「南瀛三大代天府」。相傳於明朝末年，當地漁民在海上拾獲載有五府千歲的王船，於是便建廟祭拜，後因神蹟顯赫而廣為流傳，後因廟毀，信徒另擇棟榔山建廟；據傳王爺選地建廟時，與當地的神靈「囝仔公」起了爭執，雙方大戰數日依舊難分勝負，遂請觀音佛祖會同眾神調停，後以「王爺公起大廟，囝仔公建小廟，大廟來進香，小廟必有敬。」尊囝仔公為「萬善爺」，一同享用香火。（節錄自臺南市美術館數位典藏）

● 連橫（1878-1936）

字雅堂，號慕陶；及長，改名橫，字天縱；一字武公，又號劍花；顧喜自署雅堂。生於福建臺灣府臺灣縣寧南坊馬兵營（今臺南市府前路臺南地方法院對面）。畢生盡瘁於保存臺灣文獻，其著作除巨著《臺灣通史》外，尚有整理臺灣語文之《臺灣語典》四卷，《臺灣贅談》、《臺灣漫錄》、《臺灣古蹟志》、《雅言》，臺灣第一部文學史《臺灣詩乘》六卷，刊行《臺灣詩薈》二十二期；復又蒐集先民有關臺灣著作三十餘種，編為《雅堂叢刊》。（資料出處：《臺灣歷史人物小傳—明清暨日據時期》，臺北：國家圖書館，2003，頁 466-468。）

作品創作理念

釋文：弧帨雙輝映竹城，鹿車鴻案久知名。曠開大衍花齊放，節過中春月兩明。孝友傳家推碩望，文章華國足長生。百齡仇儷稱殤日，還向高堂介兒觥。

款文：良臣先生暨德配陳夫人五秩雙慶，愚弟連橫敬撰。

鈐印：海外連橫（朱文）。

● 郭柏川（1901-1974）

出生於臺南打棕街（今海安街），臺北師範學校畢。1928 年進入東京美術學校西洋畫科，從岡田三郎助習畫。留日期間曾三度入選臺灣美術展覽會。1937 年前往中國北平任教。定居北平十二年是繪畫生涯中重要的轉捩點，加上日籍畫家梅原龍三郎數度到北平，均由郭氏結伴寫生，因此受梅原的影響頗深。1948 年返臺後一直定居於臺南。郭柏川取材臺灣民間，自器物、刺繡與廟宇紅牆中，尋求與他風格相融的色彩，擷取成熟圓融的東方精神在自己藝術上，影響臺南藝術發展甚深。（節錄自臺南市美術館數位典藏）

● 陳永森（1913-1997）

出生於臺南。1935 年赴日本美術學校繪畫科和東京美術學校油畫科進修，在日求學時，攻讀了日本畫科、油畫科、工藝科、雕刻科，涉略範圍甚廣。於日展期間一度同時入選日本畫、油畫、書法、雕刻及工藝等五項作品，故獲得萬能藝術家之雅號，曾二度榮膺日本最高藝術大賞——白壽獎。1949 年再考入東京藝術大學附屬工藝技術講習所。不斷追求創新與突破，其膠彩作品融入油畫用色原理與技法，如後印象派秀拉點描法，以及中國水墨畫「墨分五色」的思考層面。（節錄自臺南市美術館數位典藏）

● 陳玉峰（1900-1964）

本名陳延祿，人稱「祿仔師」、「祿仔仙」或「陳畫師」。漢學啟蒙於堂哥陳延齡，畫藝由臨摹畫譜入門，後求教請藝於兼有文人畫與民間風俗畫特長的呂璧松，受其影響深遠。臺灣現存著名彩畫作品包括嘉義新港水仙宮、臺北保安宮、高雄旗後天后宮及臺南三山國王廟。門神作品包括嘉義城隍廟、臺北艋舺清水祖師廟與北港朝天宮。（資料出處：李乾朗，《陳玉峰〈郭子儀厥孫最多〉美術家傳記叢書歷史·榮光·名作系列》，臺北：藝術家，2012，頁 19-21、24。）

作品創作理念

款文：時甲子歲仲夏月既望，畫於赤崁，居士玉峰陳延祿本。

鈐印：玉峰（朱文）、陳延祿印（白文）

● 陳英傑（1924-2012）

本名陳夏傑，出生於臺中大里，長兄為臺灣雕塑家陳夏雨，1949 年定居臺南，任教於成大附工建築科。臺灣光復後入選省展多次，1956 年提出〈思想者〉雕塑以免審查會員身分參展。從 1956 年到 2010 年期間，在寫實與造型之間迂迴前進，呈現「思想者」各種樣貌，顯示雕塑家的創作策略與藝術理念，被視為是陳英傑重要系列代表作品。1953 年加入南美會，對南部雕塑發展影響甚深。2010 年以 87 歲高齡製作〈思想者〉大型雕塑創作，進駐成大校園。（節錄自臺南市美術館數位典藏）

作品創作理念

〈迎春〉為陳英傑於 1954 年獲得第九屆全省美展最高榮譽獎作品，並在當年受薦為首位榮獲省展雕塑部免審查會員。陳英傑於 1953 年創作此件作品，這年他與妻子剛結婚，是結婚前以妻子為模特兒所作。此作女人頭部傾斜，雙手上舉抓著領巾，身體略呈 S 型，顯現優雅體態，均勻而富韻律感，臉部表情則呈現女性因新婚而羞澀的樣貌。此雕塑無論對作者的家庭或藝術，皆具有重要意義，象徵著陳英傑人生一個新階段的開始。（節錄自臺南市美術館數位典藏）

● 陳澄波（1895-1947）

出生於嘉義。1924 年陳澄波赴日就讀東京美術學校師範科，1926 年以〈嘉義街外（一）〉首次入選日本第七屆帝展，是臺灣首位入選日本帝展的西畫家。1929 年至中國上海任教，深受中國山水畫影響，1933 年返回嘉義，先後組織七星畫壇、赤島社、臺陽美術協會等重要美術團體。回到家鄉後，嘉義風景自然經常入畫，且期間風格變化頗為明顯，創作風格逐漸穩定與成熟，1947 年於二二八事件中遇難隕落。（節錄自臺南市美術館數位典藏）

作品創作理念

33 歲的陳澄波，在考進東美研究科這年，特地為自己畫了一張自畫像，作為人生的重要紀錄。由於他一向非常欣賞梵谷的創作熱情，所以這張自畫像，他就決定借用梵谷的手法，來表達對自我的期許。也許當時創作心中湧動的情感實在太強烈了，畫面上陳澄波臉上的表情，竟然顯露出緊張焦慮的神色，在整個色調暗沉的畫面上，游移的光線正好映照在臉上，造成強烈的明暗效果，也加強了畫面情緒性張力。畫這張圖時，陳澄波頭戴大大的寬邊帽、一頭蓬鬆的捲髮，一身陳舊的衣帽，卻掩不住瀟灑不羈的態度與一股懾人的英氣，他以炯然堅毅的目光，毫不閃避地看著觀眾，大方表達對努力奔赴未知前程的篤定。（資料出處：林育淳，《油彩·熱情·陳澄波》，臺北：雄獅圖書股份有限公司，1998，頁 48。）

● 陸鼎（1756-1838）

字調梅，江蘇吳縣人，光緒時來臺。與倪湜、蕭聯魁二人，均工於左腕月寫，並有名於清光緒年間的臺灣書壇，時人並稱「三梅」。（資料出處：黃華源，〈誌『墨潮—瀛臺先賢書畫展』〉，《墨潮——瀛臺先賢書畫展》，臺南：臺南市政府文化局，2016，頁 12。）

作品創作理念

釋文：論事者，理長拙，而勢常勝。君子處事，未嘗奪於所勝，而病於所詘。夫君子豈不欲成天下之事哉。天之興廢不可取。必時之得失不可強為。以其不可強為而取，必though橫於中。則顧畏觀望之釁漸生，而貞固迫切之誠日損。固有。假雖死無益之言，以文其過而逃其譏。接失於（後文缺漏）

● 曾茂西（道光年間）

道光年間寓臺畫家，精人物，亦擅翎毛走獸，此領域題材近似徐渭之筆趣。

作品創作理念

款文：口戊午曾茂西。

鈐印：曾光美印（白文）、茂西（朱文）。

● 黃本淵（道光咸豐年間）

道光咸豐年間書法家。

作品創作理念

款文：歸途近處鄉心切，勝地遊來野望難。傍晚人煙趨市急，隔江燈火雜星寒。江煙筆去詩思老，口楚樓高酒夢殘。為問辛勤成底事，俗情坐怕對魚竿。

款：虛谷黃本淵

鈐印：臣黃本淵（白文），辛巳徵士（朱文）。

● 黃明賢（1943-）

出生於臺南。師承傅狷夫、胡克敏，曾獲青溪美展國畫金環獎、南美展國畫市長獎。黃明賢的水墨作品以花鳥、農村景色為主要題材，其所繪之走禽，姿態活潑、翼羽輕盈而生動，栩栩如生；農村景象作品，則繪出恬靜而清雅之意境，正如其樸實淡泊的個性。（節錄自臺南市美術館數位典藏）

作品創作理念

此作品為黃明賢擅長繪製的農村景象，畫面中以稻草、竹子搭建的棚子是農村常見的景象，棚架上的紫色牽牛花亦是鄉間常有的花種。在清晨喚醒人們的雞隻，成雙成對，公雞氣宇軒昂，母雞則依偎在旁，悠閒地享受早晨時光。此作筆法細緻，用色清新淡雅，道出作者對於臺灣農村的深刻觀察與眷戀。（節錄自臺南市美術館數位典藏）

● 楊鵬摶（1871-1922）

本籍福建泉州，1890 年舉秀才，1902 年任臺南第一區街長，1910年任東區區長，1915 年任臺南廳參事，1920 年任臺南州首任協議會員。為臺南南社社員，詩作多登於報刊，擅長行草。（資料出處：楊建成《日治時期臺灣人士紳圖文鑑》[稿本]）

作品創作理念

釋文：千山鳥飛絕，萬徑人蹤滅，孤舟簑笠翁，獨釣寒江雪。

款文：壬戌春日，雪嶤仁兄雅屬，楊鵬摶書

鈐印：楊鵬摶印（白文）、錐園（朱文）。

● 葉文舟（生年不詳 -1827）

字晴帆，號藕香，福建海澄縣人。乾隆五十一年（1786）舉人。乾隆年間來臺，長於指墨松柏。歷任連江、晉江、嘉義教諭。晚年寓臺邵，指墨松柏尤長。目前在嘉義留有「嘉義市孔廟修復碑」，文末刻有「臺灣府嘉義縣儒學教諭加三級海澄葉文舟謹書 嘉慶二十年歲在乙亥皋月穀旦立」。（資料出處：國立清華大學圖書館《日治時期日人與臺人書畫數位典藏計畫》）

作品創作理念

款文：東崗夭矯雨蒼龍，千尺盤空黛色濃。六十餘年松若比，誰知我更老於松。庚辰春，仿青藤居士畫意，藕香，葉文舟指畫。

鈐印：臣文舟印（白文）、藕香指畫（朱文）。

● 廖繼春（1902-1976）

出生於臺中豐原農家，自幼家境清苦。臺北國語學校畢業後，任教於豐原公學校，後在未婚妻資助下，於 1924 年赴東京美術學校深造，返臺後先後任教於臺南長老教中學、臺中師範學校、臺灣省立師範學校。1927 年以〈裸女〉與〈靜物〉分別獲得入選與特選，1928 年以作品〈芭蕉之庭〉入選帝展。曾組「赤陽會」、「赤島社」、「臺陽美術協會」。曾在 1962 年獲得美國國務院的邀請訪問美國，接著經由歐洲返臺，期間遊歷各大美術館，成為影響他日後畫風改變的轉捩點，1976 年因肺癌逝世。（資料出處：潘潘，《廖繼春〈有香蕉樹的院子〉美術家傳記叢書歷史·榮光·名作系列》，臺北：藝術家，2012，頁 13-15、21、27。）

作品創作理念

此作以鮮豔的色塊，畫出遠山、海面與河岸，畫家自由自在的表達個人主觀的審美態度，並不在乎交代時間和距離的關係，繽紛的色彩，雖向奔放的音符，其實一切都在畫家的掌握之中，有節奏的互動呼應。

● 蒲添生（1912-1996）

生於嘉義市美街，1919 年進入嘉義玉川公學校（現崇文國小）就讀，導師為日後的岳父陳澄波。十四歲時以膠彩畫作品〈鬥雞〉參加新竹美展獲得首獎，展現其藝術才華。1931 年進入日本東京川端學校，1933 年考取日本帝國美術學校（現武藏野大學），課餘之暇進入朝倉文夫私塾學習雕塑，奠定創作的基礎。以人體雕塑為主要鑽研題材；創作多直接以手捏塑造型，甚少借重工具，他認為如此才能捕捉人體的肌理感。（節錄自臺南市美術館數位典藏）

作品創作理念

〈詩人〉被認為是東方的〈沉思者〉，除了外貌的相似外，在選用的模特兒也有所關聯。蒲添生的〈詩人〉原形為魯迅，而羅丹的〈沉思者〉則是以但丁（Dante Alighieri）為藍本，魯迅與但丁雖然相隔了五、六百年，但他們對當時的社會與人性的批判卻相當一致。蒲添生曾說：「這尊像我用了許多想法來呈現，主要是表現中國人的風度。」所謂的風度是什麼？或許就是千年沉積下來的文化底蘊。裸體具有豐富的意義，然而〈詩人〉的那身衣袍則是中華文化傳承的象徵，深沉卻溫潤。〈詩人〉的那雙眼沉靜地凝視著前方，靜靜地看著天下人，從過去到現在到未來。（資料來源：蒲添生雕塑紀念館）

● 劉啟祥（1910-1998）

出生於臺南柳營，上公學校時受到美術老師陳庚金的賞識，引發他學習繪畫的興趣。1928 年考入東京文化學院美術部洋畫科。畢業後返臺，曾在日日新報社舉行首次個展。隨後與楊三郎同船赴歐。歐洲的藝術氣氛與大師作品激發出他的雄心，孜孜不息於繪事，繪畫融成他生命的一部分。臺灣光復後攜眷回到臺南定居，曾組成「高雄美術研究會」，對臺灣的美術教育、美術風氣推動給予熱誠的關心與贊助，逐漸成為南臺灣畫壇的靈魂人物。（資料出處：文化部《臺灣網路美術館》網站）

作品創作理念

雖然畫幅尺寸不大，但此作卻把最高峰玉山冷冽險拔的氣勢表現得淋漓盡致。冷色調的藍與白，讓空氣中的分子似乎都凝結了起來，陽光照射的部分把白雪照得發亮，而陰影的部分，畫家則是用湛藍色；這一明一暗的強烈對比，讓山勢看起來更加挺拔陡峭。沒有過多的筆觸與肌理的變化，完全任由畫刀粗放自在的運用揮灑，表現出臺灣山脈的生命力。（節錄自曾媚珍，《劉啟祥〈成熟〉，美術家傳記叢書 II 歷史·榮光·名作系列》，臺北：藝術家，2014，頁 50。）

● 劉銘傳（1836-1896）

字省三，安徽合肥人。詔任督辦臺灣事務大臣、臺灣省任巡撫，擅行書。於光緒十八年十一月二十七日（1896 年 1 月 11 日）病卒，年六十。著有《大潛山房詩集》二卷，《奏議》二十四卷。（資料出處：《臺灣歷史人物小傳—明清暨日據時期》，臺北：國家圖書館，民國 92 年 12 月，頁 680-681。）

作品創作理念

釋文：般若波羅蜜多心經。觀自在菩薩。行深般若波羅蜜多時。照見五蘊皆空。度一切苦厄。舍利子。色不異空。空不異色。色即是空。空即是色。受想行識。亦復如是。舍利子。是諸法空相。不生不滅。不垢不淨。不增不減。是故空中無色。無受想行識。無眼耳鼻舌身意。無色聲香味觸法。無眼界。乃至無意識界。無無明。亦無無明盡。乃至無老死。亦無老死盡。無苦絕滅道。無智。亦無德。得以無所

得故。菩提薩埵。依般若波羅蜜多故。心無罣礙。無罣礙故。無有
恐怖。遠離顛倒夢想。究竟涅盤。三世諸佛。依般若波羅蜜多故。
得阿耨多羅三藐三菩提。故知般若波羅蜜多。是大神咒。是大明咒。
無上咒。是無等等咒。能除一切苦。真實不虛。故說般若波羅蜜多
咒。即說咒曰。揭諦揭諦。波羅揭諦。波羅僧揭諦。菩提薩婆呵空。

款文：雨孫仁兄大人雅屬，省三劉銘傳書。

鈐印：劉銘傳印（白文）、省三（朱文）。

● 潘元石（1936-）

出生於臺南，臺南師範學校藝術科畢業後，即長期耕耘藝術教育、
推動文化工作，在臺南府城擁有極高聲望。早年，服務於臺南啟聰
學校，全力投入特殊兒童美術教育及幼兒美育的推廣，並出版專書，
對兒童版畫教學，著力尤深。後進入信誼基金會、臺南市文化基金
會，對臺南地區文化工作推展，貢獻頗巨。潘元石個人在創作上，
以版畫為主，其中尤其用心於「藏書票」的研究與推廣，長期與日
本藝壇交流，成為臺日民間友誼的橋樑。（資料出處：臺灣南美會）

作品創作理念

〈臺南寧南門〉

寧南門又稱為大南門，建於 1725 年，是清領時期臺灣府城十四座
城門之一。寧南門是一座甕城，早期是用來加強城門防守而修建的
小城，上方設有防禦設施，能使來犯的敵軍無法輕易的揮軍直入。
臺南原有寧南門、大北門、小北門、小東門、小南門五座甕城，而
寧南門是現今僅存的一座，現為直轄市定古蹟。（節錄自臺南市美
術館數位典藏）

〈安平民房〉

安平區位於臺南市西南方，區內北邊為老安平聚落，是漢人最早的
開發地之一。安平早期被稱為「大員」，明朝中葉開始聚集了來自
中國、日本的走私客，以及來自葡萄牙、西班牙等歐洲商人，並在
此與臺灣的平埔族進行貿易，今日安平的延平老街漸漸形成市街。
老安平聚落旁有安平舊港，清領時期至日治初期曾為南臺灣第一大
港，後因淤積嚴重，日治時期便另修築臺南運河供城內船隻進出安
平舊港。今日的安平是歷史悠久、古蹟眾多的知名觀光區，由六個
角頭（海頭社、王城西社、灰窯尾社、港仔尾社、十二宮社、囝子
宮社）組成，而舊街道依然保有些許清代的建築樣式；而許多古代
居民的生活習俗仍在安平沿襲著。（節錄自臺南市美術館數位典藏）

● 潘春源（1891-1972）

原名聯科，人稱「科司」，字進盈，早年字邨原，春源為號，後以
號行，並為日後畫室之名。1909 年，十八歲自修有成，在府城三官
廟旁，開設「春源畫室」。1928 年第二屆「臺展」，使用膠彩為媒
材，取「寫生」手法，〈牧場所見〉獲得入選。此後至 1933 年，
持續入選，直到 1933 年的第七屆「臺展」。（資料出處：林保堯，
《潘春源〈婦女〉美術家傳記叢書歷史・榮光・名作系列》，臺北：
藝術家，2012，頁 14-15、18-19。）

作品創作理念

款文：丁卯夏四月上澣日，畫于赤崁觀瀾山房之靜軒，春源寫。

鈐印：潘進盈印（白文）、春源（朱文）

● 蔡茂松（1943-）

出生於嘉義縣義竹鄉，畢業於國立臺灣藝專美術科國畫組，臺灣師
範大學美術研究所結業。曾任長榮大學視覺藝術系主任、臺南師
院美教系教授、臺南美術研究會理事長，以及全國美展等評審委員。
蔡茂松承傳狷夫一派山水畫風，筆墨功夫紮實，是將傳統筆墨轉
於詮釋臺灣本土風光的傳系傳人之一，其投身藝術教育近四十載，
作育無數優秀門生，在臺灣地區形成重要的水墨教學體系，是府城
中壯一輩水墨畫家當中，頗受矚目的一位。（節錄自臺南市美術館

數位典藏）

● 蔡草如（1919-2007）

出生於臺南，原名錦添。早年隨舅父陳玉峰習畫，1943 年赴日本川
瑞學校日本畫科夜間部習畫。1946 年自日本返回臺，協助陳玉峰廟
宇彩繪工作，同年，以〈伯樂相馬〉入選第一屆省展。1964 年與畫
友成立「臺南市國畫研究會」，並擔任首屆理事長，曾獲臺南市最
高榮譽藝術獎。蔡草如一生繪製許多廟宇彩繪、道釋畫及肖像畫等
常民藝術作品，亦醉心於膠彩與水墨畫創作，更活用水彩、蠟筆、
油畫等各種不同材質特性，是位傑出的全方位畫家。（節錄自臺南
市美術館數位典藏）

作品創作理念

此件作品的構圖是從赤崁街仰眺赤崁樓，於夏日清晨捕捉旭日東升
時刻之情景，文昌閣聳立畫面正中央，成為畫面焦點，朝陽宛如急
速旋轉的火球一般，從文昌閣左後方綻射出漩渦狀金芒，其逆光照
射的光影氛圍，籠罩整個畫面，或許了為凸顯光影效果之考量，這
件作品的線條表現機能頗為低調，利用色彩和明暗之變化來烘托光
影效果。也由於清晨的逆光表現，因而依照現場視覺經驗而降低彩
度及景物細節之清晰度。左側翹脊者是蓬壺書院建築體，遠處盛開
鳳凰花處是成功國小，也點出了夏日時節。此作品同時紀錄了戰後
初期赤崁樓之原貌。（節錄自臺南市美術館數位典藏）

● 蕭聯魁（1839-1898）

字占梅，另字嘯期，又字筱鵬，名甲庚，別字性中，號康齋。鳳山
縣港東裏人。原姓張，為蕭家抱養。咸豐四年（1854）秀才，咸豐
八年娶府城許吉為妻。光緒十六年（1890）恩貢。乙未割臺，仍居
府城。1898 年去世，年六十。為有名的左腕書法家，酒醉時作書更
佳。列入臺南十大書法家之列。並與幕客陸鼎（字調梅）、倪湜（字
筱梅）三人，均以左腕書著稱，時人並稱「三梅」。（郭啟傳）（資
料出處：《臺灣歷史人物小傳—明清暨日據時期》，臺北：國家圖
書館，2003，頁 748-749。）

作品創作理念

〈行書 -2〉

釋文：出門見南山，引領意無限。秀色難為名，蒼翠日在眼。有時
白雲起，天際自舒卷。心中與之然，托興每不淺。何當造幽人？滅
跡棲絕巘。

款文：蕭聯揆左書

鈐印：蕭聯魁印（白文）、左手翰墨（白文）、氣象萬千（朱文）。

● 薛萬棟（1911-1993）

出生於高雄，自小就喜歡畫畫，雖然非藝術科班出身，但無師自
通，作品深得公學校老師欣賞。1928 年移居臺南府城，在火車站
擔任驛夫，1928 歲拜膠彩畫家蔡媽達為師，1931 年拜賴蒙呈學國
畫。1932 年及 1934 年分別以膠彩畫〈姐妹〉和〈夏晴〉入選第六
和第八屆臺展，1938 年以膠彩畫〈遊戲〉榮獲府展特選、總督賞，
1947 年至 1972 年多次獲得省展入選與優選。早期從事膠彩創作，
光復後改以水墨創作，晚年創作題材主要以「火雞」寫生為主。（節
錄自臺南市美術館數位典藏）

作品創作理念

火雞是薛萬棟晚期以單一主題創作數量最多的作品，無論是手稿、
草圖皆是他以嚴謹的態度構圖，掌握火雞的自然樣態。薛萬棟用火
雞表現家庭、夫妻、親子的關係，雄雞表現壯闊的氣勢，身旁有母
雞跟雛雞結伴而行，從畫面中不難感受作者借物詠情和賦予深遠寓
意的表現手法。（節錄自臺南市美術館數位典藏）

子題三

● **方偉文**（1970-）

出生於汶萊，國立臺南藝術大學造型藝術研究所畢業。

重要展覽經歷：2008年捷克布爾諾市國立摩拉維亞美術館聯展「泡沫紅茶：臺灣藝術‧當代演繹」、2016年臺南東門美術館「遠方、靜物和其它的」、臺南文化中心「城內／城外：臺南當代藝術初探」、2017年中國銀川當代美館聯展「非常持續」、2018年國立新加坡博物館聯展「Signature Art Prize」。

作品創作理念

〈野生花園〉的原初意象是築於橋道上的住居；裝置以虛擬實境進駐的形態，試圖作個人世界狀態的呈現和探索。如作品名稱所示，拆成兩個部分。「野生」做為一種自然機制的現象，而「花園」則是人工的意向結果，兩者在基礎上看似衝突，實則在「園」的存在上不然。這裡不企圖在處理自然／非自然的二元對立，最終作品是完全人為的結果，而是試圖提出兩種併存的處、模式和過程。裝置主要的立體結構為木製的桁架橋，以它為出發點，向周圍衍生。「住居」以人類的屋子或類建築呈現，以物件尺寸上，做為意象的出現，或其它物種的居所。作品中的自然與人造物做為視覺元素以隨機的方式出現，與主結構也許融合也許突兀，最終各有位置。（藝術家提供節選）

● **方惠光**（1952-）

出生於臺南，美國舊金山藝術大學雕塑碩士。

曾任美國舊金山藝術學院雕塑研究所教授、臺灣藝術大學美術系、雕塑系教授。

重要獲獎：1993年美國舊金山藝術學院最高榮譽獎、2007年中華民國行政院文建會公共藝術獎、2013年中華民國文化部公共藝術卓越獎、2015年中華民國故宮博物院邀請創作「古今華表」。

專業著作包含《二十世紀新藝術的浪潮》、《現代青銅雕塑脫蠟精密鑄造的理論與技術》、《青銅雕塑氧化顏色處理的理論與技術》。

作品創作理念

〈唐吉軻德〉本作品在表達唐吉軻德為了追求理想奮鬥不懈的精神。〈憐憫〉作品旨在表達對於人世間苦難的關懷與慈悲為懷的珍貴情操。

● **李昆霖**（1965-2009）

出生於臺南。

重要展覽經歷：1995年臺南文化中心個展「咖啡屋裡的冥想」、2005年臺南東門美術館個展「騎士與木馬」、2008年上海世貿商城聯展「上海國際藝術博覽會」、2009年臺北黎畫廊個展「山賦」、2016年臺南文化中心聯展「城內／城外－臺南當代藝術初探」。

作品創作理念

生活於臺南，卻不囿於臺南。創作媒材為平面、裝置為首。創作系列「憂嫩的風和景」、「咖啡屋裡的冥想」、「銘印」、「平行飛行的雲朵」、「騎士與木馬」、「獨腳仙行旅圖」、「山賦」。孤獨一直是所訴說的重要主題。創立了獨腳仙，不止獨腳、也是獨行。

作品題材與生活有關，例如：爬山、游泳。一生愛山、畫山，最後以身殉山，驗證了人類脆弱的本質；但一生思索所建構的作品，也印證了藝術永恆的真理。名言：人生產人，人生產作品；作品生產意念，意念生產精神；精神生產生命，生命生產存在。

● **李俊賢**（1957）

出生於臺南麻豆，紐約市立大學藝術碩士畢，現職高苑科技大學建築系副教授。

曾於臺北、臺中、高雄市立美術館，國立歷史博物館，各地文化中心，畫廊、閒置空間，以及巴黎、北京、紐約等地參與聯展多次，近年來也參與多次地方藝術節慶。

重要展覽經歷：2010年臺北小室畫廊個展「賢仔‧臺北‧Palafan」、2011年臺南加力畫廊個展「賢仔‧臺南‧Palafan」、2013年臺北南畫廊「南方三劍客I－李俊賢2013個展」、高雄荷軒新藝空間個展「五花‧雜色‧讚」、2015年高雄小畫廊聯展「現狀與未來I：郭振昌、蘇旺伸、李俊賢三人展」、高雄新思惟人文空間個展「港都好男兒」。

作品創作理念

關於臺灣，李俊賢曾經用十年的時間完成了龐大的「臺灣計劃」，一部無數作品羅織的島嶼實錄。那是一種說故事的方式，也可能是自傳的一種方式。「台」這個字是李俊賢創作自述裡非常顯眼的關鍵，藝評也曾以巨大篇幅、國臺語雙聲帶闡述了他的作品如何體現俗又有力的南方風格。他自己也曾經說得明白：「『台』應該是腳踏實土，站在臺灣的土地上，體受臺灣的一切，然後面向未來的。」李俊賢筆下這些帶刺的色彩和線條也絕對有專屬於臺灣土地的親近感。這樣的氣息像是南島燠熱夏季的午後大雨，唰唰地從高空落下，打在每一個細微的臺灣經驗之上。

● **李錦繡**（1953-2003）

出生於嘉義。

重要展覽經歷：1987年法國巴黎見那諾畫廊「旅法藝術家聯展」、1988年法國法國巴黎大皇宮「新青年繪畫沙龍展」、1993年臺北市立美術館「李錦繡個展」、2005年臺北市立美術館「竹凳的移動－李錦繡紀念展」、2013年臺北市立美術館「臺灣現當代女性藝術五步曲」。

作品創作理念

李錦繡在師大四年級時喜愛以人為題材，以帶有非合理性的思維，並帶有佛洛伊德潛意識說精神性的表現人有時被變形、扭曲，在她的自畫像就是明顯的例子，畢業後畫了許多以家族合照為題材的畫作，人與人之間常以黑色塊來聯繫，帶有些許的淒冷和脆弱。

1983年到法國巴黎深造，人依然是她的最愛，人在巴黎這階段，已不再孤寂，人時常會融入人群裡，也常和現代的建築環境結合，或是金屬反射，或是透明穿透，非常精采。回國之後，她的畫風更加廣泛多樣，風景也常被納入她的畫面，很是獨特。家庭空間擺設被她化成畫作，非常生活，但很深刻。（黃步青代述）

● **林鴻文**（1961-）

出生於臺南。

重要展覽經歷：2002年加拿大魁北克 Silex's Gallery 個展「新山水二」、2003年美國 red mell gallery 佛蒙特藝術村個展、2004年波蘭 Lodz 雙年展、2009年紐約臺北經濟文化中心個展「Journey / through Time」、2018年高雄市立美術館個展「林鴻文創作研究展」。

作品創作理念

物始？在有限的知識堆裡能力總是微不能極，自小生活在乘載萬物千載的大地之上，我也總是呆如木雞。

幽微的感知隨著生命匍匐前行，縱容所有的一切無以復加，遂行著他所謂的可能的或許被應證於未然而也在未然鄰近時，我思及的一切同時也茫然了於續行，在時間跌進歷史的陳跡層裡，我也是被壓入刻痕於往後。說著是我踩踏過的生命鑿痕拼湊出的思緒碎形在倉穹無度間。那是我能力上的心思視覺說法，當下。

● 洪根深（1946-）

出生於澎湖。

重要展覽經歷：2007 年波蘭客拉客夫美術館典藏「穿越國立臺灣美術館山水畫」、2012 年國立台灣美術館「刺客列傳三年級」、高雄市立美術館「殺墨洪根深創作研交展」、2013 年臺灣創價學會建構臺灣美術全省巡迴展、2017 年高雄市立美術館「水墨曼陀羅韓全南羅道國際水墨展」。

作品創作理念

新的媒材與新的形式、新的圖像解碼實驗中，透過基本的遊戲性，去顛覆、裂斷藝術本身，這才是藝術創造自由的本質，真正的意涵。……由於創作主題和創作形式都有顛覆性新思維，後現代水墨創作在臺灣，在題材上的渲染性與技巧的繁複變革，多元變動，是自由的倡議，更期待臺灣水墨畫界重做領域上的探索研究。

我的後現代水墨畫思維，從 1984 年的「繃帶人性」系列，1987 年更種材質的混搭交錯，1991 年的都會空間「黑色情結」，探視解碼人性幽暗的不同層面，1994 年「人形人形」試圖與環保共鳴，也從 2003 年「心墨無法」的觀念發展到「殺墨」的絕對自由，減諸法性斷尾重生的創作觀，企圖臺灣水墨畫的另一心領地。（藝術家提供節選）

● 許自貴（1956-）

出生於高雄，美國紐約普拉特學院藝術研究所畢。

重要展覽經歷：2015 年高雄駁二藝術特區「亞細亞現代雕塑展」、2017 年臺中軟體園區 Dali Art 藝術廣場「許自貴」個展、新光三越百貨臺北／臺中／臺南／高雄巡迴展「新光三越大師系列──這夏動物趴趴走」、臺南市文化局臺南／臺北／臺中／宜蘭／高雄巡迴展「赤焱府城：許自貴、曾英棟雙個展」、2018 年高雄市立美術館個展「左腦×右腦：許自貴的混世哲學」、臺南大新美術館「巷弄裏的靈光──兩岸當代藝術展」。

作品創作理念

〈史前柱子〉

化石都是史前生物遺留下來的生命形體，該作品以化石、石子，還有如洞窟文化中的壁畫刻畫動物形象，把遠古意象重塑而出，色彩亦是以泥土自然色彩。

〈海洋文明史〉

人類理直氣壯把地球各種資源視為自己豢養的，不管海洋或陸地。此作品是以海洋敘述，各種海洋生物是以翻模製成，所謂文明即是滅亡。

● 陳水財（1946-）

出生於臺南。

重要展覽經歷：2012 年高雄市立美術館個展「流動風景──陳水財創作研究展」、2015 年臺南大學香雨書院個展「看不見的旅程」、2016 年高雄市立美術館聯展「沉默風景」、2017 年高雄新浜碼頭藝術空間個展「島嶼風景」、2018 年高雄醫學院藝文空間個展「行過高雄」。

作品創作理念

鄉親的容顏在記憶中揮之不去，烙印在他們臉上的皺紋，並不因時間而模糊，而在綿密的追憶中，反而更加清晰。冷對流光，咀嚼歲月，追憶流逝的時光；「叔公系列」中，我刻畫滄桑、刻畫往事、也刻畫心境，苦澀中帶著甘醇，也充塞幾分淒迷。

● 曾英棟（1953-）

出生於臺南。

重要展覽經歷：2015 年臺南甘樂阿舍美術館個展「雙城個展」、2016 年中國哈爾濱黑龍江省美術館個展「新桃花源記」、2017 年中國北京愛慕美術館個展「共時」、2018 年美國西雅圖 A/NT Gallery 個展「春雨沐財」、德國柏林 Galerie-Kuchling 個展「第五元素」。

作品創作理念

「海洋」系列為其 1997 年作品，除使用厚重的油彩之外，又加入砂與石膏以造成粒子般的質地，以斑駁的痕跡刻畫出並列的魚，海是億萬年的歲月再現，而土地是生物的反覆輪迴，相互層疊出兩者所經歷的流逝跡軌，羊角落在方格上的烙印，是生命所帶不走的記痕。

● 黃宏德（1956-）

出生於臺南。

重要展覽經歷：1987 年韓國漢城國立現代博物館聯展「中華民國現代繪畫展」、1995 年臺北伊通公園個展、1999 年北京中國美術館聯展「複數元的視野──臺灣當代美術 1988-1999」、2000 年臺北誠品畫廊個展、2004 年臺北市立美術館聯展「當代水墨與水墨當代」。

作品創作理念

擁有極高的書寫辨識度，早期的繪畫在空間的安排上，以大比例的放空呈現一種極為宏觀的視覺空間效果。畫作經常只是錯落、豪放、奔走、拙樸的線條。在半醉似醒間，將「我」化身為線條，就連畫作年份在畫面上也成為了不可忽視的部分，一樣影響著畫面的構成，因此，在作品中，只有少數的作品存在著符號。不刻意的以純形式的方式表現創作，而是以恣意應在狀態進行創作，應用就用，隨畫之性而順勢為之。讓書寫本身說話，讓線條本身呈現線條本身的性格。

● 黃步青（1948-）

出生於彰化鹿港。

重要展覽經歷：1999 年義大利威尼斯「第四十八屆威尼斯雙年展」、2000 年中國上海美術館「海上·上海─上海國際雙年展」、2012 年英國倫敦英國文化學會「雙凝，空間裝置展 國際建築暨設計展」、2014 年台北當代美術館「門外家園：荒蕪的邊緣 黃步青個展」、2016-2017 年臺南耘非凡美術館「當代臺灣抽象經典展」。

作品創作理念

1976 年自師大美術系畢業，油畫為主要創作的媒材，在臺北求學時期以大都會的生活背景做為創作的泉源。……1981 年去法國求學之後，我開始嘗試各種媒材的應用，同時也以巴黎都會文化為新的探討背景，巴黎的人文，再度回到我做為一個外國人創作的焦點，生命依然是我想要探索的核心目標，我的作品也逐漸從平面轉向半立體的作品，媒材以巴黎的報紙及各種木頭、金屬材料來表達。這持續到我從巴黎回國。

回國後，回到自己生長的國度，我更加自由的以我們自己的社會文化當成我要探討的目標，報紙、日常生活的棄物廣泛的被我應用，後來，植物的種子也成為我創作的重要元素，我的作品詮釋，更從物件發展到大型的空間裝置，諸如〈追逐水草〉、〈野宴〉、〈雙凝〉等之作品。（藝術家提供節選）

● 黃金福（1969-）

出生於臺南。

重要展覽經歷：2014 年國立台灣美術館「臺灣美術雙年展：臺灣報到 YES, TAIWAN」、2016 年臺北好思當代藝術空間「津夫個展：奇觀城市物語 影像拼貼繪畫研究展」、2017 年臺南東門美術館「奇觀城市物語：影像改變的世界 津夫個展」、中國杭州兩岸交流中心

「奇觀城市物語——杭州西溪溼地：影像與心靈之間」、2018 年中國廣州大新美術館「『創作能動』Art in Initiative-2018 臺灣當代藝術家駐村計畫成果展」。

作品創作理念

對於一個生活在古老城市中的現代藝術創作者而言，1990 年代的臺南，無疑是充滿著車水馬龍、空氣污染、緊張現實、紛雜景觀等的文明禍水，這些現實環境其實也皆是自詡能在城市裡悠遊自如的藝術家所需去面臨的種種問題。……城市中原本美麗而迷人的人類原始質性或開發前的文化歷史痕跡，也無庸置疑地漸漸離我們遠去；作品藉由回歸城市文明原點來進一步省思我們所謂生活環境惡劣的課題，試圖表達出人類文明與自然生態之間的相斥（或相容）性。大自然早期孕育了人類文明的發展，而今人類文明建設的過度開發卻已漸漸侵蝕大自然的生態平衡，兩者之間的容忍度極限在哪裡？我們對於自然資源的使用態度和原則似乎是如此地模糊。（藝術家提供節選）

● **葉竹盛**（1946- ）

出生於高雄，西班牙馬德里最高藝術學院繪畫教授畢。

重要展覽經歷：1992 年臺北縣立文化中心「環境與藝術系列 5——人與自然的關係」個展、1993 年臺北悠閒藝術中心個展「秩序與非秩序」、1994 年臺北悠閒藝術中心個展「素顏」、1995 年臺北悠閒藝術中心個展「南方性格」、2007 年臺南亞帝畫廊個展、2008 年臺中由鉅藝術中心個展「變遷與共生海洋‧種子‧未來」。

作品創作理念

秩序與非秩序一直是我追求的，象徵宇宙的生生不息。生、死、幻、滅、自然萬象，人類的七情六慾，無可避免的大循環。含有自然與人為，感性與理性。故我希望由實物本身的屬性和形式的特徵，在畫面的自然結合，由其現身說法，也許非常熟熱、冷卻；若即若離。

● **盧明德**（1950- ）

出生於高雄，日本國立筑波大學藝術研究所畢。

曾任國立高雄師範人學美術系系主任、國立高雄師範大學藝術學院院長、國立高雄師範大學跨領域藝術研究所教授兼所長。

重要展覽經歷：2013 年臺北名山藝術個展「如果歷史由植物書寫」、2014 年高師大藝術中心聯展「高師藝樣風華 2014 藝術學院教授聯展」、2015 年臺北關渡美術館聯展「啟視錄：臺灣錄像藝術創世紀」、高雄市立美術館個展「媒體是一切——盧明德創作研究展」、2018年臺南加力畫廊個展「文化擬態」。

作品創作理念

擅長以複合媒體來進行創作，繪畫對他而言等同於閱讀的運作，經常引入出人意料的視覺記號，並於之間相互的撞擊產生了一種有益的疏異化（Aliénation）作用，這是他個人自由意志的展現，亦是對被禁錮已久的意識型態之反駁、決裂，特別希冀在實際生活和精神生活之間拆卸去虛假的對立。盧明德在創作時也涉及到身體觸感的愉悅。觸覺的材質感和筆勢的速度、走向，在在都印證了心物之間的時空契合，一種意識和身體行為的聯繫來強調其與身體較諸與意識的關係更為密切。盧明德使用身體力行正是對傳統美學的語言文字思考系統進行質疑。（藝術家提供節選）

● **顏頂生**（1960- ）

出生於臺南。

重要展覽經歷：1991 年臺北誠品畫廊個展、1997 年臺北誠品畫廊個展、2010 年嘉義泰郁美學堂個展「邊界」、2012 年臺北非畫廊個展「鵑‧華　秋‧色」、2016 年臺北非畫廊個展「仮境」。

作品創作理念

藝術傳達我的情感，記錄我的生活，且緊密的使我與這土地有所聯繫。對我而言，若無藝術，存在之於我的苦悶，我不知從何宣洩。

佛教經典《楞嚴經》裡提到一句話——入流亡所，那是觀音聽海潮時所悟出的道理。「入流」是指進與出，「亡所」是指無所駐留。遭逢困挫是人無法避免的，面對困挫對我而言，我所需學習的，是如何讓困挫的苦悶不於心中有所駐留。藝術之於我的意義價值就在於此，它讓因潮水聲而波動的心境，能隨著潮退後與其共同消失。

「重新詮釋中」

日本

● 十一代 大樋長左衛門（年雄）（1958-）

出生於日本石川縣金澤市，波士頓大學大學院修士課程結業，2016 年襲名為十一代大樋長左衛門。

曾任國立臺南藝術大學客座教授、金澤大學客座教授、東京藝術大學講師、上海工藝美術學院客座教授、文化廳長官諮詢委員。

重要展覽經歷：2015 年東京銀座和光 Hall「工藝未來派展」、東京 KH Gallery「大樋年雄 × 小篠弘子 宇宙‧土‧器」、美國紐約藝術設計博物館「工藝未來派展」、2016 年美國華盛頓特區日本大使館文化中心「日本工藝展」、日本京都／東京高島屋個展「襲名記念十一代大樋長左衛門展」。

● 久米 圭子（1985-）

出生於日本千葉，金澤美術工藝大學美術工藝研究科工藝專攻、金澤卯辰山工藝工房結業，現居住、工作於金澤市。曾獲韓國第八回清州國際工藝公募展特選、2017 年金澤市工藝展金澤美術工藝大學學長賞、2014 年金澤市工藝展金澤市長最優秀賞。

重要展覽經歷：2013 年與 2016 年於日本東京 Gallery Okariya Ginza。

● 山村 慎哉（1960）

出生於日本東京都調布市，金澤美術工藝大學大學院畢業，現為金澤美術工藝大學教授。

重要展覽經歷：2007 年英國 V&A 博物館「Collect 2007」、韓國首爾 Nanum Gallery「安德春、山村慎哉二人展」、2008 年中村邸金澤中村記念美術館聖誕夜茶會、2009 年金澤 gallery「點 61 in 3+1/8」、美國紐約 Ippodo Gallery。

● 山岸 紗綾（1981-）

出生於日本石川縣，金澤美術工藝大學工藝科之漆‧木工課程畢業，金澤卯辰山工藝工房結業，現於自宅工房進行制作。

重要展覽經歷：2013 年東京 O-Jewel 個展「Blooming Voice」、2015 年日本東京日本橋島屋個展「山岸紗綾：景色を纏う」、2016 年荷蘭阿姆斯特丹 Lloid Hotel & Cultural Embassy (C&)、「FIRANDO Japan's Island of Sweets」、統營漆藝美術館「國際當代漆藝展」、東京小出由紀子事務所個展「山岸紗綾──植物採集」。

● 中川 衛（1947-）

出生於日本石川縣金澤市。金澤美術工藝大學產業美術學科卒業，人間國寶─重要無形文化財「彫金」保護人。

重要展覽經歷：1995 年英國 V&A 博物館「日本工藝『現代與傳統』」、1999 年法國巴黎日本工藝「今」百選展、2004 年丹麥哥本哈根「當代日本金工展」、2007 年英國大英博物館「工藝之美：日本傳統工藝 50 年」。

● 木瀨 浩詞（1980-）

出生於日本滋賀縣，東北藝術工科大學大學院藝術工學研究科之藝術文化專攻修士課程、金澤卯辰山工藝工房結業，曾於 2008 至 2011 年間於公益法人宗桂會月浦工房進行制作活動，現於石川縣金澤市進行製作活動。

重要展覽經歷：2008 年第二十二回工藝都市高岡工藝展（漆媒材賞）、第二十六回朝日現代工藝展（準優勝）、第四十七回日本工藝展（丸之內大樓賞）、2010 年第十八回 Tableware 大賞（大賞‧經濟產業大臣賞）、2017 年金澤世界工藝競賽（大樋陶冶齋審查員特別賞）。

● 石山 哲也（1973-）

出生於日本琦玉縣，東京設計與藝術大學碩士畢業，曾任臺南藝術大學客座藝術家、曾於印度 Uttarayan Art Center 駐村、2015 年於香港浸會大學擔任駐校藝術家、景德鎮陶瓷藝術家工作營。

重要展覽經歷：2016 年香港巨年藝廊「Story Teller」、2017 年荷蘭歐洲陶藝中心「URNEN」、韓國廣州昆池岩陶瓷公園「京畿世界陶瓷雙年展」、十和田市現代美術館「村上隆的超扁平當代陶藝考」、2018 年日本京都艸居個展「ICON」。

● 池田 晃將（1987-）

出生於日本千葉縣，金澤美術工藝大學工藝科之漆‧木工課程畢業、金澤美術工藝大學大學院修士課程結業，現為金澤卯辰山工藝工房研修藝術家。

重要展覽經歷：2014 年石川 Café&gallery Musee「池田晃將漆展──微觀裝飾」、2015-17 年東京伊勢丹新宿本店 5 樓 West Park「池田晃將：漆飾小工藝展」、2017 年日本東京日本橋三越「漆之結晶」（Essence of URUSHI）、香港港麗酒店「Asia art contemporary Hong Kong」、新加坡新達城新加坡國際會議展覽中心「Asia art contemporary Singapore」

● 竹村 友里（1980-）

出生於日本愛知縣名古屋市，愛知縣立藝術大學美術學部設計‧工藝科之陶瓷專攻畢業、財團法人金澤卯辰山工藝工房結業。曾為滋賀縣立陶藝之森駐村藝術家，現居於石川縣金澤市。

重要展覽經歷：2007 年日本京都高島屋京都店美術工藝沙龍、2012 年愛知松坂屋名古屋店美術畫廊、石川金澤 21 世紀美術館「工藝未來派」、2013 年日本東京日本橋三越本店美術沙龍、三重 Paramita Museum 第八回 Paramita 陶藝大賞展。

● 坂井 直樹（1973-）

出生於日本群馬縣，東京藝術大學院博士後期課程鍛金研究室結業，曾於金澤卯辰山工藝工房研修，現於金澤市內進行制作活動。

重要展覽經歷：2012 年財團法人美術工藝振興佐藤基金淡水翁賞、2015 年傳統工藝日本金工展──宗桂會賞、2016 年 Tableware 大賞、大賞‧經濟產業大臣賞、2017 年傳統工藝日本金工展──宗桂會賞、傳統工藝日本金工展──朝日新聞社賞。

● 村本 真吾（1970-）

出生於日本石川縣，東京藝術大學美術學部工藝科、東京藝術大學大學院漆藝專攻結業，金澤卯辰山工藝工房研修藝術家。

重要展覽經歷：2015 年東京東銀座 Galerie Pousse 個展「村本真吾展──搖曳 II」、2017 年美國明尼蘇達明尼阿波利斯美術館「Hard Bodies：當代日本漆雕刻」、日本東京 Gallery Okariya Ginza「Urushi‧Jewelry vol.4」、金澤 21 世紀美術館「金澤 21 世紀工藝祭『工藝建築』展」、2018 年日本東京日本橋三越「漆的現在 2018 展」。

● 松永 圭太（1986-）

出生於日本岐阜縣多治見市，畢業於名城大學建築學科，多治見市陶瓷器意匠研究所結業、金澤卯辰山工藝工房結業。

重要展覽經歷：2016 年埼玉 Utuwa Note「Mars Gravity」、大阪

Gallery Tosei 桃青「松永圭太作陶展」、岐阜 ishoken gallery「松永圭太展」、東京 Pragmata「Void of Space」、北海道 kamo kamo「松永圭太展」。

● 桑田 卓郎（1981-）

出生於廣島縣，現居於岐阜縣土岐市。京都嵯峨藝術大學短期大學部美術學科陶藝課程畢業、多治見市陶磁器意匠研究所結業。

重要展覽經歷：2012 年金澤 21 世紀美術館「工藝未來派展」、2013 年紐約 SALON94「Flavor of Nature」、東京 8 / Art Gallery / 小山登美夫畫廊「桑田卓郎展」、2015 年紐約 SALON94「Dear Tea Bowl」、2017 年十和田市現代美術館「村上隆的超扁平當代陶藝考」。

● 奈良佑希（1989-）

出生於石川縣金澤市，2013 年畢業於東京藝術大學美術學部建築科，2016 年畢業於多治見市陶磁器意匠研究所，2017 年於東京藝術大學大學院美術研究科建築專攻首席畢業。

重要展覽經歷：2018 年法國 Pierre-Yves Caër Gallery「Les Promesses du Feu / 炎の同心」、2017 年瑞士 Art Basel、2016 年菊池寬実記念智美術館「菊池雙年展」、2016 年多治見市美濃燒博物館「美濃陶芸の明日展」、2016 年東京都日本橋三越本店「うつわ その先に陶──魂のかたち」。

中國

● 吳光榮（1961-）

出生於安徽淮南，南京藝術學院美術系碩士。

現為中國美術學院陶藝系講師、中國美術家協會會員、中國古陶瓷學會會員。從事陶瓷史、工藝史研究及陶藝創作。

重要展覽經歷：2005 年日本「中、日、韓三國陶藝交流展」、2006 年廣東「壺非壺」宜興紫砂藝術展、北京中國美術館「陶瓷藝術邀請展」、法國瓦洛里國際陶藝雙年展、杭州「當代中國青年陶藝家作品雙年展」。

● 吳昊（1970-）

出生於安徽，日本京都市立藝術大學大學院美術研究科工藝（陶瓷器）專攻畢，現任中國美術學院陶藝系講師。

重要展覽經歷：2013 年杭州「一脈相承──中國美術學院當代陶藝作品聯展」、日本滋賀「THE TANUKI ─たぬき・狸・タヌキ─陶藝展」、杭州「『淘』瓷生活──杭州當代陶瓷器物」、杭州「第一屆交杯幻盞千杯展」、新北市「新域──東亞當代陶藝交流展」。

● 李海霖（1974-）

出生於江西餘江，中國美術學院陶藝系畢（博士在讀）、美國夏威夷大學陶藝系訪問學者，現為中國美術學院陶藝系教師，中國美術家協會會員。

重要展覽經歷：2017 年中國美院民藝館「『白石』人在草木間──中國茶文化展」、韓國「『林中路』韓國骨灰盒展」、日本愛知「『白石』亞洲現代陶藝交流展」、中國山東博物館「『幽』中國美協 2017 界・尚──第四屆中國當代陶藝實驗作品邀請展」、中國西安美院「『禮』空間・轉換：2017 西安國際當代陶藝交流作品展」。

● 陸斌（1961-）

出生於北京，南京藝術學院工藝美術系畢，現為南京藝術學院設計學院教授。

聯合國教科文組織陶藝協會會員（ICA）、中國美術家協會會員，中國藝術研究院特約研究員、中國美協陶瓷藝委會委員、江蘇省陶瓷行業協會陶藝委員會副主任。

重要展覽經歷：2000 年香港世界畫廊「陸斌陶藝雕塑展」、臺南索卡藝術中心「陸斌陶藝雕塑展」、2006 年美國堪薩斯尼爾畫廊「陸斌陶藝雕塑展」、2013 年中國南京「陸斌當代陶瓷藝術作品展」。

● 黃永星（1988）

出生於江西宜春，中國美術學院畢，目前任教於泉州工藝美術職業學院陶藝系。

重要展覽經歷：2016 年藝術 8 中法文化論壇、德化縣陶瓷博物館「探索──首屆德化陶瓷雙年展」、中國美術學院美術館「第十屆中國當代青年陶藝家作品雙年展」、臺北「福爾摩沙國際藝術博覽會」、2017 年光州「GICB 世界陶瓷雙年展主題展」。

● 浮雲堂

以當代視覺闡釋中國東方之美，通過文化活動、茶會雅集、茶道教學、茶博會、茶道藝術品展覽、各媒體宣傳來宣導智慧、閒適和覺醒的藝術人生態度，和雅致的生活方式，做忠於原創，忠於傳統工藝的茶生活品牌。

● U+ 傢俱

U+ 傢俱是一個獨立品牌，於 2008 年在山東濟南創辦。沈寶宏是 U+ 傢俱的董事長兼設計總監。

U+ 傢俱創建之初，即確立了以「中和之美」作為美學標準的設計理念──「尊重材料、人文和美學，出於善意，歸於平和，追求中和之美」。

臺灣

● 方柏欽（1976-）

澳大利亞墨爾本皇家理工大學藝術學院（RMIT University, School of Art）藝術創作博士畢，現任國立臺南藝術大學材質創作與設計系助理教授。

重要展覽經歷：2011 年鶯歌富貴陶園「Deuteragonist ──方柏欽實用陶瓷創作個展」、2012 年新北市立鶯歌陶瓷博物館「新域──東亞當代陶藝交流展」與「第四屆臺灣金壺獎陶藝設計競賽展」、2013 年京畿道江南大學韓國陶藝協會「2013 KSCA 國際交流展」、臺北一票票藝術空間「路陸溜溜」聯展。

● 吳偉丞（1976-）

出生於臺中縣烏日鄉，國立臺中商專商業設計科畢業。

重要展覽經歷：2008 年新北市立鶯歌陶瓷博物館「陶瓷與異質媒材特展」、2010 年與 2012 年新北市立鶯歌陶瓷博物館「臺灣陶瓷金質獎邀請展」、2014 年新北市立鶯歌陶瓷博物館「大器非凡──容器、藝術、跨界特展」、2015 年京畿陶瓷博物館韓國京畿世界陶瓷雙年展「本色共感：東亞傳統陶藝邀請展」、2017 年新北市立鶯歌陶瓷博物館「形塑無疆──臺灣當代陶藝進行式」。

● **卓銘順**（1968-）

出生於新北市鶯歌，國立臺灣藝術大學工藝設計學系碩士畢，1995年成立陶藝工作室、專業作陶。

重要展覽經歷：2014年臺中市立大墩文化中心「茶壺不只是茶壺，一起玩吧！」個展、澳門理工學院「臺澳陶藝交流展」邀請展、上海工藝美術博物「第四屆國際現代壺藝雙年展」邀請展、2015年韓國「世界陶藝雙年展」韓國陶藝基金會邀請展、2016年立法院「茶壺幾何學──卓銘順陶藝創作個展」邀請展。

● **陳逸**（1981-）

出生於宜蘭，國立臺南藝術大學應用藝術研究所金工與首飾創作組碩士畢，現職金工與首飾創作者。

重要展覽經歷：2007年美國密蘇里州Pottery藝廊「陳逸、陳峙傑──金工、陶瓷雙個展」、2008年國立臺南藝術大學南畫廊「敲·痕」陳逸金工創作個展、2013年臺北爆炸毛頭與油炸朱利工作室「自畫像／陳逸金屬器物創作展」。

● **黃天來**（1958-）

出生於臺中大甲，1974年習傳統玉器雕刻，1978年師從林昌德教授門下，正式接觸中西繪畫、1985年隨雕塑家許維忠學習人體雕塑。

重要展覽經歷：1997年臺灣省手工業研究所臺北展示中心個展、「藝術薪火相傳：第十屆臺中縣美術家接力展」、1999年法國巴黎臺北新聞中心「臺灣傳統工藝展」、2000年臺北車站文化藝廊「匠心獨運：黃天來的現代鐵器美學」。

● **趙丹綺**（1966-）

英國倫敦市政廳大學應用藝術及視覺文化碩士畢，英國皇家寶石學會珠寶鑑定院士（FGA）、重要工藝競賽評審委員、金銀細工技能檢定命題與監評委員，現任國立臺灣藝術大學工藝設計學系專任副教授。

重要展覽經歷：2010年日本奈良「Sailing to the Future」中、日、韓當代金屬藝術展、2011年北京「互動·創新── 2011國際金屬藝術展暨學術論壇」展覽、2012年臺南文化中心「2012當代女性金工藝術展」、2013年高雄市歷史博物館「穿出時代的容顏──典藏織品金工特展」、南韓首爾弘益大學當代藝術館「第一屆韓國首爾國際珠寶藝術展」。

● **劉世平**（1965-）

出生於高雄鳳山，中華民國工藝發展協會並成為永久會員，2007年獲選為臺灣工藝之家，現職為陶、石、木為主要媒材之專業藝術創作者。

重要展覽經歷：2000年臺中縣立文化中心個展、2003年臺北車站文化藝廊個展、2005年嘉義市文化局個展、2011年臺北「心境作茶器 森／CASA」、2012年臺南「心境作茶器 森／CASA」、2014年臺北「慢慢作茶器 森／CASA」。

● **劉榮輝**（1972-）

出生於臺北，協和美工陶藝組畢，師從於劉瑋仁老師。

重要展覽經歷：2003年日本「益子陶庫三人聯展」、2011年臺灣富貴陶園「大氣初現」陶藝個展、2012年富貴陶園藝術創作聯展、2017年臺灣富貴陶園「鶯歌『尋味、暖心』茶器創作聯展」、2017年臺灣富貴陶園「三義『花舞』花器創作聯展」。

● **鍾雯婷**（1984-）

出生於臺灣。金澤卯辰山工藝工房、東京藝術大學美術專攻（陶瓷）博士課程結業。

重要展覽經歷：2013年金澤「鍾雯婷個展──冰肌玉·愡」、2015年東京「鍾雯婷個展──薄光」、2017年大阪「鍾雯婷作陶展」、臺北與東京「鍾雯婷個展──恋果物語」、金澤「鍾雯婷個展──白華の詩」。

● **羅濟明**（1981-）

出生於臺中，大甲高中陶瓷科畢，師事趙勝傑老師及李幸龍老師。2009年成立「土丕匋坊」陶藝工作室。

重要展覽經歷：2005年臺中縣港區藝術中心「陶壺千秋」聯展、2012年大墩文化中心「Nature 羅濟明陶藝展」、2017年方圓美術館「臺灣陶藝壺藝展」、臺中市海線社區大學「砌匋人」陶藝展、2018年當代陶藝館「羅濟明陶藝展」。

● **蘇保在**（1968-）

出生於高雄，陶瓷乙級技術士，現任雲林科技大學文物資產維護系陶藝講師。1996年成立「雲白天青」工作室。

重要展覽經歷：2005年臺北造居藝術中心陶藝個展、2006年逢甲大學藝術中心陶藝個展、2007年臺北造居藝術中心陶藝個展、2010年臺北造居藝術中心「香韻」陶藝個展、2011年當代陶藝館「器韻生動」青瓷創作展。

● **任大賢**（1977-）

2004年國立臺灣藝術大學雕塑系畢業。2010年國立臺南藝術大學造型藝術研究所畢業。2006年曾獲台北美術獎。現居住及創作於臺南。

重要展覽經歷：2007年於台北當代藝術館個展「放設線」、2015年新竹智邦藝術基金會「灰階」、2016年臺南總爺藝文中心「無設線」、2018年匈牙利Tatabanya museum，「Jen Ta-hsien solo exhibition」。

謝誌
Acknowledgments

臺南市美術館感謝下列單位與人士對本展之貢獻與協助：

（以下依筆畫順序排列）

Tainan Art Museum wishes to thank the following people and organizations for their efforts and assistance in making this exhibition possible:

林柏亭 先生	Lin, Po-Ting (Mr.)
吳佳蓉 女士	Wu, Chia-Jung (Ms.)
郭為美 女士	Kuo, Wei-Mei (Ms.)
劉俊禎 先生	Liu, Chun-Chen (Mr.)
楊文富家族	Yang Wen-fu Family
文化部	Ministry of Culture
加力畫廊	Inart Space（新生態藝術環境 New Phase Art Space）
甘樂阿舍美術館	Asir Art Museum
大樋美術館	Ohi Museum
東門美術館	Licence Art Gallery
阿貴美術館	Akui Art Museum
原型藝術	Prototype Art Space
泰郁美學堂	Taiyu Beaux Arts Salon
財團法人大牛兒童城文化推廣基金會	Louitech Children's Culture Progressive Foundation
財團法人何創時書法藝術基金會	HCS Calligraphy Arts Foundation
陳澄波文化基金會	Chen Cheng-po Cultural Foundation
凱倫偉伯畫廊	Karin Weber Gallery
順益臺灣原住民博物館	Shung Ye Museum of Formosan Aborigines
黑森林藝術空間	The Black Forest Art Center
臺南市政府	Tainan City Government
蒲添生雕塑紀念館	P.T.S. Sculpture Memorial Museum
德鴻畫廊	Der-Horng Art Gallery
邊陲文化	Border Culture
蘇菲亞.C 藝術空間	Sophia. C Art Gallery

Felita hui Wai Yin

KOSAKU KANECHIKA

Yuri van der Leest

國家圖書館出版品預行編目資料

府城榮光──臺南市美術館1館開館展
/ 潘襎總編輯-- 初版. --

臺南市：臺南市美術館, 2019.01
256 面；22.8×30公分
ISBN 978-986-05-8270-3（平裝）

1. 臺南市美術館 2. 美術館展覽

906.8   107023378

府城榮光

臺南市美術館 1 館開館展

The Glory of Tainan—Tainan Art Museum Grand Opening

指導單位	臺南市政府		Supervised by: Tainan City Government
發 行 人	陳輝東		Publisher: Chen, Huei-tung
總 編 輯	潘襎		Supervisor: Pan, Fan
總 監	林育淳		Artistic Director: Lin, Yu-chun
監 督	溫淑姿		Executive Supervisor: Wen, Shu-tzu
編 輯	關秀惠		Editor: Kuan, Hsiu-hui
策 展 人	白適銘、李思賢、張清淵、潘安儀		Curator: Pai, Shih-ming / Li, Szu-hsien / Chang, Ching-yuan / Pan, An-yi
展覽執行	莊東橋、徐嘉晨、常鴻雁、蕭楷競		Exhibition Coordinators: Chuang, Tong-chiao / Hsu, Chia-chen / Chang, Hung-yen / Hsiao, Kai-ching

展場設計	一禾設計規劃	Gallery Design: Yi-He Design
資料提供	展覽企劃部	Information Provide: Exhibition Planning Department
校 稿	莊東橋、徐嘉晨、常鴻雁、蕭楷競、余青勳、沈明芬	Proofreader: Chuang, Tong-chiao / Hsu, Chia-chen / Chang, Hung-yen / Hsiao, Kai-ching / Rita Yu / Shen, Ming-fen

封面設計	株式會社日本設計中心	Cover Designer: Nippon Design Center
美術編輯	藝術家出版社	Graphic Designer: Artist Publishing Co.
地 址	台北市金山南路（藝術家路）二段 165 號 6 樓	Address: 6F., No. 165, Sec. 2, Jinshan S. Rd. (Artist Rd.), Da'an Dist., Taipei City 106, Taiwan (R.O.C)
電 話	(02) 23886715	Tel: (02) 23886715
版 次	初版	Edition: First Edition
發行日期	2019年1月	Publication Date: January 2019
發行數量	2000本（平裝）	Copies Printed: 2000 Copies
定 價	新臺幣1800元	Price: NT $1800
I S B N	978-986-05-8270-3	ISBN: 978-986-05-8270-3

發行單位	臺南市美術館	Published by: Tainan Art Museum
地 址	1 館 70049 臺南市中西區南門路37號	Address: Building 1 No.37, Nanmen Rd., West Central Dist., Tainan City 70049, Taiwan (R.O.C.)
	2 館 70041 臺南市中西區忠義路二段1號	Building 2 No.1, Sec. 2, Zhongyi Rd., West Central Dist., Tainan City 70041, Taiwan (R.O.C.)
電 話	(06) 2218881 、 傳真：(06) 2235191	Tel: (06) 2218881 、 Fax: (06) 2235191
電子信箱	public@tnam.museum	E-mail: public@tnam.museum
網 址	http://www.tnam.museum	Web Site: http://www.tnam.museum